Crucifix Lane

Kate Mosse

FLAME
Hodder & Stoughton

First published in 1998 by Hodder and Stoughton
A division of Hodder Headline PLC
First published in paperback in 1999 by Hodder and Stoughton
A Flame Paperback

A CIP catalogue record for this title is available
from the British Library

ISBN 0 340 69292 8

Typeset by Palimpsest Book Production Limited,
Polmont, Stirlingshire
Printed and bound in Great Britain by
Clays Ltd, St Ives PLC, Bungay, Suffolk

Hodder and Stoughton
A division of Hodder Headline PLC
338 Euston Road
London NW1 3BH

For Ruth Picardie
1 May 1964 – 22 September 1997

We shall not cease from exploration
And the end of all our exploring
Will be to arrive where we started
And know the place for the first time.

T. S. Eliot
Little Gidding, Four Quartets

1

Saturday 2 August 1997

Five o'clock. A wet and grey London morning. A light drizzle was falling like confetti. Melting into the empty pavements. There were few signs of life. Just the occasional shriek of a taxi taking the corner with Tooley Street too tight or the blistering shunt of goods trains pulling out of London Bridge Station. Each sound echoed briefly, then was swallowed up by the silence.

Shand Street was deserted. A few parked cars and random bits of rubbish blown in by the wind, discarded sweet wrappers and crisp bags and the front page of a newspaper with an ad torn out. There was even an old car battery, pushed neatly out of the way against the wall of the railway arch. The tarmac on the road had been worn away in places, revealing the older, grey cobblestones of the road underneath. It wasn't worth repairing. There was too little traffic and, like so many of the tiny roads snaking under the railway tracks, it led nowhere. No one came up here by accident. Even the lads with their illegal fly posters hadn't bothered to waste their glue. Only one notice clung defiantly to the wall, a cheap white poster with red print advertising gigs during August at the club opposite. The names of the resident DJs and guests had been half covered by the words 'The Leviticus Eleven' scrawled across the bottom in blue Biro. A band? A film? Victims of a miscarriage of justice? The graffiti gave nothing away.

A large board hammered into the brickwork itself was the

only clue Reboot actually existed. Like so many clubs, it would have a short shelf life. Opening, a brief flash of fashionable glory, then shut down all inside six months. The wooden sign looked as if it had been painted by hand, a yellow Celtic cross, set inside a purple circle and surrounded by blue and pink stars. The black bubble writing was uneven. Someone had scribbled the word 'entrance' with a black marker pointing to a flat, green sheet of reinforced steel. There was no handle on the outside of the door. No need. After one a.m., nobody got in this way.

Down below, the chemical generation danced to the sounds of summer 1997.

The bouncer pushed the door open and Annie slipped out into the street.

''Night, then,' she said.

The man took no notice. Once she was out of the club, she was no longer his responsibility. He'd no need to be nice. She heard a clatter as the exit door banged shut behind her, then a sharp click of the lock. The party was over.

Annie looked around her and took a deep breath. She could still feel the repetitive thudding of the music deep in the pit of her stomach and her ears were ringing. But even though she was a little dizzy from lack of food and sleep, the buzz hadn't worn off yet and she felt fantastic. Like she could do anything.

After a night of being in an overcrowded space with people she'd never seen before and probably would never see again, it was good to be outside in the fresh air. Annie felt most at home in London at this early time of the day. Always had. When she was younger, it had worried her grandad sick, waking up to the flat empty. He'd tried to frighten her into staying in. Listing in graphic detail the things that could happen to girls out on their own in the city between dusk and dawn. But his scare tactics hadn't worked. If anything, his opposition had made her night excursions all the more glamorous. As she got older, he gave up trying to stop her. It wasn't worth the fight. Just told her to be back in time for school.

She didn't have to creep out any more, but she still loved watching the city come to life. The clink of crates being unloaded from the backs of lorries, the smell of fresh bread and the sharp aroma of roasted coffee. The incessant chatter of birds balanced in rows on the telephone lines and the shriek of gulls over the Thames. Sometimes, when the tide was low, she would clamber down the defence walls by William Curtis Park and sit on the exposed mudflats listening to the sound of the water lisping on the shingle. Not this morning, though. Annie knew she was too exhausted to climb back up.

It had been a good night. They had only had to queue for forty minutes to get in and she'd scored virtually the second she was through the door. There was the usual scrum in front of the mirror in the ladies' toilets, everyone elbowing each other out of the way as they fiddled with combs and lipstick and knocked back their doves or pinkies. Since Annie loathed make-up and her black hair was no more than half an inch long all over, she travelled light. When she stared in the mirror, she saw pale skin, oval-shaped brown eyes, wide mouth and silver stud in her nose. It was a handsome face, someone once described as a cross between a medieval knight and Skunk Anansie on a bad day. The comment had been intended as an insult. Annie took it as a compliment.

The night had passed without any help from her. Her only distinct memory of the five hours was an up-close juggler standing in front of her, throwing and spinning his silver and gold beanbags in the air before her eyes. She'd thought they looked like tiny planets orbiting the moon, although she hoped she hadn't said that out loud. She certainly had said she loved him. Annie winced. The great thing about drugs was how uninhibited they made you feel. The bad thing was how fucking embarrassing it was afterwards.

She was shivering. For the first time in weeks, there was a slight chill in the air and her sleeveless white vest and faded baggy army fatigue hipsters were nowhere near warm enough for the real world. She squatted on the kerb and rummaged until she found the blue fleece she'd shoved to the bottom of her rucksack the right before. Ignoring the flakes of tobacco and the suspicious brown stain around the neck, she tugged it out and slipped it over her bare arms and midriff. The sound of the chunky zip was satisfyingly loud in the silence of the street.

She hadn't got a clue what time it was. Five o'clock? Half past? Not that it mattered. She could do with a coffee or something, though, and she was pretty sure there was nothing back at the flat. She'd not been shopping since, well . . . Dan had been the one who kept the fridge well stocked, not her. Annie scowled at herself. The whole point about going out in the first place had been to put men out of her mind.

She stretched her arms above her head. If she couldn't find a café, then the general store round the back of Snowsfields might be open. Failing that, there was probably somewhere on Weston Street. She'd get a bit of breakfast, do some shopping, then go back to the flat and give it a good clean out. All part of her major life overhaul.

She had only been back once in the past two weeks to pick up some clothes. It had been a mistake. Everything smelled of Dan. His ghost was everywhere. She wasn't hurting, really. She knew it wasn't going anywhere. It was just a matter of pride and the fact that he'd got in first. Dan was a complete bastard and it was the same depressing story. She was good at falling for people, brilliant at sex, crap at sustaining relationships. Friends or lovers. A familiar pattern. If she was honest with herself, the main reason she didn't want to go to the flat was that it made her feel a failure. But the longer she left it, the worse it was going to be. She couldn't crash on other people's floors for ever.

Annie stood up, hitched her bag over her shoulders and walked decisively out of Shand Street and right into Crucifix Lane, humming 'No Surprises' under her breath without thinking about it. The boys' ultimate suicide song, it was predictably Dan's current favourite track on the new Radiohead album. The CD was the last thing they'd bought together before he left. He had taken it – and a lot more besides – with him. When Annie realised what she was doing, she immediately stopped singing.

At the corner of Crucifix Lane and Bermondsey Street,

Annie paused to look in the window of Astrocat, the New Age bookshop. The name was painted down the door in elaborate white handwriting and the windows on either side were crammed with books, crystals, zodiac necklaces and joss sticks. She cupped her hands over the glass to get a better look inside. She could just make out all sorts of ribbons and sticks and stars, mobiles and moons hanging from the ceiling. Even some peacock feathers with huge blue and green eyes. Annie smiled. She must have walked past the shop a thousand times before and somehow never bothered to go in. She read the sign. Open at ten. Maybe she'd pop back later. It might be a laugh and it was something to do.

The drizzle had given way to proper rain now and Annie realised she was getting wet. In the distance, she could hear the whoosh of spray trapped in the wheels of buses and cars as the traffic started to move. Everything was beginning to get going. Children waking up and creeping towards television sets to watch holiday cartoons with the volume turned down. People were putting the kettle on, making tea. Suddenly, the ordinary, domestic things seemed very appealing. Annie turned her collar up and hurried across the road towards the grocery shop.

It was shut.

'Bummer,' she muttered to herself.

Annie doubled back down the side of the multi-storey car park, her trainers slithering on the greasy pavements, then cut through the playground past the old shelter where that girl from Tyers Estate had been attacked. Nobody knew if it was true. There'd been no conviction. It was just one of those stories that everybody told. Each time, the number in the gang got bigger and the injuries to the girl got worse. The boys were white, the boys were black. The girl was just engaged, the girl was still a kid. The facts were irrelevant. In one way, Annie knew it didn't actually matter if it was true or not. If not that incident, then another. Her grandad would have told them that for nothing.

The playground was dead quiet now, though. The metal frames of the swings looked like two giant iron spiders. Most of the seats were missing. There was no one about. By mid-afternoon, local kids would be swarming all over them.

Annie was starting to feel more together now and realised she was making mental notes of things to do under the heading of 'Life After Dan'. Top of the list was going down to Deptford to see her grandad. Tomorrow, definitely, if not today. Not that he'd recognise her, of course, but a visit was long overdue and she felt bad about it. The nursing home had rung a couple of weeks ago, but she'd never called them back. She'd put money on it that there'd be a stack more messages waiting for her at the flat. This was who she was going to be from now on. Responsible, caring, decisive. Yeah, right, she thought.

Annie suddenly noticed that a thick fog had come down out of nowhere. A penetrating swirl of smoky grey cloud that had sucked the sounds and shapes out of everything. Already, she couldn't see more than a couple of feet in front of her. Could no longer work out where the earth stopped and the sky began. Even the tower blocks, fixed points on the landscape of south-east London, had disappeared.

Her heart began to thump. She knew she had to get her bearings. She couldn't make out even the bench or the rubbish bin, though they had to still be there. She carried on in the same direction, no longer knowing exactly where she was, walking faster and trying not to pay attention to the way the light from the streetlamps had smothered everything with a sinister orange glow. There was no sound, just the squelch of her soggy soles and the thump of the rucksack against her back. It was all too still. When she stretched out her arm, her fingers vanished into nothing as if they didn't exist any more. Out of sight, out of mind.

Now Annie was properly scared, could taste the fear in her mouth and throat, smell the malice in the air. With every step she took, she became more convinced there was someone stalking her in the fog. Several times she spun round, hoping to catch them out. But there was never anything to see.

'Who's there?'

Nothing. Just her own words bouncing back at her.

She started to run, the terror snapped at her heels like a dog. If she could get to the main street, she'd be all right. Her breathing was jagged, burning in her throat as the muscles pulled tight in her legs. She didn't slow down. Head for where the people are was the first rule of self-preservation. Every woman knows that.

Without warning, the fence surrounding the playground suddenly reared up at her out of the fog. Annie put her hands out to protect herself, felt the sharp wire cut into her palms as she smashed into it. She thought she'd been heading for the exit, but her sense of direction had got scrambled and she'd gone too far to the left. Desperate to get out, Annie pulled herself along the wire, hand over hand over hand, until she found a gap in the fence and was out through the gate. Keep running.

Her legs had a mind of their own now. She wouldn't have been able to stop herself if she'd wanted to. Past La Salette Presbytery, its doors padlocked shut, past the derelict warehouse and Arthur's Pentecostal Gospel Mission, with its decayed wooden boards. The burnt-out car was still up on bricks in front of the Victorian Ragged School.

As she fled through the walkways of White's Grounds Estate, out of nowhere Annie heard a voice. A single, enchanting line of melody, floating high above the ugly buildings. Something about it pierced her, made her shiver. She wanted to stop and listen, but she was too frightened. She had to keep running. Up the steps, round the garbage shed where someone had sprayed 'Stacy is Fat' on the bricks, and out into Crucifix Lane.

Only at this point did Annie notice she'd gone round in a circle. She was almost back at the club, where she'd started. The realisation took the wind out of her sails and, as she started to slow down, she heard the singing again. Still faint, but closer now. She turned her head to see if she could work out where it was coming from.

The tramp was lying half in and half out of a cardboard box at the junction of Crucifix Lane and White's Grounds, with a couple of empty bottles for company. Annie didn't see him until it was too late. She stumbled on the kerb, caught her right foot on the edge of the box and twisted up in the air. Then somehow she was outside herself. She watched her body falling down to the ground, as if it was happening to someone else. All in slow motion. She knew it was going to hurt, but there was nothing she could do to stop it.

The left side of Annie's head took the full force of the collision. She felt no pain as the skin on her cheek split open. As she slipped down the wall, she left a trail of blood smeared on the bricks. Like a line on a map to show where she'd been.

In the final seconds before she lost consciousness, Annie thought she saw a sequence of figures carved on the soot-stained bricks just above the the pavement. A pattern of thin vertical and horizontal lines, like some sort of hieroglyphics.

'What the fuck?' she muttered.

Her voice came from miles away, as if it was nothing to do with her at all.

2

Saturday 2 August 2008

Leah stood on the foreshore, waiting for the ferry that crossed from the northside to the south.

The sun was still low in the sky. To her right, she could see the Barrier, its silver gates shining in the early morning sun. They looked like a line of wrecked rowing boats, up-ended and half-submerged in the water. From this distance, it seemed tiny. Like a child's construction toy.

Despite the August heat, Leah shivered. Sometimes, the whole of the last four months seemed like a blur. Being so close, back right where it had started, reminded her of quite how far she had travelled. Scientist to saboteur in ten easy lessons. Leah patted the netputer she was carrying in her bag, as if to reassure herself it was still there, then pulled up her sleeve to check the time: 07:40:05. Later than she thought. She didn't have long to take the readings Michael needed, drop the data off at the Weston Street headquarters and still make it back to the Pen before she was missed. It all seemed a hell of a risk. The best she could hope was that no one spotted her and reported it to Kellen.

Leah had gone through the school system at a time when the agenda had focused on raising boys' achievements at the expense of the girls. In her rough school, she had learned the lesson that she could either be popular or high-flying. Not both. Deciding she would rather do without friends than exam results, she had put all her energy into work. It was the only way to escape an unhappy home life and the otherwise drab future mapped out for her. She made it through university, postgraduate college and, because hydrology and hydrogeology were growth industries, she found the opportunities were there for those prepared to take them. She'd quietly beavered her way up the career ladder and so was now back in London at the age of thirty – independent, self-sufficient and reliable. Dr Leah Bennett, hydrologist, with a business card to prove it. Where others sat behind a desk, she ignored the benefits of seniority and chose to spend as much time on fieldwork as she did in the office.

When a position had come up at the Thames Barrier, Leah had accepted it. It was what she had been aiming for ever since she was old enough to know that life was what you made it. It was the final proof that she had made it. To be working in the very place she'd passed every day on the bus on her way to and from school. Not a woman stuck behind the till like her mum, but in charge. A respected professional.

However, that was not how it had gone. It had been the worst six months of her life, living under a constant pressure to find ways of concealing the acute problems affecting the river and surrounding area. The simple truth was that the Barrier was no longer adequate for what was required of it and the entire flood defence system was under strain. Leah had spoken out, tried to make the new management take her comments seriously and do something. Nothing happened. Their prime concern was with their public image, not the public interest.

When her dissatisfaction and concern was at its worst, Michael Searle had appeared. One of the driving forces at the Ministry of BioProspecting and Patenting, the government authority responsible for controlling biotechnological activities in Britain and enforcing legislation, Leah knew his name. He was brilliant, solitary, uncompromising, single-minded and, while many people claimed his acquaintance, few claimed to like him.

Michael made contact out of the blue in April. After a couple of calls, which left Leah none the wiser as to what he wanted from her, he had suggested they should meet. Leah felt comfortable with him straight away, warming to his lack of small talk and his evident passion for what he did. He explained he was in the process of establishing an Industrial Intelligence Unit under the auspices of the Ministry. It would be highly confidential and designed to undertake surveillance and undercover work that could not be handled by other departments. Answerable only to him, the Unit would focus on particularly complicated cases of suspected illegal bioprospecting, where evidence was hard to come by. He was looking for a hydrologist to complete his team, he said, and her name had come up. Was she interested? Leah had listened carefully, asked lots of questions – hardly any of which Michael would answer – then accepted the job on the spot.

Without pausing, he had started to brief her immediately. As if he'd never doubted for a moment that she'd come on board. The Unit's first project was to monitor a voluntary organisation called the People's Network, based in a large warehouse on the south side of the river, known as the Pen. The Network consisted of a core of five people, including the leader, Kellen Harris. Other volunteers and helpers came and went. There was no membership, no salaries.

On the surface, it appeared to be a humanitarian group which provided food, medicine and advice to people living in some of the swamp estates in the eastern suburbs. However, Michael suspected the whole operation was a cover for biopirating activities and that the Network was interested in a group of people known as the Lightermen, who lived in the Marsh Projects just beyond the Barrier. The Unit's job was to find out everything it could about Kellen Harris and the People's Network. If there was anything illegal going on, they were authorised to attempt to stop it in the most appropriate manner. What was extraordinary about this case, Michael explained, was that there was a chance that the Lightermen possessed some sort of unique gene, a super-gene that could have important medical properties. Since virtually no unique genes had been discovered in Europeans, it would be an incredible breakthrough and one that would have enormous ramifications for the biotechnological industry worldwide. From start to finish, the meeting had taken less than an hour. Leah had left, her head swimming with names and facts and figures, wondering what the hell she'd got herself into.

Four months ago. Leah shook her head. She could hardly recognise the person she'd been back then. So much had changed.

She pulled herself together and then turned her attention to what was going on around her. Even though it was early, there was quite a crowd waiting on the jetty. Leah could sense their impatience and anxiety about getting a place on the first boat. Most of them had worked all night on the northside and now wanted nothing more than to get home and spend the rest of the day with their families.

A smartly-dressed man with a palmtop caught her eye. He looked out of place among the exhausted workers in their uniforms, unusual enough for Leah to wonder who he was and what he was doing on this part of the river. She edged nearer. He was talking very softly, as if he didn't want to be overheard.

'One. Number-1075.'

The image of a bottle flashed up on the tiny screen.

'Confirm.'

Wine? Vinegar? It didn't matter. Just a man self-conscious about doing his shopping in public. Nothing to worry about. Leah smiled at how suspicious she was nowadays, then turned away before he noticed her watching him.

It was already very humid. Swarms of mosquitoes were hovering over the banks and Leah was glad of her protective clothing. Most of the regulars, like her, were wearing hats with nets and had covered their arms and legs in spite of the temperature. Nobody bothered to flick the insects away. There were too many to make it worth the effort. However often Leah came this far out, she still couldn't get used to the fact that the area had more in common with the swamps of the

Northern Territories now than the Thames of her childhood. A rumour had even reached the Unit of a case of dengue fever being treated at the Princess Alice Malaria Hospital at Tripcock Point, although the administration there denied it.

A ferry came close and turned, ready to dock and let people aboard. The colony of kites, perched on wooden posts jutting out of the water, took flight, then settled again slightly further away from the human activity. Leah shuffled forward with the others. It was only four weeks since she'd last been here, but she could see that things had deteriorated. The land was more saturated, there were pools higher up the banks and thick residues of blue dye were clinging to the woody stems of the reeds at the water's edge. Some of the grassflats were stained permanently, no longer green at all but a washed-out turquoise.

Leah found herself crushed in the middle of the crowd. She was very small and, with her long, thick plait, she looked like a child from the back. Trying to get a bit of air, she pushed through to the railings, letting the spray fly up into her face and cool her down. Somewhere round Limehouse or Wapping, a helicopter took off. She watched it follow the line of the river, then suddenly swoop right and head out over Kent. It looked like a giant insect. By the end of the day, the sky over London would be thick with them.

Leah felt a sharp prick on her skin. Looking down, she saw a mosquito was stationed motionless on the one patch of exposed flesh where she'd not pulled her sleeve down properly. She slapped her wrist sharply, killing it dead. Red blood spluttered out. Fresh blood.

3

The regular Saturday basketball session was taking place in William Curtis Park. Every few minutes there was a thump as the ball hit the backboard and rattled through the hoop, accompanied by shrieks and yells of encouragement. Some of the residents of the flats in Barnham Street found the noise irritating and complained. This morning, given the court was in direct sunlight, they wouldn't have to wait long before the game was wrapped up. Somewhere, a dog barked. Commentaries from the sightseeing cruisers blared out over the river as usual. Japanese, French, Spanish, any language you wanted was available at a price.

All the shops in Crucifix Lane were open, but there was nobody much about. Anyone who could afford it abandoned London in August for the coast. Britain or abroad, it made little difference. The climate and prices were much the same. The chemist, perhaps hoping to scare his customers into spending money, had hung cardboard models of various insects in his window – mosquitoes, flies, roaches – to advertise his comprehensive selection of preventative medicines and over-the-counter treatments. The publican of The Horns, taking advantage of a free five minutes while trade was slow, was spraying the geraniums in her window boxes. It was the same every summer. If the flowers survived the bugs and pollution, the combination of heat, wind and flash rainstorms tended to finish them off. But she persisted. One of the massage workers from Karma's on the corner waved good morning, but she took no notice, just gathered up her equipment, and went back into the cool interior.

Only the security specialists were doing good business. Alarm systems, human surveillance resources, flood protection warnings, personal safety devices, everything and anything to reassure the modern urban dweller. All above board, of course. Nothing illegal was displayed. An expanse of dark glass protected customers from the casual glances of people passing by outside. The electronic bleep of the door as it opened was familiar to everyone who lived nearby. It drove everyone mad.

Nobody noticed the young woman lying on the pavement in White's Grounds. Even if they had, it was unlikely they'd have done anything. She might be sick. Dead, even. You could never be too careful. Better not to get involved.

The sun climbed higher in the sky.

When Annie came round, she had no idea where she was. Very carefully, she rolled over and propped herself up against the wall of the railway arch, legs spread out in front of her. The light was dancing in front of her eyes and everything was out of focus, all woolly and ragged round the edges.

Gradually, it started to come back to her. The club, the fog, running, the tramp. There was no sign of him now. Even the cardboard box and bottles had gone. If she hadn't been in pain, she would have smiled at the idea of him conscientiously putting his rubbish in the bin before moving on.

Her trousers were ripped on one knee, the green material gaping like a wound, and her hands were grazed and sore from where they'd made the acquaintance of the playground fence, but otherwise not too bad. Cautiously, she put her fingers up to her cheek. It felt a mess. There was a lump the size of a conker and a deep cut, all sticky and rough where the blood had dried. Her lips tasted salty, as if she'd been crying while she was unconscious.

Leaning her throbbing head against the bricks, Annie tried

to persuade herself she was lucky. There didn't seem to be any serious damage. So she'd got a headache, sure, but nothing that a couple of Panadol and a plaster wouldn't fix. She reached into the side pocket of her trousers for her cigarette packet, then remembered she'd run out last night. That was where she'd been going when all this started. To pick up some fags. She reached into her bag for her lucky cigarette, to be smoked in emergencies only. Careful to move as little as possible, she lit up. The nicotine went straight to her head.

'Fuck-ing hell . . .'

The sound of her own voice reverberated in her skull. Annie closed her eyes, trying to remember when she'd last felt this bad. She was very hot. Perhaps she was running a temperature. No sleep, no food and now this. She didn't think she'd be going out again tonight, not in this state.

All she wanted to do was sit quietly on her own on the pavement for the rest of her life. Do nothing. Say nothing. The main thing was that there couldn't have been anybody after her, otherwise she wouldn't be here, but carved up in an alleyway somewhere with more than a headache and a few cuts to bother her.

Was it possible she'd imagined the whole thing? Not the accident, obviously. But the fog and the stalker? It wasn't beyond the bounds of possibility she had imagined she was being followed when there was no one there, even though it was totally out of character for her to get so spooked for no reason. Given the chemicals that had gone up her nose and down her throat, she knew you couldn't always trust the evidence of your own eyes. But fog? That was something else. Annie couldn't believe she'd dream up something like that.

In the end, though, she guessed there was no point getting bothered about it. It didn't actually help matters and she ought to be concentrating on getting herself home and cleaned up. Using the wall as a support, Annie tried to put her weight on her legs. It didn't feel too bad. Without making any sudden movements that might cause her to lose her balance, she slowly pulled herself to her feet. OK. Her arms and legs were stiff, but still in working order and she actually felt less dizzy now she was up. All she needed to do was to check she had enough money for a cab. One was bound to come down Crucifix Lane sooner or later.

What was so outrageous was that in all the time she'd been lying here – however long that actually was – no one had come to her rescue. Seriously bad. Somebody must have walked past and seen her. It was like the time she'd fainted on Embankment Tube Station. Nobody had helped then either, simply stepped over her and carried on about their business.

As she started to feel more herself, Annie suddenly remembered the hieroglyphics she'd seen on the wall as she was passing out. Ignoring the sensible voice in her head telling her to leave it and go home, she thought she might as well take a quick look. She examined the bricks, but found nothing. Nothing at all.

Annie was surprised at how disappointed she felt. Of course, it was hardly likely there'd be something so intricate on a dirty railway arch under London Bridge. But it was odd. She didn't usually have a particularly active visual imagination and her memory of the pattern was so clear. She reckoned she could even put it down on paper if she put her mind to it.

She couldn't find traces of blood on the wall either. That absence was harder to account for. She didn't think she was going crazy, but a bit of corroborative evidence would have been nice, to prove it wasn't all in her imagination. Her cuts and bruises were real enough, sure, but even so . . . Annie had another good look around, just in case she'd missed something. Still nothing.

'Displacement activity,' she said out loud. 'Classic case of. Either that or I've finally lost it . . .'

Her voice sounded reassuringly normal. Not mad at all. Annie stood up. No more excuses. She had to go back to the flat and get it over with.

The heat of the sun hit her as soon as she was out of the shade of the arch. It was incredible, easily as bad as Tunisia had been last summer. She took off her fleece, and tied it round her waist. There was a very strong wind and there were flies everywhere. Annie felt uneasy. Nothing she could put her finger on, just an instinct that something was wrong.

The streets seemed surprisingly empty, even for a Saturday in August. She could hear traffic in the distance, but not a single car had gone by in all the time she'd been in Crucifix Lane. In fact, now she came to think about it, she'd not seen a single person of any description. It was like three o'clock on Cup Final day, everyone indoors, watching the game. And the shops. Crown Security was still there, but it was much bigger than she remembered it. She had no recollection of there being a chemist along here and, although the pub looked much the same, she hadn't noticed all those window boxes earlier when she'd come out of Reboot. It was possible the landlord took them in at night, she supposed.

But it was only when she reached the corner that Annie became seriously worried. Instead of the bookshop, with its ribbons and peacock feathers, there was a sign offering massage. Both the windows had been covered over with black paint and the door by a wrought-iron grille. The name Astrocat had been replaced by Karma's, written in red.

Annie had no idea what the fuck was going on, but she was genuinely jumpy now. Perhaps she had concussion? She rubbed her eyes with her dirty fingers, as if that would get things back to normal. Maybe she was hallucinating? It didn't feel like an illusion, though. More like someone had been messing with the furniture while she was asleep. It was still London, but everything was now in a different place.

It was then that Annie heard the singing. She'd forgotten all about it. It was the same voice, but a different meolody. The purity of it, the beauty of it, made Annie catch her breath, made her remember words a lover had read once to her: 'Music begins when words end.'

Annie forgot all about the missing bookshop and, without questioning her motives, started walking towards the sound.

Like a child of Hamelin, she felt she had no choice but to
follow the music. Along St Thomas Street, down Joiner Street
and under the station, past exotic buildings made of blue, red
and green glass

4

After a few minutes, Annie found herself at the top of a concrete staircase that spiralled down under London Bridge itself. She hesitated, a natural reaction to going down into a secluded place, and asked herself what the fuck she thought she was doing wandering around London when she should be heading home. But it would be a waste to give up now, when she'd come this far. She'd give it another five minutes, find out where the music was coming from. It couldn't hurt.

At the bottom of the steps was a long and dusty subway. It was cooler than up at pavement level, but there were just as many flies and also a disgustingly sweet burning smell. Cheap incense? Grass? Pools of stagnant water lay on the ground near to the walls, although there didn't seem to be any pipes leaking. Annie felt edgier down here, less sure, and the tunnel seemed to just go on and on, leading nowhere. Nonetheless, once her eyes were accustomed to the gloom, she carried on. A little more cautious, a little more slowly, but no less curious.

She kept expecting someone to appear and challenge her, but no one did. She'd got no reason to believe the subway was private, but at the same time the lack of posters and signposts was unusual. At last, the ground started to slope upwards. A few seconds more and she could see daylight again.

The street was cobbled and quite wide and there were still no cars or people. Looking around, she tried to work out precisely where she was. There was a footpath on her right that appeared to lead down to the river, although not to a bit that she recognised. She could just pick out the swathe of bright green rushes along the banks. In the glare of the sun, the water seemed to be a brilliant blue rather than its usual silted brown.

The singing had stopped. Instead, there was a low and syncopated drumming, all a bit weird. Not sure why she was creeping about like some sort of guilty kid, Annie sneaked up to the entrance to a narrow dead-end street where the noise was coming from. On one side, was a high and half-demolished wall, its bricks dangling and gaping like rotten teeth. On the opposite, was a huge warehouse packed with people. Even from several feet away, Annie felt the heat coming off the crowd jammed tightly inside. She moved a little closer. She couldn't see any faces, just the backs of heads, but it all seemed perfectly harmless. Their clothes were a bit unusual, though. A few of them were wearing long tunics with matching trousers.

Annie wasn't sure she liked the look of it. They appeared to be having a good time, but maybe it was some sort of cult. Not that it was likely in a public place in the middle of London on a Saturday morning, but then how would she know? Everything was strange today.

She hesitated for a couple of seconds, not sure what to do, but as usual nosiness won out over sense. She edged up the street, then nipped through the wide cargo doors at the back. The incense she'd smelled in the tunnel was clearly coming from here. Annie couldn't see much, but from the reactions of the men and women closest to her, she worked out there was probably some sort of stage in the middle from where the service or rally, whatever it was, was being conducted.

A single, massive thump, then the drumming stopped. A moment's silence. Then a voice rang out over the crowd, the most beautiful voice Annie had ever heard. Deep and clear and gentle.

'In the name of the spirits of the Earth, the Seas and the Skies . . .'

Annie felt a shiver up her spine. For some reason, she

desperately wanted to get a look at the man with the voice. She stood on tiptoe, straining her neck to see if she could catch sight of him, of anything, in fact, but there were too many people in the way. She couldn't just push past them all. And she didn't want to draw attention to herself. She'd talked her way out of hundreds of awkward situations before, but this was different. Apart from anything else, she looked a total state, with her injured head, ripped trousers and filthy clothes.

Without warning somebody grabbed her arm. Spun her round and pinned her back against the wall. A hand clamped down over her mouth. Annie's heart leaped against her ribs, like an animal against the bars of its cage.

'How did you get here?'

She was too shocked to speak. The man's fingers were pressing her bare arm roughly and she could smell his breath. Common sense told her not to struggle, that he was certainly stronger than she was. Even though she was tall, his body loomed over hers. She couldn't see much of his face under his sports cap, just a glimpse of pale skin and peculiar green eyes. Annie turned her face sideways so as not to meet his gaze.

'Tell me who you are,' he hissed.

'I just . . .'

Although he didn't step back, he loosened his hold on her. Annie was conscious of his physical presence and the urgency behind his questions. Then, for some reason, he put his fingers to the wounds on her head. Gentle. Annie winced as he touched her, knowing that tenderness could be more threatening than violence.

'When did you come through? Please tell me.'

Annie took her chance. She spat into his face and jerked her knee up into his groin. As he doubled up, she twisted out of his grasp and ducked out under his arm.

The service had ended and the crowd was already streaming out through the door. Running against the tide, Annie charged into the mass of people, keeping her head down. No one seemed to be paying her any attention, but she kept going, feeling the tension in her neck and back as she had earlier in the fog. The pricking of her skin, the anticipation, just waiting to be caught. Any second now.

There was a flight of stairs in the corner. Annie sprinted across the hall, then up the steps two by two. There were more than she'd expected and she could feel the strain on her knees as the cut on her leg split open again. At the top, she found herself in a long, narrow gallery that overlooked the hall. She scanned the area, looking for the blue baseball cap, but she couldn't see it anywhere. She took no relief from that. He could be on the stairs already.

Annie knew she'd fucked up big time. She should have got out of the warehouse, not trapped herself inside. She'd have a hard job explaining what she was doing up here, especially if the man who'd grabbed her turned out to be in charge. But the bottom line was that he was down there, in that big, emptying space. She couldn't risk it. She'd have to go on. The corridor looked the same to both left and right. Wooden floors, small square windows with shutters, no doors she could see. Which way? Eeny, meeny, miny, mo. She went left and walked quickly along until she reached a door. She turned the handle, then slipped inside.

The room was very hot and stuffy, but it felt safe. Annie leaned back against the wooden door, her chest burning and listened to the sound of her blood pounding in her ears, before noticing a chair just a few feet in front of her. Too tired to think about what she was doing, she just had to sit down before she fell down. She had no physical reserves left.

Annie lost track of the time. Let herself drift. She knew she should not be letting her guard down, but kept bargaining with herself for just a few more minutes rest. A clicking sound in the corner of the room brought her to her senses. In the shadows, she hadn't noticed the second door. She was suddenly completely wide awake and alert, turned in the direction of the noise. To her horror, she realised someone was walking into the room.

'Hey,' he said, sounding surprised.

Annie leaped up, knocking the chair flying, and tried to get hold of the door handle. But her palms were slippery and her panic make her clumsy. She couldn't get out. He was coming towards her. She could feel him getting closer and closer.

'Hey,' he said. 'It's OK.'

This time she recognised the voice. It was the man who'd conducted the service, not the one who'd been after her. Her legs almost gave way with the relief of it.

'Downstairs,' she started to explain. 'Someone attacked me.'

He put out his hands to hold her up. 'Ssh. Don't try to talk.'

'His eyes were too green. They were all wrong.'

'It's OK,' he repeated gently. 'You're all right.'

Annie allowed the man to guide her across the room, without a fight, thinking she was going to pass out. Somehow, she managed to put one foot in front of the other until they got to the bed. Annie was aware of his tight black curls brushing her cheek and the faint scent of vanilla on his skin.

She was now so far gone that she let him remove her shoes and lay her legs on the sheets without arguing. Stupid to put herself in the hands of a man she didn't know the first thing about, but she was too exhausted to care. Annie let him clean the cuts on her head and knee, then wipe the palms of her hands. She half-heard the strike of a match and the hiss of candles. The last thing she remembered before falling asleep was his fingers slipping something between her lips and then a wonderful sweetness, like honey, in her mouth.

'Sleep well, traveller,' he whispered.

5

The block in Weston Street was not prepossessing. A tall, faceless concrete development, built in the lean years of the new century, it had not appealed to the people for whom it was intended. A bit too far away from the river to be exclusive, it was now filled with men and women passing through. Nobody talked to anyone else in the hallways or took in one another's packages. The place smelled of misjudgement and disappointment.

It was perfect for Michael Searle's purposes. He needed a private and safe base for his new Industrial Intelligence Unit, away from the glasshouse environment of the Ministry of BioProspecting and Patenting. Not only was it essential to keep the identities of the six members of the Unit confidential, but he wanted somewhere secure for briefings and for storing files and data concerning the Unit's operations, somewhere that could not be accessed by anyone within the Ministry. Weston Street was within striking distance. It was also less than half a mile away from the target of the Unit's first case, the People's Network.

Once the necessary paperwork had been dealt with – none of it in his own name – Michael had installed the security system, which allowed access to members of the Unit and no one else, taught the computer to recognise their voices and got an intranet system up and running. He even worked out a route for getting in and out which avoided the building's CCTV cameras.

By the end of the first week in April, everyone in the Unit had been trained to use the systems and was ready to go. The only thing Michael hadn't taken into account was what the flat might be like in the height of summer. And if it had been hot in June and July, August looked like breaking all records and the air conditioning was less than efficient. Already, Michael had lost count of how many times it had broken down.

The light came on automatically as he walked through the front door into the featureless white hall. No attempt had been made to humanise the environment with pictures or rugs or books. The kitchen had the bare essentials, nothing more. Fridge, ralentisseur, microwave, a few jars of coffee, tea, water and a couple of bottles of good malt whisky in the cupboard. The bathroom was the same – a bar of soap, towels, toilet paper. Even the bedroom was anonymous. Three single beds and a mattress propped up against the wall. The pillows and sheets were stored in the built-in cupboards which filled one side of the wall. They were rarely used.

Leah had left his netputer neatly on the floor outside the sitting room so he couldn't miss it. He picked it up, deactivated the alarm on the door, then went in, kicking the door shut behind him. This was the heart of the flat, the command centre where everything happened. A screen and speakers took up most of one wall and there were additional speakers in the ceiling above the cupboards. Everything was silver and black. Someone had once remarked that it looked more like the bridge of the Enterprise than anything you'd expect to find in Weston Street, of all places.

Michael was still struggling to keep his temper under control. Clutching the netputer in one hand, he dropped his head and forced himself to take deep breaths. He was furious with himself. To have gone to the Pen at all was stupid enough. But to be so taken by surprise by the unexpected appearance of the traveller as to approach her directly . . . Christ, what in hell's name had he been thinking of?

There were two possible explanations for her arrival, neither particularly reassuring in the circumstances. The first – which assumed she was genuine – was that her presence signified something. Michael didn't know what, how, why or even if, but he nonetheless remained convinced that there had to be a reason behind the arrival of another traveller. Was it a coincidence that she had turned up at such a sensitive time? The day before the Unit were to launch a counter-attack on the Network?

However, if she wasn't a genuine traveller, then Michael had to face the fact that he'd been set up. If Kellen Harris suspected the People's Network was under surveillance – and that someone else besides Harris himself knew about the travellers – he might have planted the woman as bait. Either to flush his opponent out, or, more likely, to try to divert attention away from the Network's visit to the Marsh Projects in the morning.

Michael put the netputer on the thin silver workcounter in front of him, knowing that he had to put the tall, dark-haired woman out of his mind and concentrate on tomorrow. Nothing else mattered at this point. He had to finalise the timings of each stage of Operation Bayoux, download the data Leah had gathered this morning on the increasing destabilisation of the river environment, and revise entry and exit routes and areas of cover if necessary. The last thing he needed was anyone getting trapped.

'Activate.'

The blank screen flickered into life at the sound of Michael's voice.

'Log on.'

The date and time flashed up and the computer greeted him in its precise and emotionless tone.

'Welcome. Please enter your password.'

He wrote it on the pad in front of him – b a y o u x – and waited for the computer to accept the code and his handwriting.

'Password verified. Which software do you require?'

'Voice recognition.'

Michael paused as the computer booted up, then punched the transmit function key.

'Since your last download, you have created . . . two new files. Continue?'

'Confirm,' he replied.

It took less than a second for a text version of the first file to appear on the screen. Michael took a quick look at it.

'Save *kh/08.02* to kellendirectory.'

'Saved as *kh/2008.08.02*. Exit file?'

'Confirm.'

Moments later, Michael was scanning the second file. Leah had succeeded in acquiring all the information he'd asked for. As always, her efficiency made his life a hell of a lot easier.

With one eye on the time, he got to work incorporating the new material. He didn't have long. He was due at the Ministry to report to his European Consortium partners at twelve-thirty. The agenda had been circulated already and the discussion documents were tabled, but Michael knew it was still going to be a difficult meeting.

Within half an hour, he'd finished everything he needed to do.

'Save *md/08.02* to marshdirectory.'

'Saved as *md/2008.08.02*. Exit file?'

'Confirm.'

Michael walked to the safe, put his hand on the wall and waited.

'Identity confirmed.'

The panel opened. Putting the netputer inside, he took out a small box containing a pair of blue lenses and swapped them for the green pair in his eyes. The whole process took less than a minute and totally altered the look of his face. Even his own brother wouldn't know him.

Outside on the street, the lunchtime crowd was heading for restaurants and bars. It reminded Michael he'd not eaten in a while. He took out his smart card and joined the queue outside the deli on the corner to buy a sandwich and an iced tea. As he waited, he discreetly observed the people around him. A couple of young women stood in the line smoking, a dispatch rider in black leathers, a few medical types in whites from St Claire's Hospital and the Coma Hospital round the corner. Just people going about their normal Saturday business.

'Afternoon, Kaleb,' he said at the counter.

'Sir. The usual?'

'Yes please.'

'Sir. To go?'

'Yes. Thank you.'

Michael watched in silence while his food was prepared and his card debited, then walked fast along the river path eating as he went and up onto the bridge. He tasted nothing. As he approached the north side of the river, he looked at the digital clock on the side of the Ministry as he always did. *2008.08.02/12:36:02/+ 35°c.* Christ. No wonder he felt bad. The sooner he was inside, the better.

The security procedures occupied him no more than a matter of minutes, then he was through to the cool outer lobby. The receptionist stood up as he entered.

'Good afternoon, sir.'

'Afternoon, Steve,' he replied. 'Have my guests arrived yet?'

'I've put them in the Conference Chamber, sir.'

'Are we waiting for anyone?'

'No, sir. They're all here.'

'Thank you.'

He walked briskly up the escalator and headed along a walkway corridor towards a glass door marked 'Code Area 3 – Restricted Access'. Michael placed his hand flat against the recognition panel.

'Identify.'

He leaned towards the wall to answer.

'MS/028.'

The door slid open. He carried on right to the end of the corridor. The Conference Chamber was to his left. Michael paused outside to straighten his jacket and tie. Over the past couple of weeks, he'd grown suspicious that one of the members

31

of the Consortium was not playing straight. He'd had the strong feeling that at least one person, possibly two, was using the Consortium in order to gain information to advance their own private business interests, legal or otherwise. There was an obvious candidate, but he was trying not to let personal antipathy influence his thinking.

Michael hated partnerships of any kind, particularly when several countries were involved, but as usual he'd had no choice. Without business sponsorship, the Unit simply couldn't function. It was Consortium money that was paying for the Lighterman project and the last couple of months of surveillance of the Network. Despite this, Michael had still told them very little. He wasn't prepared to jeopardise the success of the operation if there was even the slightest chance of a leak.

The Consortium had no idea how far advanced his plans against the Network actually were. In fact, he hadn't even mentioned the Network to them by name so far. When he walked through the door in a couple of seconds time, not only was he going to have to justify the amount of Consortium money he had already spent monitoring the Lightermen, but he was also going to have to come up with a plausible explanation as to why – if he was asking for their support for an operation on the Marsh Projects – he wouldn't tell them anything about it.

Michael took a deep breath, then opened the door.

'Ladies and gentlemen,' he said, 'please accept my apologies for keeping you waiting.'

6

Annie's dream was a collage of her day. Like a sheet of card covered with tiny scraps of paper, feathers and silk. She remembered shapes, faces, snatches of all the things that had happened to her, everything magnified and distorted by sleep, at once familiar and unrecognisable. The ribbons from the bookshop were hanging around the Celtic cross painted on the sign for the club. Hundreds of flowers were covering the pub, but when she reached out to pick them, they all turned into notes of music and flew away. Tiny black dots in the sky. Then it was raining and the world was getting darker and she was being chased by a snarling dog wearing a baseball cap, its mouth red and vicious. At the moment it pounced, she woke up with a start.

Annie lay on the bed with her heart thudding and her eyes wide as saucers, wondering if it really could be true that she was in a strange man's bed, in the middle of a warehouse, with a bad headache and no idea of the time. Once the room stopped spinning, she sat up and looked around. One of the candles had blown itself out, but it was just light enough to see that the walls were covered with tapestries. Templar crosses, gryphons, heraldic animals. No people. Thin strips of cream and white hung from the ceiling, like a field of streamers, and there were four or five sand-coloured mobiles – yellows and transparent browns and the lightest of greys – surrounding wind chimes, which swayed very slightly. As she turned her head, she could see the chair she'd sat on was back on its feet. Next to it, there was a small table carved from a pale grained wood. A pretty weird bedroom.

Annie flopped back on to the bed.

'Shit,' she said.

For a while, she did nothing. She was comfortable watching the moon through the high casement window casting its white shadow on the floor. In any case, she didn't have a clue what she ought to do. The air smelt slept in and it was much cooler now, so she must have been asleep for hours.

Wondering where the man who'd taken care of her had disappeared to, Annie dangled her feet over the edge of the bed. The wooden boards were deliciously cold. She hesitated, then decided that she might as well be clean and presentable when she said her thank-yous and goodbyes. She could see a shower, toilet and basin through a third door, next to a chest of drawers, so she went to investigate. It all looked promising, although she didn't want to take liberties. Quickly pulling off her clothes, she laid them in a heap in the doorway, to alert anyone to the fact that she was in there and hoping he wouldn't mind.

Annie worked out the controls, then stood in the shower letting the cool water splash over her. When she'd finished, she wrapped a towel around herself, then wandered back into the bedroom rubbing her hair dry. At that point, she noticed someone had laid out a pair of trousers and matching light-blue tunic at the end of the bed. For her? She felt a bit strange about putting on someone else's stuff. In any case, she'd always had a bit of a problem with clothes that made everyone look the same and half the people at the service earlier had been done up in this get-up. Like it was some sort of uniform. When she was six, she'd been chucked out of the Brownies for defacing her tie and cutting holes in her beret because she didn't want to look like everyone else. One of those rare occasions when her grandad had laughed, although he was supposed to be telling her off.

Annie looked at her torn trousers and her vest, which reeked of sweat and fear and London pavements, and thought she'd rather be comfortable. Even though the trousers were a bit tighter than she liked, the tunic was pretty good. They probably belonged to a man. At five foot ten, Annie had to look hard for women's clothes she liked that fitted her.

Feeling much better, she decided she might have a quick snoop before someone came to get her, but there was nothing much more to see. There were no books, no sound system or CDs, no television. She tried the handle of the small door in the corner of the room, but it was locked. So was the ward-robe. She poked and prodded around, peering half-heartedly at the tapestries and the furniture, but within ten minutes she was bored.

It was beginning to worry that no one was going to come to get her. Perhaps he'd gone out and no one else knew she was here. For the first time since waking up and finding herself in this bizarre situation, Annie started to feel nervous. Her bag and trainers were nowhere to be seen either.

She decided she'd better go and find out what was going on. She picked up a candle, padded across the room in her bare feet and went out into the corridor. It was completely dark and she couldn't find a light switch anywhere, so she tiptoed along with the flame throwing up long, distorted shadows on the wall. Outside, she could hear low growls of thunder. Inside, it was completely silent, except for the whine of something that sounded like a mosquito. Obviously it couldn't be. Britain's biggest selling point? No serious biting bugs . . .

The warehouse didn't feel deserted. There was a warmth to it that suggested people were somewhere about. Annie supposed that if the worst came to the worst, she could just walk out. But she didn't want to go without retrieving her shoes and her bag with her purse and keys in it. Mrs Hunt next door had got a spare, but Annie couldn't face the thought of her. She'd want to quiz her about Dan and ask how her grandad was, even though she'd hated his guts until he got ill. Thinking about the conversation helped strengthen Annie's resolve to stay until morning.

The hall where the service had been was empty now. She could still smell traces of incense in the air and she could just make out the marks on the ground where something heavy had stood. She cast her eyes around, until she spotted a crack of light over in the far corner and found herself standing in front of a huge wooden sliding door. Her grandad would have known what sort of cargo would have been stored in this warehouse, just from the shape of the doors and windows. She had no idea.

It was too heavy to open. Putting the candle down on the ground, she tried again with both hands. She heard a click, like a switch being thrown, then the next time she tried the door it opened without any problem. Feeling somewhat like Alice in search of the White Rabbit, Annie walked through an empty room to another door which was clearly not part of the original warehouse structure. It was made of white metal and completely flat. She ran her fingers over the smooth surface, feeling for a catch or handle, when she felt it sliding open beneath her. She snatched her hand back as if she had been burned.

Annie was blinded by a brilliant light shining right in her face. She lifted up her hands to shield her eyes.

'Hey. Look who's woken up.'

She couldn't make out where he was, but it was great to hear a familiar voice. Second time today he'd rescued her.

'Where are you?' she said. 'I can't see a thing.'

Straight away, there he was. Right next to her.

'Everybody,' he said, taking her hand, 'this is Annie. Annie Jones.'

7

Annie felt at a total disadvantage, standing like an idiot in the doorway with a load of strangers staring at her. She didn't know whether to say hello, just smile or do nothing. She felt very tall and very conspicuous.

'I'm Kellen,' he said. 'I don't think we've been properly introduced.'

'Hi.'

'And you won't remember any of the names,' he continued, 'but this is Leah, Jonas, Malik, Vicky and Lonnie.'

Annie looked around the room and smiled awkwardly.

'You're right,' she agreed, 'I won't remember. But, hi, anyway.'

One of the women shoved up and made room for her on the sofa.

'Vicky,' she said, introducing herself. 'I see the clothes are OK then.'

Annie looked down at her arms and legs.

'The trousers are a bit tight, but otherwise they're fine, thanks.'

'Good.'

'Was it you who brought them up for me?'

Vicky shook her head. 'I think Kellen did.'

To her utter astonishment, Annie blushed.

'I couldn't find my shoes, though,' she added, talking to cover her embarrassment. 'Or my bag, for that matter.'

'Sorry. Don't know anything about it,' replied Vicky. 'I've only just got in. I didn't even know you were here until about half an hour ago.'

'What time is it?'

'About ten.'

Vicky didn't show much inclination to talk further, so Annie was able to sit back and observe. Someone got her a beer and, a little later, some draw came her way. Nobody hassled her, just left her alone and carried on with their conversations around her. People came and went, changed the music. Every now and again Annie recognised a track, although nothing sounded quite right. A dance version of 'Orinoco Flow', something appalling by Belinda Carlisle, a bit of Fairground Attraction with a manic bass line. All pretty old stuff. Vicky got up and her place was taken by the skinny Indian guy, who turned out to be Jonas. Little by little, as the grass started to take effect, Annie stopped feeling like the girlfriend being taken home to meet the parents and started to relax.

It was a bizarre room, a most peculiar mixture of ancient and modern. There were tapestries on the walls, just like the ones she'd seen in Kellen's room upstairs. The sofa and chairs were nothing special. She couldn't see a television or music system here either, but the sound quality, wherever it was coming from, was incredible. There were four massive black speakers in each of the corners of the room and a load of computer stuff, although Annie couldn't quite work out what she was looking at. What she could see was that one entire wall was covered by a large screen, at least ten foot by ten. Watching videos on that must be like going to the cinema.

The more she relaxed, the harder she was finding it to keep her eyes off Kellen. He was one of the most beautiful men she'd ever seen. Very pale skin, piercing brown eyes, blue–black curly hair to his shoulders and an insolent, sexy mouth. His fingers were exceptionally long and thin. Annie became conscious of every move she made, sure that he was watching her too. She could feel her skin prickling all over with anticipation.

At last, he came over. Jonas moved to let Kellen squeeze

himself in next to her. For a moment he said nothing, just gazed at her as if he'd never seen anyone quite so wonderful before.

'What?' she said. 'Why are you looking at me like that?'

'Because you're beautiful.'

Annie raised her eyebrows. 'That's a bit . . .'

He shrugged. 'I've been waiting all day to tell you that.'

'Well, thank you then.'

'For what?'

'Your patience.'

He laughed. 'It's no problem.'

'Seriously, though,' she said after a moment, 'I'm sorry about earlier. I'm not usually like that and it's so embarrassing, passing out like some, well . . . But I've had this weirdest day. I even got knocked out for a while.'

Kellen just looked at her.

'Then – and I know this is going to sound completely ridiculous – I heard this singing. And, I don't know why, I just decided to find out where it was coming from.'

'And did you?'

'Well, obviously. That's why I ended up here. It was coming from here.'

Kellen frowned. 'Singing,' he repeated. 'I'm not sure that—'

'Just before the drumming started,' Annie continued. 'In the hall earlier.'

He still looked confused.

'I came in to get a better look and that's when I heard you talking. Then this man grabbed me, for no reason at all. He kept asking me how I'd got here.'

Annie noticed a shift in Kellen's expression.

'Can you remember what he looked like?'

He was suddenly watchful, interested, as if the answer was important.

'Tall, white, wearing a blue baseball cap so I didn't get a good look at his face. But he had these weird green eyes. Synthetic, almost.'

She hesitated, then added, 'Why? Do you think you know him?'

'Just interested,' he replied. 'Anyway, that's how you ended up in my bed.'

Annie nodded, amazed they were flirting so outrageously. 'And very nice it was too.'

'After all that, I'm not surprised you were feeling bad.'

'No.'

The sexual tension between them sparked like electricity. Annie couldn't remember being so immediately physically attracted to a man. She was no longer aware of the others, only of Kellen. The desire to reach out and touch him was so overwhelming that she put her hands under her legs, so as not to do something she'd regret.

As if Kellen had been thinking the same thing, he leaned across and started to stroke her cheek with the back of his hand.

'Annie,' he said quietly. 'I think we need to talk.'

She looked at him, surprised by the tone of his voice. The last thing she wanted right now was to talk. She simply wanted to kiss him.

'Talk?'

'I need to ask you something.'

The expression on his face made her pull back a little.

'OK. Ask away?'

Kellen hesitated. 'Do you know where you are?'

Assuming the question was not supposed to be taken literally, Annie was surprised. Could it be she'd finally stumbled across a responsible man, who didn't want to go for it until he was absolutely sure that a) she knew what she was doing, and b) wasn't still suffering from the after-effects of the bump on her head. A miracle . . .

'Near enough,' she said. 'Somewhere near London Bridge.'

He looked serious now, as if trying to read the message behind her words.

'I didn't mean it quite like that. Let me put it another way. Do you know what day it is?'

'Saturday,' she said, a bit puzzled. 'Unless it's later than I think. In which case, I guess it's Sunday. But look, this is sweet of you, but you don't have to worry. Promise. I'm not going to change my mind in the morning.'

The expression on Kellen's face threw her, then she went cold. Maybe she'd misread the signs and he wasn't interested in her in that way at all.

'Shit,' she said. 'I'm sorry, I . . . I'm really embarrassed.'

'Hey, don't.' said Kellen quickly. 'It's me. I'm doing this all wrong. But I — we — didn't want to freak you out.'

Annie was suddenly aware that the atmosphere in the room had changed. The music was still playing, but the background hum of voices had stopped. As if everyone was listening, waiting for something.

'Freak me out about what?'

'Have you looked in the mirror since you got here?'

'This is getting worse,' she said under her breath. 'Are you trying to tell me I've got something stuck in my teeth?'

She didn't mean to sound so defensive, but couldn't help it. The way the conversation was going was too humiliating.

'Now I've offended you,' he said. 'I'm sorry.'

He reached out and touched the skin above her right eye with his fingers, at exactly the same point as the man who'd gone for her earlier.

'I wondered if you'd seen this?'

Annie was starting to get pissed off. Intense was good, but this was going too far.

'I told you how I got that, Kellen.'

Instead of answering — or apologising again — he got up, went and said something to one of the other women, then came and sat back down. Annie could feel his leg pressing against hers and the heat of his skin through the thin material of her trousers and felt a kick at the base of her stomach. She leaned back, the material of the sofa rough on her bare neck, and wondered what the fuck was going on.

The woman reappeared holding a small mirror.

'Thanks, Leah,' said Kellen. 'Can you all give us a moment?'

Without a word, everybody stood up and went out. Some-one killed the music as they left. Annie heard the slide of the door, then a sharp click as it shut. Silence. Except for the very loud thumping noise in her head.

'Here you go,' he said. 'You need to see.'

Annie didn't want to take the mirror. She was rarely fazed, but partly because she liked Kellen, she resented being manipulated into playing some sort of game when she had no idea of the rules. She just didn't know how to read the situation.

'You're making me nervous . . .'

He didn't answer. Just kept looking at her with an expression of such concern that, in the end, it seemed rude not to take the mirror. Keeping her hand steady, Annie lifted it up to her face. She was slightly paler than usual, sure, but there was the same wide mouth, same nose and brown eyes. Only one thing was different. On her temple, just above the cut on her cheek, was a small black symbol. A thin crooked cross, like a tattoo.

It didn't feel like a scratch or cut. She rubbed at it with her fingers.

'It won't come off like that,' said Kellen.

'What the fuck is it?'

'Annie—'

She felt seriously angry now. Didn't bother to hide it.

'How did you know my name anyway?'

'I looked in your bag. It didn't seem right, with you sleeping upstairs, not knowing who you were.'

'There wasn't anything with my name . . .'

She broke off. The 'this-isn't-working-out' letter from Dan was in there. When she'd first read it, she'd been more hurt by him putting her name in full on the envelope, than by what it actually said. Annie L. Jones. As if they hardly knew each other.

'Look,' Kellen said. 'If I shouldn't have done that, then I'm sorry. But forget your bag for now.'

Annie looked mutinous. Like she might swing for him any minute.

'If you say so.'

'I know what I'm about to say is going to sound crazy, like

I've lost it. All I can say is that I am telling you the truth. Even though it sounds totally impossible.'

'I still haven't a clue what you're going on about,' she snapped. 'And to tell *you* the truth, you're getting on my nerves.'

'OK. The mark you've got on your head? I swear I've got nothing to do with it, but I have seen something like it before on somebody else.'

'I don't know why you're making such a big deal of this, Kellen. It's just a simple scratch.'

The words were barely out of Annie's mouth when she knew, somehow, that it wasn't a simple anything. She shivered.

'A few months ago,' he continued, 'another woman turned up here out of nowhere. Mary Royle. Just like you, she had this odd black mark on her head. Not quite the same as yours, but near enough.'

'Hardly out of nowhere,' Annie said. 'I was only round the corner in Crucifix Lane.'

'Annie, I can't think of a better way to say this. It is Saturday the second of August. But this is 2008. Not whenever you come from.'

'2008?' she repeated. 'You mean, the year 2008?'

Kellen nodded. There was no trace of a smile on his face. 'I said it would sound crazy.'

Annie burst out laughing.

'Yeah, right, and – no wait, don't tell me – you're a reincarnation of a tree spirit from an ancient forest and we met in a former life. Shit, Kellen. I've had some lines in my time, but give me a break . . .'

Annie didn't know how she was expecting him to react, but she was unprepared for the coldness in his voice.

'Don't laugh at me,' he said.

'Hold it,' she yelled suddenly. 'You've obviously been sitting here all this time laughing at me, for fuck's sake. Like I'm some sort of gullible kid. So, look, I'm sorry if I've offended your delicate sensibilities. But I reckon the score's just about even.'

She was furious now, not altogether sure whether she was embarrassed or upset or both. Whatever, she needed to stop shouting and leave before things got nasty. She got up and tried to give the impression of being in control.

'I'm going to go now,' she said, still not really wanting to. 'So if you could just get me my bag and shoes?'

'I'll prove it to you.'

'Shit, Kellen. Don't you ever give up?'

Taking her by surprise, he cupped the back of her neck with one hand, the other on her waist, parted her lips with his tongue.

It wasn't that her resolve crumbled. She didn't want to go, anyway. Not really. It was more that, like so many times before, Annie let her body do the thinking for her.

They kissed.

8

Sunday 3 August

Annie and Kellen walked slowly along the river path holding hands, like any other couple. Their body language was the usual first-date mixture of intimacy and awkwardness, but they were a perfect physical match. Both dark, both tall, both pale.

The thunderstorm earlier had driven the flies away. Now, the air smelled clean and washed, as if it had been laundered. The sky was purple, peppered with stars, and the reflection from the streetlamps shimmered on the surface of the river like a string of white pearls. An owl's brown wings flashed brightly in the moonlight, before swooping back into the shadows.

The city looked like a painting. All the Londons it had been – and would be – superimposed one upon the other. Shadows becoming light, new buildings taking the place of old. The skyline was forever changing. Architecture was higher and thinner and sharper now, making familiar landmarks look squat, overweight. In time, the fashion would change again. Nothing is contemporary for long.

There had been an enormous amount of building in the frenzied years leading up to the Millennium. A tower had been erected to the south of Southwark Bridge, but no one could remember why it had been put up, or who owned it. It had already been empty for years, standing like a sentry by the river as if its sole purpose was to guard the bridge itself.

A little downriver, a new bridge spanned the water like an arc of quicksilver and on the bank opposite, an intimidating square glass building, the colour of blood, dominated the landscape. The Ministry of BioProspecting and Patenting, bearing witness to the new god Science. The digital display on the river side flashed out the date and the time and the temperature, come rain or shine. Constant reminders that life moved on.

The inhabitants of the twenty-first-century city understood – as their earliest ancestors had understood – that the heart of the city was the river. The difference was that they believed they had tamed it.

'It's weird how the light makes the water seem to look blue,' said Annie, after a while.

Kellen smiled. 'It is blue. Blue dye, pumped in on a regular basis. Not toxic, they tell us . . .'

'Yeah, right. It never is. But what a bizarre thing to do. Doesn't it leave horrible stains all up the walls and the boats and stuff when the tide goes out? It must look awful.'

'No more tides.'

'What do you mean, no more tides?'

'The river was stabilised about five years ago or so.'

'You're kidding me.'

'Would I lie to you?' he said. 'Anyway, it's not that big a deal. They'd been talking for ages about converting it from a tidal to a non-tidal river. Years before they actually got around to doing it.'

'Well, I never heard anything about it.'

'Don't you come from London?'

'Yes, I do. Obviously I wasn't listening to the right radio station.'

Annie and Kellen had spent hours talking, sitting close together on the sofa in the Pen. Actually, Kellen had done most of the talking. Annie wasn't sure how to react to Kellen's announcement that it was now 2008. She'd never been remotely interested in physics or astronomy, but she knew enough to know that time travel was not scientifically possible. Parallel universes, flying machines belonged in books and sci-fi movies and anything involving Michael J. Fox. She'd always thought of it as a boys' thing really. Not aimed at her. She'd gone with

Dan to see *The Fifth Element*, and quite liked it. But the almost total absence of women in those sorts of films always irritated the hell out of her. And it pissed her off even more that nobody seemed to notice. She had tried explaining her feelings to Dan once, asked him how he'd feel watching a movie with only women in it. After he'd finished making obscene comments and realised she wanted a serious answer, he'd accused her of being paranoid.

The thing was, Annie believed Kellen was serious about it. Either that or he was a fucking brilliant actor. But she had a good feeling about him – he was attractive, funny, sensitive – and she wanted to get to know him better. He didn't seem manipulative or deceitful or, for that matter, mad.

While he was talking, she had been trying to come up with a rational explanation. She'd narrowed it down to four options, all of them ridiculous. One: she was the victim of a massive conspiracy to persuade her, for some unknown reason, that she had gone forward in time – that would mean the different London and everything around her was an optical illusion and Kellen and the others were all in on it. Ridiculous theory number two: someone had slipped her something and the whole thing was a chemically-induced hallucination – but she knew what it felt like to be tripping and this was not it. Everything was far too physically real and normal. Three: she was dreaming – the same arguments applied as in the drug option. None of them made sense. And none of them accounted for the weird climate. Or the flies and mosquitoes. Which led to option four: she was in the future.

In the end, Annie realised she could either have herself sectioned or roll with it, treat Kellen like any other guy she was interested in and see how things developed.

'Hey, you look like you're in a world of your own. Are you OK?'

She smiled. 'Fine. Just thinking.'

'We can go back if you're tired.'

'No, really. I'm fine. Tell me about the river and the tides. It sounds very dramatic.'

'Actually, the whole Canute thing did happen on the banks of the Thames. Not at the seaside at all.'

Annie raised her eyebrows. 'Very impressive . . .'

'I aim to please.'

She smiled. 'So, go on then. Wow me some more.'

'You're serious?'

'Absolutely.'

Kellen moved to a bench overlooking the river, then sat down and put his arm around her. Annie snuggled in close.

'OK?'

She nodded.

'Good. Even as far back as the 1980s, town planners and architects and developers, some politicians too, thought London could be transformed if the Thames was sorted out. The idea was to regenerate it – new housing, leisure stuff, proper cruisers – make it productive and usable twenty-four hours a day rather than just this north/south dividing line. Everyone had their own ideas, but the one thing they agreed on was that nothing substantial could be achieved if it remained tidal. There were problems with silting, the flats at low tide were ugly and it always looked dirty, because the tides stirred up the mud all the time.'

'I can't believe I never heard anything about all this?'

'How old were you in the mid-80s?'

Annie laughed. 'Good point. No more than ten or eleven.'

'There you go, although that was just the beginning of it. There were big objections, from environmentalists, council tenants, you name it, but it made no difference. In 2003, or thereabouts, a deal to permanently dam the river was put up by an alliance of investors, politicians, planners and men with deep pockets. It went through on the nod.'

'Fucking amazing.'

'You said it,' said Kellen. 'And fucking fast work. Less than three years from start to finish.'

'So who decided how high the water should be?'

Kellen shrugged. 'Don't know. But it's set at approximately midway between the highest ever and lowest ever recorded levels. If you're really interested, you should ask Leah about it.'

'Leah?'

'She was at the Pen earlier. Small woman. Long blonde plait. Serious.'

'Yeah, of course. The one who wasn't Vicky.'

'Right. Vicky's the fierce one. Leah is a hydrologist and knows anything there is to know about the river and how it functions, if you're interested. As part of the stabilisation of the river, the Thames Barrier had to be raised to control the level of the water. She worked there for a while.'

Since Annie's interest in the Thames was limited to Kellen telling her about it, she thought it unlikely she'd be taking up his suggestion.

'And does it work?'

'It depends who you ask. And, more to the point, what your priorities are. Money or people.'

Annie was surprised by the edge to Kellen's voice. One minute, he was laid back and flirting, the next, he'd gone all zealous on her. Not sure what was going on, she turned and saw he was gazing into the middle distance as though he had the cares of the world on his shoulders.

'What is it?'

At first, she thought he hadn't heard her. Then she felt him pull her closer.

'I'm sorry,' he said, giving her a quick kiss on the cheek. 'There's just such a lot of bad stuff going on. Stuff you wouldn't believe. It gets to me sometimes, that's all.'

Annie looked at his expression and her heart gave a lurch.

'Do you want to talk about it?'

He shook his head. 'Don't worry. I'll be OK in a minute.'

For a moment, Annie was quiet. Trying to think of something to recover the mood.

'My grandad used to work the river,' she said, after a while.

No response. Resting her hand lightly on his leg, to let him know she was there if he needed her, Annie let her own thoughts free-fall too. It was ironic, all things considered, to find herself here on this particular stretch of river. Her grandad's favourite bit. When she was a kid, he'd brought her down here from time to time, to get out in the fresh air and away from the noise of the flats. It was the only time she remembered him being happy. Most of the river frontage to the south was derelict back then, the windows all blown out. No glass, no shutters, just rows of blind eyes trapped behind black iron railings. Everywhere there was a sense of dispossession, the smell of time suspended.

Slipping her child's hand into his, Annie would listen as he pointed at the huge loading doors of the warehouses and told her of the days the clippers sailed upriver on the tide to unload their cargoes. Tea from India, sugar from Barbados, fruit and spices and oils and meat, stories about the shiploads of bones that arrived from Africa, ready to be boiled into glue and soap and the poisonous spiders hidden in the straw. How, when they started digging in Rotherhithe, whole skeletons of whales were found in the mud, a bizarre testimony to the once powerful presence of the Icelandic shipping fleets. He remembered the men from when he was an apprentice, big, burly sailors who spoke no English but knew how to work. Sometimes, when she was feeling especially brave, he'd scare her with the story of the time he unpacked a crate of lion skulls and was nearly bitten by a deadly snake.

But she had grown up and lost interest in his old man's stories. Even before his mind had started to wander. First, he stopped going out at all, not even to the shops. Then he stopped being able to care for himself. By the time they took him into the home, the modern world had ceased to exist for him. The only thing left in his head was memories of the river. Everything else had been erased.

Annie wondered what he'd think of the blue water and the flat surface? If he'd approve. She doubted it. But it seemed wrong, somehow that all that remained of the history he'd helped to make were a few exhibits in museums and some street names: Cinnamon Street, Jamaica Road, Deadmen's

Dock, Tiger Bay, Greenland Passage. Not much to show for a life. To her surprise, Annie felt her eyes pricking with tears. She hadn't thought about him with such affection for a long time. He'd been a cold man, totally unsuited to bringing up a child, but at least he had been there. She'd forgotten how much he'd meant to her. She swallowed and took a deep breath.

'Hey,' Kellen said. 'Not you as well?'

She half laughed, half sniffed.

'I was just thinking about my grandad. I don't know why it's made me all weepy.'

'Did something happen to him?'

'He's senile and he's in a home. Doesn't even recognise me when I go to visit.'

'Were you close?'

Annie shook her head. 'Not really, to be honest. But he was the one who brought me up.'

'What happened to your parents?'

'Mum was only fifteen when she got pregnant – some foreign student on an exchange trip, who fucked off back to Hong Kong without knowing a thing about it. She had me, but resented being stuck at home with a baby, so started going out more and more and leaving me with Grandad. In the end, predictably she met a man she liked and wanted to marry. The only problem was, he wasn't interested in having a kid about. She chose him.'

'That's bad,' murmured Kellen. 'Are you in touch with her at all?'

'No.'

'Does that bother you?'

Annie paused. 'I can't really remember her. I was only about two when she went.'

'What about brothers and sisters?'

'Just me. Although I suppose there might be a load of half-brothers and sisters running around somewhere.'

He leaned across and kissed her on the cheek.

'It sounds like no fun at all to me,' he said.

She gave a wry smile. 'It could have been worse.'

KATE MOSSE

Annie felt his fingers slip through hers. His face was so close now that she could feel the heat of his breath on her skin. They did not kiss as Kellen reached out and put his hand over her breast. Annie felt her nipple harden under the thin material of the tunic. And the thump of desire between her legs, as he pushed her back against the wooden struts of the bench.

9

Half a mile away, Michael poured himself a whisky and sat down in front of his computer screen. It had been a very long and frustrating day.

The meeting with his Consortium partners at the Ministry of BioProspecting and Patenting had lasted for over four hours, despite his attempts to wrap things up, and had been even worse than he'd anticipated. Almost all of them were unhappy at the continuing lack of information about the Lightermen and unimpressed at Michael's inability to produce an adequate breakdown of how the money – their money – was being spent. Pierre Cordou had been particularly outspoken, raising the issue of the viability of the project in the first place. He considered it a waste of time and argued that they would do better to concentrate their resources elsewhere.

In the end, Michael had got what he wanted from the meeting, although not without making concessions. He had agreed to provide a detailed budget for their next meeting on Monday and to produce hard evidence to justify the monitoring of the Lightermen. In return, the Consortium had given its approval – in principle – to continuing work on obtaining DNA from the Lightermen for screening. Which was just as well, thought Michael, given that this time tomorrow the samples should be in his hands.

The over-run had repercussions for the rest of his day. Michael was late for his following appointment and the next one. He'd been due at yet another tedious government sponsorship dinner, but because the rainstorm had grounded the Ministry helicopter – and the traffic was at a standstill in the resulting flooding – he'd not arrived until the end of the first course. He was always being reminded to show appropriate gratitude to the money men by turning up when required, and his lack of punctuality would be noted. But then he'd always been bad at singing for his supper. Black tie, cigars and small talk with people who knew nothing and cared even less, were not his idea of fun.

'Activate.'

He was surprised to see there was some mail from Leah. He checked the time code. Eleven twenty. He frowned. He'd not expected to hear from her again today. Hoping it didn't mean there was a problem with the arrangements for the morning, Michael punched the transmit function key to see what she had to say.

urgent
re: traveller

second traveller – Annie L Jones – arrived at Pen today
physical characteristics (approx):
age: 22–25 yrs
height: 1.76m
weight: 55k
hair: v short black
eyes: ?brown
ethnicity: white, but poss recessive Asiatic genes
imprimatur/letter: Muin
found by KH in his room after end of service v upset
injuries: cut & bruise r/h side head; grazed palms; cut on r knee
KH told group & me at approx 20:00. Said he put her to bed at 10:30 (suspect K gave her Lethe to help sleep!) but didn't talk to her
AJ came down approx 21:00. She talked to V & J – neither thinks AJ aware of whats happened to her

KH asked everyone to leave approx 22:45
assume he is finding out how much she knows & will explain
if necessary – no idea how AJ will react

thought youd want to know soonest

I think shes genuine

Michael sat back in his chair.

'Well done, Leah,' he muttered, taking a sip of his drink. Despite tomorrow being such a big day, she was still efficient and conscientious enough to pass on information she knew he'd want. Leah was the only one in the Unit who knew about the travellers. She'd never said anything, but he suspected she knew how obsessed he was with the subject, although she didn't realise it was *Kellen*'s interest in the travellers that concerned him most, not the travellers themselves.

Michael stretched his arms and rocked his head from side to side to ease the stiffness in his neck as he read the document through again. At least he had a name now. Annie Jones. It was so typical that she'd somehow found her way to Kellen's room, of all the places in London she could have ended up . .

Michael took a deep breath. As always, things played into Kellen's hands. What were the odds on him being in the right place, at the right time, to witness the first traveller coming through? A thousand to one? A million? Then Mary Royle three months ago. And now Annie Jones. He just drew luck to him, men and women, it made no difference. Sooner or later, he always seemed to get what he wanted.

Michael looked down and saw that his fists were clenched. He mustn't let Kellen get to him. Count to ten. He couldn't think straight if he was angry. He took a large gulp of whisky and waited for the burn in the back of his throat.

It was a simple decision. Either get some rest and forget about the travellers, or use the time to do something productive. Despite building up exhaustive files on the scientific and theoretical possibilities of time travel – and analysing and cross-referencing the social, genetic and temporal data he had on the travellers from every angle in the hope of finding a pattern – Michael had got nowhere. He simply couldn't find an interpretation of the facts that made sense. But if he added Annie to the equation? There wasn't much information, but maybe something would jump out at him now if he looked hard enough.

He checked the on-screen clock: 02:53:00. Enough time to take another look at the footage on the first traveller. When Michael had first started monitoring the People's Network in January, Kellen was still working as a Processor at the Monitoring and Surveillance Unit. All the job involved was watching a bank of closed circuit screens for twenty-four hours a day, seven days a week. If anything happened in a particular division it got reported to the Duty Manager, who decided whether it was serious enough to warrant follow-up action. Muggings, fires, hit-and-runs, floods, vandalism, illegal vehicles. It was a dead-end job and Michael had always assumed Kellen had an ulterior motive for being there. Blackmail? Selling information? Supporting the Network's other activities in some way?

In the event, it didn't matter because, after the traveller came through in February, Kellen handed in his notice and left. What was relevant, from Michael's point of view, was that it meant that his own microcameras, set to record Kellen's movements, were already in place at the point when the traveller appeared in Crucifix Lane.

Michael had edited the film to make it appear that he was watching the CCTV screen live, rather than watching it through the lens of another camera. He'd frozen certain frames, magnified others, until he had as clear a picture as technically possible.

'Load video player – drive E.'

'Software loaded.'

'Load file *kh/02-cl*.'

'File is loaded.'

'Play,' Michael instructed.

The MSU cameras gave one hundred per cent coverage. There were no blind spots. But one minute, Crucifix Lane was empty – no cars, no people, no rats – the next there was a man dying on the pavement. As if he had simply walked through the wall. At first, it looked as if his clothes were on fire. But when you looked closer, you saw it was his skin itself. He was clawing at his neck and shoulders, as if he thought he could somehow pull the flames off. There was nobody to hear him scream.

Suddenly, the screen was flooded with a bright, blue light, almost obscuring the man altogether. Michael could just see him jerking like a puppet, as if being charged through with lightning. After a couple of minutes, he fell to the ground. Smoke belched around him. There were scorch marks on the pavement and the bricks in the tunnel were streaked black. Tiny orange flames, blue at the base, flickered on the side of the man's head. And there, on the right side of his head, was a thin, vertical line. At first, Michael had dismissed it as an exit wound. It was only when he'd magnified it as much as he could that he noticed the four short strokes cutting across it. It looked like a tattoo, just like the small, black mark on Annie's head.

Michael pushed his fingers back through his hair. What he couldn't figure out was why this man had died when the two women had made it through? After this first incident, Michael had immediately hacked into the Central Registry of Death in the City of London Morgue. He was right to assume the body had been taken there, but learned little he hadn't worked out for himself. The date was the third of February. Unfortunately, because the forensic surgeons were not looking for anything out of the ordinary, they'd done a minimum cut-and-stitch autopsy rather than a more detailed genetic and physiological post-mortem. It was just another unclaimed body among the thousands that came through their doors every year.

Several of the classification boxes were blank. No name, no colour of eyes or hair, no address or occupation. They assessed him to be a white Caucasian man between the ages of forty-five and fifty. State of the teeth and internal organs suggested alcohol abuse and a poor diet and, although the notification was death by fire, they had been unable to identify the source. Internal not external, possibly some form of spontaneous combustion none of them had witnessed before. A sentence added at the end of the report said the injuries were consistent with temperatures in excess of 200 degrees centigrade.

Many times Michael had found himself wondering if anybody had missed this man. Would he have died anonymous and unmourned in his own time? Had it made a difference dying in the future? Perhaps not. But it was not much of an epitaph. A classification number and a few notes stored on a computer.

Michael glanced at the time. Gone four o'clock. Nothing new had occurred to him watching the film, so he might as well call it a day and get a couple of hours sleep.

'Exit file,' he said, draining his whisky. 'And log off.'

Kellen was also sitting in front of a screen, in silence except for the faint crackling of a joint burning in the ashtray. Everyone else in the Pen had long since turned in. Annie too. He was very aware of her, lying in his bed on the other side of the wall.

It had been a real struggle. Kellen was more attracted to her than he had been to any woman for a very long time. Her incredible mouth, the smell of her, her strong arms. It would have been the most natural thing in the world to forget his priorities, let go and make love to her for the rest of the night.

Kellen took a drag from the joint and watched as the white smoke spiralled up into the air. He'd stopped it from going too far. The time wasn't right. Besides, he knew how women respected men who could wait and a bit of anticipation would only increase their appetites for one another. More to the point, he had a few things to check before the morning. He hadn't told Annie much about the Network's expedition to the Marsh Projects tomorrow – today now – other than that it was something they did every month. They took food, medicine and bedding for the people who lived there. Tomorrow, they were also going to administer vaccinations to anyone who wanted them. After his explanation, Annie had been completely sympathetic. Totally understanding about why he had to work rather than come to bed.

Kellen was more interested in her story of a man attacking her at the service. From what she had said, it sounded as if the mark on her head had been recognised by someone. It all fitted together. For months, now, Kellen had realised that the Network was being watched. Rumours, odd questions being asked. He had assumed it was to do with the Marsh Projects and had warned everyone to keep their eyes and ears open, told them to be on the alert for anything out of the ordinary. There was always some official or other sniffing around the Network trying to cause trouble.

But if someone else knew about the travellers – and was also aware of Kellen's involvement – then it put an entirely different complexion on things. Perhaps the surveillance was nothing to do with the Lightermen. In a way, that would be a relief. Everything would be a lot less complicated when the time came to sell the DNA if he didn't have to keep looking over his shoulder.

Kellen leaned back and pushed his fingers through his hair. He looked at the time. Right now, he needed a shower and a little something to wake him up and keep him going. It was nearly dawn and in a couple of hours the volunteers would start arriving, all wanting a slice of his time and attention.

As he stood in the shower, being as quiet as possible so as not to wake Annie, he realised that he'd better get Leah to keep an eye on her during the expedition. He'd be too tied up to do it himself. But he didn't want her to get lost or hurt, and she was going to find it all quite shocking. He'd sort something out with Leah.

Twenty minutes later, Kellen was sitting outside, watching the last pink remains of the night fade from the sky. The clouds looked like strips of white tissue paper against the red of the rising sun. It was going to be another hot day. In less than half an hour, the whole of this side of the street would be in direct sunlight. By midday, it would be too hot to be out here unprotected. He picked up a small cup of black coffee and took a gulp. Looked at his watch again.

Time to go.

10

The main hall of the Pen was alive with people and provisions and noise.

There were boxes everywhere. Flat grey oblong containers that opened out to hold an enormous amount of stuff. Food parcels were being stacked on the table nearest the main door, ready to be taken down to the boat and, beneath the tables, was row upon row of bottles of water. Vicky was checking the contents of each container, then giving it a number. Another table was covered with smaller white boxes. The basic medical kits of bandages, plasters and bog-standard drugs. Ibuprofen, water tablets, anti-malarial drugs such as Paludrine and Chloroquine. Vaccines and other notifiable drugs were packed separately.

The whole business was well organised, a contemporary version of the old-fashioned human factory line. A constant rustling of plastic and Cellophane, the dull pop of lids being sealed, the thud of crates taken off tables and stacked. There was an air of excitement and purpose.

Annie stood on the gallery looking down at the scene below. The noise had woken her up. There'd been no sign of Kellen and no note to say where he might be, so she'd splashed some water on her face, got dressed and come out to see what was going on. She was totally stunned by it all. He'd told her something was planned for today, sure, but she'd imagined nothing of this size. She began to realise he'd rather undersold the Network and quite how big its operation was.

'Annie,' someone shouted.

She leaned over and scanned the faces below, trying to identify the voice.

'Annie. Over here.'

Finally, she picked out Leah in the crowd, gesturing at her to come down.

Annie smiled, aware of the irony of being pleased to see someone she'd never even spoken to. But then, everything was odd.

When she'd first woken up – and found she was still here – she'd actually pinched herself to prove to herself she wasn't dreaming. She didn't have a clue what the fuck was going on, but as she lay there in Kellen's bed, hearing the wind chimes chink lightly, she'd decided simply to treat the whole thing as time out of real life. It wasn't so different from how she spent most weekends anyway. Dancing in the company of strangers, developing an immediate and intense intimacy that lasted only as long as the drugs did. It didn't matter that it was all an illusion. They felt like your best friends, like you'd known each other all your lives, but everybody understood that when the night was over, the real world would come crashing back. Jobs, families, arguments, responsibilities. That the experience would be a fading memory the second you walked through your own front door. It just about summed up Annie's philosophy of life. One of the get-it-while-you-can generation, she lived in the present and did not bother to think about where she was going or where she had come from.

Shaking the thoughts from her head, Annie waved back at Leah and headed for the stairs.

Leah kissed her twice on each cheek when she'd made it through the crowd. 'Very French.'

'So much is now,' replied Leah. 'Did you sleep well?'

'Great, thanks.'

'I'm Leah, by the way. I didn't get the chance to introduce myself last night.'

'Kellen told me.'

'We're a little behind schedule this morning,' she said. 'Kellen was hoping to be loaded and ready to sail by nine.'

'Is it always like this?' Annie asked.

'It depends where we're going. Most of the Network's operations are smaller than this, but the Marsh Projects is not only one of the largest housing projects on the river, but it's also in the worst state.'

Despite being small, Leah walked very fast and efficiently. Annie struggled to keep up and not lose sight of her in the crush.

'How do you mean?' she said, half out of breath.

'I'll fill you in on the boat, if that's OK,' Leah replied over her shoulder. 'There's not really time now.'

'Fine. I don't want to get under your feet.'

'You won't. Anyway, why don't I take you to get something to eat now? We've got about half an hour before we'll need to leave.'

'Food sounds brilliant. My stomach's complaining it's not been fed for days.'

Leah went through into a large kitchen, not far from the room they'd sat in the previous night listening to music. A long table ran along the entire side of one wall, groaning under the weight of breakfast. Annie didn't know where to start. There was an enormous earthenware dish filled with ruby grapefruits, kiwis, nectarines and other fruits she couldn't identify. There were croissants and *pains aux raisins* and steaming white rolls in a basket, wrapped in blue linen to keep them warm. Next to the pastries, was a glass bowl of creamy white butter and several smaller dishes containing honey, jam and syrup. Lime green, gold, peach, crimson. It looked like a spread in a Sunday colour supplement, all colour and contrasting textures.

Leah filled a couple of cups with freshly-squeezed apple juice, then put them in what looked like a microwave for ten seconds. When she handed the glass to Annie, it was ice-cold.

'How the hell did you do that in a microwave?'

Leah laughed. 'It's a ralentisseur not a microwave. You've not come across them before?'

Annie shook her head. 'Never heard of it.'

'The principle's pretty much the same as a microwave. The difference is that a ralentisseur slows molecules down, to make the food colder, instead of agitating them to make it hotter. All very straightforward.'

Annie looked sceptical.

'It is,' Leah smiled. 'Anyway, I'm afraid I'm going to leave you to fend for yourself for a while. Help yourself to as much as you want and I'll come back and get you in about twenty minutes or so.'

'No problem.'

Leah was clearly anxious to get moving. 'Great. I'll see you—'

'Just one more thing . . .' said Annie.

Leah stopped. 'Sure.'

'You haven't seen Kellen anywhere about this morning, have you? I wanted to thank him for the loan of his bed.'

Annie hoped she sounded casual. If she at least knew if he was around, she could be ready for him. Otherwise, she knew she'd be turning around every time anyone came into the room, just in case it was him.

'I haven't seen him for a while,' Leah replied. 'He's probably down at the pier and I don't expect he'll come back up here now before we go. Is there a message you want me to pass on?'

'No,' she said quickly. 'No. It's not important. I'll catch up with him later.'

Once Leah had gone, Annie felt a bit self-conscious. There were a few people milling about, but she didn't recognise any of them from the night before. In any case, she hated eating on her own in public. It was stupid, but she always got paranoid about people looking at her and wondering why she had no friends. But she was hungry, so she helped herself to coffee, a roll, two croissants and an obscene quantity of butter, sat down at the large refectory table in the middle of the kitchen and started eating.

'Can I join you?' said a man, as he sat down next to her. 'I'm Lonnie. We met last night.'

Annie remembered him. Short blond hair, looked like he worked out, smoked a lot.

'Hi.'

'How are you this morning?'

'I'm good.'

For a moment, they both concentrated on their food. Then he shifted and smiled at her. 'Must be kind of weird? Being here.'

'I guess so,' she replied vaguely, not sure which particular 'weird' he meant – the preparations for such a expedition? Or the fact that everyone kept telling her it was 2008. Not wanting to make a fool of herself by reacting in the wrong way, she avoided answering his question, just nodded vaguely.

'So,' she ventured, after another few moments. 'Are you looking forward to this visit thing this morning?'

'You must be joking. It's a total pain in the arse.'

'You don't make it sound like it's going to be much fun.'

'It's not.'

'So why are you going?'

'It's what the Network does. And I'm in the Network, so . . .'

'How did you get involved then?' she asked. 'If you don't really like this sort of stuff. Did you know Kellen from college or something?'

'College,' he laughed. 'Yeah, right.'

'Well, what then?' she said, keen to get a conversation going. 'School? Work?'

'We go way back, me and Kellen. Maybe we met at some party? Through friends? Can't remember. I thought Kellen was sound, he thought the same about me and I liked the set-up here. End of story.'

'So you live here?'

'Yeah. So do Vicky, Malik, Leah and Jonas. Other people come and go, depending on what's going on.'

'Don't any of you have jobs?'

He laughed. 'Most of us work from time to time, when the spirit moves us. It's all casual now. Short-term contracts. In and out.'

'Doing what? Don't you need money?'

'We've got quite a few bits of paper between us, in fact,' he replied. 'Not that you'd imagine it from looking at us. Vicky's got a bit of legal training, Malik does computer programming, Jonas has a medical background and Leah . . . well, Leah's a seriously clever lady.'

Annie winced at his use of the word 'lady'. For some reason, it sounded as if he was being rude rather than complimentary.

'But if you've all got qualifications, I don't quite understand what you're doing here. To tell you the truth, I'm a bit confused about what the Network is exactly. I mean, it's a church, is it?'

'Church?' repeated Lonnie. 'Why do you say church?'

'Well, all that stuff yesterday. The incense and singing. I only caught the tail end, but it seemed like some sort of service.'

He nodded. 'I can see how it might come across like that, but it's not religious. It's just a way of getting lots of people together once a week. A bit of singing, a bit of talking. Lots of people just turn up for it even though they have nothing to do with the Network the rest of the time.'

'What for?'

'Because they like the atmosphere or have got no other social life, I don't know. I don't recognise most of them myself from week to week.'

'But it sounded—'

Lonnie stood up. 'It's just a bit of fun. But, listen, I've got to make a move. Catch you later.'

Annie watched him disappear through the door, leaving her to mull over what he'd said as she waited for Leah to come and pick her up.

★   ★   ★

The flies were already out in force as the boat pulled away from the pier and headed downstream into the sun with the wind behind it.

The river was busy. Pleasure boats, river taxis, tourist charters, the whistles and sirens drowning out the sounds of the city going about its business. One short blast for starboard, two short blasts for port. Annie found the brilliant blue of the river, especially framed by the green rushes along both banks, slightly alarming. It looked so artificial, although she supposed the people around her were used to it.

Leah had settled her at the back of the boat, then apologised for leaving her again and said she'd be back in about ten minutes. Everybody, except Annie seemed to have something to do. There were about twenty volunteers aboard, all looking busy, and she kept getting the odd glimpse of Jonas, Malik and Vicky as they charged about. Talking, disappearing, coming back. Everyone seemed to be getting changed into some sort of protective clothing. Thick white trousers, long-sleeved coats with a high neck, boots. Was she supposed to have something too? No doubt someone would say.

Annie sighed. She'd barely seen Kellen. He had given her a quick hug when she'd arrived at the pier with Leah, but there hadn't been a chance to speak to him since. She was very aware of his presence on the boat, though. Kept catching the sound of his voice, encouraging the volunteers, making sure everybody knew what they were supposed to be doing, sparing a moment for everyone.

Annie leaned against the railings and looked out over the river, watching the white water trailing the boat. She could feel the spray flying up on to her face and the hot wind driving them along. Suddenly, a pair of hands circled her waist. Her heart immediately started to thump.

'Hey,' said Kellen. 'I wondered where you'd got to.'

She laughed. 'I've not moved from this spot.'

He turned her around to face him.

'Sorry I've been neglecting you,' he said. 'There's just so much happening.'

'I'm fine. I don't feel neglected at all.'

'Did you sleep well?'

She nodded.

'You looked very peaceful.'

Annie blushed at the thought that he'd watched her. 'The sleep of the just, I guess . . .'

He touched her hot cheeks with the back of his hand.

'Leah told me she promised she'd tell you what was going on. I've come instead . . .'

Annie smiled, to show she was pleased.

'You know we're going to a place called the Marsh Projects, on the southside of the river past the Thames Barrier, which was built by the London Authority Syndicate to house the people slung out of their homes by developers—'

'Hang on,' she interrupted. 'You've lost me already. What developers?'

Kellen pulled her down, so they were both sitting on the deck. Side by side. 'Sorry. You remember me mentioning that development of the riverside was part of the reason for stabilising the Thames?'

'Sort of.'

'Well, some of the stuff is amazing in architectural terms. Their dream was to develop an exclusive, innovative water front for twenty-first-century London. Only problem was that lots of the prime sites were already occupied by governmental housing blocks and council tenants, and they were not the sort of people the investors wanted around littering up the place. So, with a mixture of bribes and incentives, the developers forced through a resettlement programme. Purpose-built estates were constructed downriver with all the newest facilities. Or at least that was the idea. The developers got their land, everyone else got a brand new home for nothing. Except the sites downriver turned out to be polluted. There were problems with flooding almost straight away and because they used cheap materials to get it done quickly – stuff that wasn't resilient enough or else not designed for the use it was being put to – the Marsh Projects started falling apart. Any families who could afford to, moved out, the squatters and dealers moved in.'

'It sounds appalling.'

'The people who live there are sick, live in shit living conditions and there's nobody prepared to fight their corner.'

'Which is where the Network comes in?'

Annie loved the fact that he looked embarrassed. Smiled at his slight flush. 'We go down there about once a month with medicines and food, although it's not the only place we go. It's not much, but it's better than nothing.'

She squeezed his hand. 'The worst thing is that there should be such a contrast. Everything around the Pen, where we walked by the river last night – that all looks so fantastic. I'd even been thinking what a great place London was, a brilliant place to live.'

'It is brilliant for some people. But only if you've got money and you fit in.'

She turned to look at him. 'You,' she said affectionately, 'are a good person. If only there were more like you around.'

Kellen didn't answer, just threaded his fingers through hers. But she could tell he was pleased.

'I'd better go and get on with things,' he said, after a while.

'Yes. You must.'

'You'll be OK?'

'Of course I will.'

He didn't move.

'Go on then.'

'I'll see you later,' he said, kissing her quickly. 'I'll get Leah to keep you company. We won't be there for a while yet.'

They reluctantly stood up, then Annie put her arms on his shoulders and pointed him in the opposite direction.

'Just go. Now.'

Annie watched him walk away from her until he was out of sight, then turned back to the river. This time she was blind to the spray or the sun or the buildings on the banks. Now, she was thinking only of Kellen. His vulnerability, as she interpreted it. His compassion. The words of their conversation began replaying in her head, as she remembered each tiny gesture, each smile.

Annie smiled.

Could it be that she had finally met a man who knew what his heart was for?

11

'Here you go,' said Leah, passing the joint to Annie. 'A present from Kellen.'

'Thanks,' she said, 'although I don't know why he didn't give it to me himself. He was just here.'

Leah shrugged. 'He's rather worried about you. Thinks it might be better if you stayed on the boat rather than coming into the Projects.'

Annie shook her head. 'No way.'

'Actually, I agree with him.'

'I can look after myself.'

'I'm sure you can. But you don't know the area and you won't know what to do if things get out of hand.'

Annie was annoyed. 'I've lived in London all my life.'

'Not this London. You wouldn't walk into a town in the middle of Sierra Leone, say,' Leah continued, 'and assume you knew what was going on. You'd listen to advice.'

'Oh, come on,' she snapped. 'It's hardly comparable.'

Leah gave a quick smile. 'I suppose Africa is overstating the case a little,' she conceded. 'I didn't mean to offend you. I just don't want you to get hurt.'

'You seem very sure there's going to be trouble. Or is it always like this?'

'A bit of both.'

The two women looked at each other, not wanting to fall out. Annie took a final drag, then offered the joint to Leah.

'I don't, thanks.'

'Nobody seems bothered about getting busted. All this gear floating about the whole time.'

'It's not illegal.'

'You're kidding me!' shrieked Annie.

'Cannabis, grass, all above board now.'

'Jesus. Where the hell do you buy it?'

'Mainly over the counter in pubs and bars, 24-hour stores. Pretty much anywhere that stocks booze and cigarettes. We even sell it at the Pen.'

'Amazing,' said Annie.

If this was what the future had to offer, they could count her in.

Annie intended to use the rest of the journey downriver to play detective and see what she could identify, what appeared to be new. Even if it didn't help her to work out what was going on, it would at least help her to get her bearings.

To start with, she tried covering both banks, switching her glance from side to side when something caught her eye, and bombarding Leah with questions. But after a while, she started to get a headache. Besides, it made her realise how little she knew the river anyway. In the past, she'd written off sightseeing trips as a mixture of embarrassing tourists, wet plastic seats and the smell of diesel. In fact, the more she thought about it, the more certain she became she'd never actually been on the Thames on a boat. Not as an adult, at any rate. Her grandad must have taken her at some time, although she had no memory of it.

Finally, she gave up and plonked herself back down on the deck.

'You don't look as if you enjoyed that,' said Leah, sitting next to her.

'Well it's so fucking hot,' Annie replied, flapping her hat in front of her face to cool herself down. 'And bright. I don't understand how people in all those glass buildings can stand it.'

Leah laughed. 'Everything's air-conditioned and we do have such a thing as blinds . . .'

'All these fantastic, bright colours are incredible. That amazing green thing we passed five minutes ago.'

'*Les Nouveaux Riverains*,' said Leah. 'An office and shopping development. All very exclusive.'

'And that amazing red glass building near Southwark Bridge – just after we'd set off?'

'The Ministry of BioProspecting and Patenting. More commonly known – with a deplorable lack of originality – as the Gene Machine.'

Annie thought Leah was joking. 'And what do they do? Build perfect people?'

'Not exactly. They exist to try to stop *other* people building perfect people.'

Annie stared. 'Run that by me again.'

'The Ministry is a regulatory authority to enforce legislation and to control biotechnolgoy activities. It's supposed to make sure everything's done legally and above board.'

'Are you talking about genetic engineering?' asked Annie.

'Exactly. That's just the old-fashioned phrase for the same thing.'

'It always sounds so grim. You know, doctors playing God, pigs with wings.'

'That's science fiction not science,' sighed Leah, as if she'd had this conversation many times before. 'The thing is to make a distinction between what is technically possible and what is morally desirable. Genetic modification has virtually eliminated thousands of life-threatening genetic disorders. Through pre-implantation genetic screening – and subsequent manipulation – sickle cell anaemia, cystic fibrosis, even breast cancer are much less common than they used to be.' She hesitated, seeing the shell-shocked expression on Annie's face.

'Sorry. We don't have to talk about this if you don't want to.'

'No,' said Annie doubtfully. 'I do want to know ... I think.'

'I'll try not to use too many technical terms, but it's really difficult.'

Annie pulled a face. 'Maybe you could try a bit harder.'

Leah laughed. 'Do you think all those breakthroughs in medical science are important. That's the issue.'

'Yeah, but that's different.'

'No,' Leah replied, 'that's what biotechnology is. It's not different at all.'

Annie looked sheepish. 'To tell you the truth, I don't really know exactly what genetic engineering is. Not properly.'

'It's not that complicated. You know what DNA is?'

Annie looked dubious. 'I think so.'

Leah laughed. 'DNA is the genetic blueprint of all life and every cell contains a full complement of DNA – which stands for deoxyribonucleic acid, by the way. I won't go into lots of detail about chromosomes, genomes or genes—'

'Good,' muttered Annie.

'—suffice to say that genes act as codes as for specific proteins, which give organisms their characteristics. The smallest change in the gene sequence can make the most dramatic change in what you see in front of your eyes. The difference, say, between a mouse and a melon. Add all the genes together and that gives you the genetic code for that particular melon or mouse. Do you see what I mean?'

'No, well maybe sort of,' floundered Annie.

'Genetic engineering simply means the process of transferring genes from one organism to another or of changing genetic material within an organism.'

'I am struggling even more now you've introduced organisms.'

Leah smiled. 'OK, let me give you an example. Imagine that you want to create a carrot that glows in the dark. First, you take a glow-worm and poke around to find out which part of its DNA code "tells" it to glow. Coincidentally, the proper term is gene mapping or gene sequencing rather than "poking around".'

Annie nodded. 'Well, I'm glad you put me straight on that one!'

'Next, you gather up your enzymes – different ones cut the

DNA code in different places – and by using the right ones, you separate the gene for glowing and lift it out. You use the same trick to cut open the DNA of your carrot at a suitable point and into that gap, using more enzymes, you insert and glue the glow fragment. Occasionally you might need to use a virus to trick the carrot into accepting the glow-worm DNA, but if you're lucky—'

'You notice I'm not asking the obvious question here, like why you'd want a glowing carrot in the first place.'

'Good,' said Leah, in her most professor-like voice. 'At this point, you splice your small fragment of glow-worm DNA into the DNA of the carrot and *voilà*, you have recombinant DNA. Put this back into a cell and you will eventually produce a carrot that glows in the dark.'

'Yeah,' said Annie, shaking her head in disbelief. 'Like you say, not that complicated at all . . .'

'So let me ask you this. What's cloning?'

'God, you ask so many questions. It's like being on a school trip!'

Annie tried to look contrite. 'Do you mind?'

'Not really,' Leah said. 'Provided they're sensible questions. A clone is a collection of genetically identical organisms which have been derived from a single parent. Members of a clone show less variability than other organisms bred by traditional means.'

'Why would you do it?'

'Well, to get cows or sheep or pigs or chickens that produce wonderful milk or wool or meat or eggs, you name it. Organs for transplant. You've heard of Dolly the sheep, or indeed Polly and Molly and Tracy the sheep?'

'Tracy,' teased Annie. 'A sheep cloned to dance around a handbag . . .'

'Actually, Tracy has the protein AAT in her milk which is used for treating cystic fibrosis. Then of course there's Mr Jefferson the cloned calf and all his pharmed brothers and sisters.'

'Stop,' said Annie, putting her hands over her ears. 'It's all absolutely bizarre. I'd rather die than have a kidney shoved inside me that had been taken from something with hoofs.'

Leah looked sceptical. 'No you wouldn't.'

'But don't things go wrong? I can't believe the world's supposed to be like this.'

'Of course, there are problems with xenotransplantation – that's animal to human organ transplants – such as the risk of spreading endemic diseases from animals to humans, which may well lead to epidemics in humans, the emergence of new and robust retroviruses—'

'—animals in pain.'

'That too,' Leah agreed.

'But not people. They don't clone people.'

Leah paused. 'Officially, no. It's still considered a step too far.'

'And unofficially?'

'Personally, I've got no doubt it goes on. It goes back to what I was saying before about making the distinction between science and the way it is or is not exploited. And there are scientists for whom possibility is justification enough. Others have a moral approach and do think about the consequences of their actions. It's down to the individual.'

'Which sort of brings us back to people being perfect or not—'

'Yes.'

Annie glanced at her, hearing the change in her voice. 'I'm sorry if you're fed up with me asking all these questions,' she said.

'I told you, I don't mind,' Leah replied, although now it sounded as if she did. 'Apart from anything, it helps pass the time.'

'Well, you're being brilliant.'

'What was it you were going to ask?'

'What does the word bioprospecting actually mean?'

'It's the business of finding and taking particular genes from something or someone. In order to make money from the genes, a corporation, pharmaceutical company or research institute has to patent them. If they can't prove that the genes fulfil three criteria – novelty, inventiveness and industrial applicability – then the patent won't be issued. Hence the phrase biopatenting and hence the name of the Ministry.'

'But how can you patent somebody else's genes?' asked Annie. 'That's ridiculous.'

'A patent is simply an exclusive property right, usually lasting between twenty and twenty-five years. The original idea of patenting was to protect the rights of inventors, so anyone seeking a genetic patent still has to prove that it is an "invention". That is, something that nature cannot produce unaided. It could be a disease-resistant gene from a strain of wild tomato plant or a disease-immunity gene from a group of indigenous people. Anything and everything.'

'What are you saying? That this applies to people and animals as well?'

'Of course people and animals. The first mammal was patented before either of us was even born. A transgenic mouse that had a breast-cancer gene spliced into its genetic make-up.'

'It makes me want to throw up just thinking about it.'

'Well, you'd better get used to it. Patented animals are old news now. There are hundreds of them. More significant is human gene patenting. That's been the big battle over the past ten years.'

'What freaks me out even more,' Annie said, looking out into the middle distance, 'is that this stuff is going on under my nose, but somehow I don't know a thing about it. It makes me feel totally stupid.'

'Lots of people don't know as much as they should,' countered Leah. 'It's not just you.'

'That doesn't make me feel any less of an idiot, but thanks anyway.'

'The bare bones of the situation is that about thirty years ago, the US government filed a patent on a human cell-line of a man from Papua New Guinea which had been identified as potentially useful in treating adult leukaemia. The patent was withdrawn at the time, but the multinationals kept pushing and pushing until they got their way. Once the principle had been breached, of course the floodgates opened. It's getting to be accepted practice. Most scientists don't have a problem with it, any more than they would with, say, organ donation.'

'But it's wrong,' said Annie forcefully.

'Not necessarily. Although, until 1980, the law agreed with you. Then an American court ruled that the relevant distinction was not "between animate and inanimate" things, but whether living products could be seen as "human-made" inventions.'

'I still can't believe this all passed me by.'

'Well, it was in the best interests of the biotech industry to keep it all as quiet as possible. They knew that once campaigners worked out what was going on, there'd be an outcry. And there was, in the end. Attempts were made to slow things up, but it was too late. In 2003, the European Commission gave in to pressure and passed a law that gave the multinational corporations unprecedented legal protection, especially in the fields of cloning and genetic engineering. From the point, virtually every living thing and every one of its parts and genes – including those of humans – could be patented as long as their production incorporated processes which nature could not accomplish by itself. Which,' she concluded, 'leads us neatly back to where we started. Red glass and the Ministry.'

'So what you're trying to tell me, is that the guys in the Ministry are the good guys.'

Leah nodded. 'The Ministry isn't there to challenge the existence of biotech. Their business is to ensure scientific technology is regulated and that appropriate legislation is passed. Everybody knows that while various multi-nationals have made a fortune out of gene-harvesting, virtually none of the profit has made its way back to the people concerned. There was a famous case in the 1990s, when the US government filed patents on the cell-lines of two people from the Solomon Islands without even telling them.'

'It's outrageous.'

Leah raised her eyebrows. 'So you've said.'

'Just one more question, then I'll shut up. Why do you know so much about it? I mean, all those dates and everything on the tip of your tongue like that?'

Leah stood up. 'I'll tell you some other time.'

'Why? Why not now?'

Leah held out her hand to help Annie up.

'Because we're here.'

12

Within the Peripherique, the London skyline was a triumph of geometry and engineering. Spires and towers reached up to heaven, like a line of praying hands. The environment changed a little when you got into the urban suburbs, broadly speaking the area between the Kingston Dam in the West and the Thames Barrier in the East. Fewer new buildings, more renovation, not as many roads protected by gates or guards. Beyond that were the suburbs. Run-down, disadvantaged, squalid.

Even the sky was a different colour this far out, as if everything bad had been exiled from the city to here. A low cloud of pollution, caused by a mixture of gas from the chemical plant on the opposite bank and diesel fumes, hovered heavily over everything. In the background, the Kinetic Disintegration Technology Micronizers thudded constantly, making the banks shudder.

Because Annie had been completely engrossed in her conversation with Leah, she had not paid too much attention to the gradually changing landscape. Now, as the boat jolted under her feet as it tried to dock, she looked around and thought that they could have travelled to the opposite side of the earth. It was a totally different London. Her stomach lurched at the smell of rotten food, stagnant water and the unmistakable stench of misery.

'Here, put these on,' said Leah.

She took the pile of clothes. 'This place . . .'

'I tried to warn you. Are you still sure you want to come ashore?'

'Definitely.'

'OK, then leave your normal hat here and put this on. It's not comfortable, but the netting will help keep the mosquitoes off. The important thing is to make sure you've got no exposed skin, so pull your gloves up as high as possible. I think the boots will fit.'

'Why have I got green gloves and yours are yellow?'

'Colour coding is the best way of identifying who's who and where people are supposed to be working. Kellen, Lonnie and I have yellow gloves, so that we're easy to pick out if there's a serious problem.'

Annie raised her eyebrows. 'Don't the gloves make things a bit difficult? A bit clumsy?'

'Anybody handing out pills or giving an injection has protective surgical gloves on underneath,' said Leah, as she helped Annie to do up her protective headgear. 'Right. You're ready. Stay close and follow me. Once we arrive in the centre, I'll find somewhere safe for you to watch where you can see what's going on, but won't get caught up in anything. And I know you think I'm overreacting, but it is essential – absolutely essential – that you stay put.'

This time Annie didn't argue.

As they traipsed up the jetty onto Unity Pier in single file, Annie tried to imagine what they must look like. A slow-moving procession of androgenous creatures, faces hidden and every inch of flesh covered, each carrying a crate. The sun was already burning the back of her neck, even through the webbing of the hat, and her hands were itching inside the rough, oversized gloves. The smell of decay was getting worse. Animals shouldn't have to live in a place like this. Let alone people.

Annie felt like they were entering a total contamination zone and suddenly wondered if she was doing the right thing by tagging along. Then again, the thought of staying alone on the boat alone made her equally anxious, so she forced herself to concentrate on putting one foot in front of the other and getting to the shore in one piece. When she looked down through the wooden slats, she could see mosquitoes hovering just above the water.

The Marsh Projects were nothing like she'd imagined. She'd pictured high-rise walkways and dark corners and a sense of threat. Like any sprawling, grey London estate, in fact, simply transported downriver. But everything about this place was brown. Brown pavements, brown walls, brown low-rise houses, all a standard size and height.

But it was the natural environment that made the atmosphere so alien. Bizarre shrieking birds sitting on the obsolete electricity lines, the permanent buzzing of insects, the sudden splatterings of rats and water snakes. And everywhere ankle-deep in liquid mud, as if there had been a small landslide and no one had bothered to clear up properly. It was like pictures Annie had seen on the news, not like England at all. Later, when she looked back, she realised this was the moment when she started to accepted that, somehow, it was no longer 1997.

Leah explained that they were heading for the main square, in the centre of the development. The Glades was on higher ground and therefore usually less waterlogged. They would position six distribution points (blue gloves) for dispensing basic medicines and first aid, eight food distribution points (red) and one (green) for bedding. Kellen was going to set up his vaccination unit slightly away from the main activity, because it wasn't part of their standard routine. The residents were used to the Network turning up and knew both what to expect and where to go for what they wanted. In the event of trouble, Leah explained, policy was to avoid confrontation, pack up quietly if challenged and return to the boat. They walked slowly on, in single file.

The Glades was smaller than Annie envisioned. Four narrow roads led into it, from north, south, east and west, and there were shops on each side, all of them protected by thick metal grilles and all of them shut. There were no cars. No vehicles of any kind, in fact. Nothing got through the sludge. Leah explained that there was road access from the south, further away from the river where the ground was not so marshy. Because she was used to posters and bright billboards everywhere, Annie found the unalleviated drabness of the blank walls incredibly depressing. Presumably there was no point advertising here. Just a waste of paper and glue.

'I'm going to take you over to the far corner,' said Leah, 'right where Malik's going to set up the bedding distribution point. If you need anything, ask him. But, otherwise please—'

'I know, I know. Don't move.'

'Hallelujah. The message has finally got through . . .'

Annie pulled a face. 'Look, I'll see you later. Good luck.'

'We're going to need it,' muttered Leah as she left.

Annie found a ledge to sit on in the shade. The heat was exhausting and she felt as if she were being boiled alive in her clothes. She tried to loosen the strap of her hat with her clumsy and bulky fingers. Impossible. After a few minutes more, she decided she just couldn't bear the chafing for a second longer. She slipped off her gloves, sorted out the strap, then shoved her hands back in as quickly as she could. The last thing she wanted was to be bitten by something.

The air seemed even worse away from the river and Annie didn't have the energy to want to wander around. She couldn't get her head around what was going on. The whole idea of the Network just turning up – no official sanction, no authority – was mind-boggling. She loved the lack of bureaucracy, the effort and commitment of getting off one's arse and doing something. Brilliant. There was a niggle in her mind, though. It was all very well when it was someone like Kellen, whose motives were good and who knew what they were doing. But what if the advice was bad or the medicines dangerous? The whole situation was ripe for corruption.

The square was surprisingly empty, given the amount of noise they'd made unloading and carrying everything up here.

There were just a few kids hanging around in the shadows of the buildings, watching them in silence, although Annie sensed there were probably eyes in every dark window.

To pass time, she tried spotting who was who in their identikit white suits. She recognised Malik, of course, organising his volunteers a couple of feet in front of her. At one point, she saw Leah in her yellow gloves, running across the square and disappearing down an alleyway. Annie kept watching, waiting her to come back, but after five minutes, and still no sign, she turned her attention back to the square and tried to see if she could find Kellen. The vaccination point was in the process of being set up, just where Leah had said it was going to be. Annie could see a chair and boxes piled up next to it, but no sign of him.

Annie sighed and leaned back against the wall, a bit bored. In the distance she could see two Network people systematically working their way up and down the deserted streets and the alleys, presumably trying to drum up business. Gradually, their efforts paid off and a few people started to appear. Women with children mainly, pulling at them to hurry. A few men. Annie found it hard to see clearly through the netting around her hat, but she thought everybody seemed jumpy. As if they were waiting for something bad to happen. They'd approach a distribution point, ask for something, then scuttle away like rabbits.

As the noise level grew and more people arrived, she began to feel less self-conscious. She decided to move a little closer to Malik, to see if she could work out what was going on in his section. Most of the people were taking blankets and sheets, and a few were rifling through the baskets of clothes and hats in case there was anything that might fit them. Annie was interested in the expressions on their faces. Her instincts had been right. Everybody was frightened.

Immediately, she started to feel a bit nervous too. She could sense the tension in the atmosphere now, the air of menace. Nobody was talking, nobody was laughing, as if scared of drawing attention to themselves. In a movie, the music would give it away, the soundtrack alerting the audience that something appalling was about to happen. Here, there was only the whine of mosquitoes and the hammering of machinery in the distance.

Suddenly, loud and aggressive voices cut through the sound of the crowd. Everybody stopped what they were doing and turned to stare, anticipating trouble. In the corner, Kellen and Lonnie were surrounded by a group of men. They looked to be a different physical build from most of the people Annie had seen so far, much stockier and heavier, with black hair and less pallid complexions. Rather than plain shirts and loose trousers, they were wearing bright, patterned clothes. It looked almost like some sort of traditional costume.

Nobody seemed to know what was going on, but it was obvious that the conflict was escalating. The shouting was getting more persistent, the threat of violence more explicit. There was some pushing, then a yell as the first blow was landed.

Annie felt sick. Knuckle connected with bone, skin split open and blood stained people's hair and clothes and hands. All around her now was the sound of breaking glass and the pop of crates trampled under foot as panic spread through the crowd. Parents dragged their terrified children to safety. Some of the Network volunteers hurried to pack up the medicines and equipment and get it back to the boat, others ran to help Kellen and Lonnie.

Annie panicked when she heard the shots. A single gun, firing two rounds.

'No,' she shouted, starting to run.

She was close enough to Kellen now to see the flash of silver and the sudden movement as he threw up his arm to protect himself from the knife.

'No!'

Annie smashed into a man standing at the edge of the pack and knocked him off balance. As he swung around to confront her, she saw he had a knife too. Shock immobilised her, she somehow couldn't make her arms or legs move. Just stood there, watching, as his fist came towards her face.

The impact of the blow knocked her off her feet. She could taste blood in her mouth and nose, then all the noise seemed to fade into the background, as if she was hearing everything from underwater. She found herself wondering what it was like to be shot. Did you feel the bullet at the point of impact? Or was it only later, when the dullness and aching began?

Out of nowhere, Leah was yelling. 'Get up. We've got to get out of here.'

Annie could see two of her. 'I can't—'

'Now! There's no time. Get up.'

She felt herself being pulled to her feet. She swayed slightly, until the double Leah melted back into one, then instinctively followed. Leah pushed a handkerchief into her hand.

'It'll help stem the bleeding,' she shouted.

Annie zig-zagged down a series of identical alleys and passages, keeping Leah's white back, swinging plait, in her sights. Left, right, right again, until they reached the river. The boat was ready to sail, the thick rope looped over the mooring but no longer fast. Annie registered that most people seemed to be on board.

'They're here,' someone shouted, as Leah jumped over the gap between the pier and the platform. Annie did the same, stumbling as she landed on the edge of the boat. The metal deck was a death-trap now, made slippery by the mud and slime on people's boots.

'Go!'

Annie heard the gate thump into place, then felt the boat lurch as it swung away from the pier. It was going too fast, too close to the shore and, for a moment, she thought they were going to capsize. A box slid across the deck and smashed into the side.

Leah guided her away from the edge and sat her down on a bench at the side of the boat. The nosebleed showed no sign of stopping and the handkerchief was drenched.

Leah squeezed her hand. 'I'll go and get you something for that,' she said.

Annie didn't reply, just leaned back against the railings. Her head was spinning. As blood trickled down the back of her throat into her lungs, she found herself wondering, inconsequentially, why the sky had clouded over.

13

Another storm was threatening. Grey clouds skimmed the red roof of the Ministry of BioProspecting and Patenting and covered the tops of the buildings on the opposite side of the river. It was still nearly thirty degrees Celsius and it was getting progressively more humid and more oppressive. It looked as though another night of flooding and disruption was on the agenda.

Inside the Conference Chamber, the atmosphere was tense. Pierre Cordou had loosened his tie, Otto Bauer was wiping his forehead with a large handkerchief. Rosa Guitierez took a sip of water. She looked pale.

'Coffee, madam?' said the waiter quietly. 'Milk and sugar are on the table.'

'Thank you.'

Michael stood at the head of the table in silence as each of his guests was served. His expression gave nothing away. The only noise was the chink of spoons in saucers, the stirring of sugar in cups, the sound of papers being shuffled. There was no polite small talk, no exchange of news about holidays or summer plans.

'Thank you, Pete,' he said.

The waiter put the pots back on the table at the side of the room and left discreetly. The door clicked shut and Cordou erupted.

'That was unforgivable. There are ladies present.'

Michael was relieved. He had intended to shock. He knew he was taking a risk — showing them the film one of his agents had recorded at five o'clock that morning of one of the Lightermen being beaten — but it had paid off. He'd needed to divert their attention away from the issue of how far he had exceeded his authority, and focus it instead on his reasons for launching the raid without their prior approval. The violence had concentrated their minds perfectly.

As soon as the news came through that the raid on the Marsh Projects had been a success, Michael had called an emergency meeting of the Consortium for four o'clock that afternoon. It was only when all five partners were sitting around the table that Michael admitted that Operation Bayoux had already taken place. The uproar was immediate. He was strongly criticised for acting unilaterally, for acting without due authority and accused of deliberately misleading the Consortium. Michael's response had been to run the film. As he watched the expressions on people's faces turn from disbelief to disgust, he knew most of them would now be more inclined to listen to what he had to say before condemning his behaviour.

'And the old man?' asked Nelson Huyk. 'Is he all right?'

'He has four broken fingers, two broken ribs, a fractured kneecap and multiple bruising. However, like most of the Lightermen, he is extremely resilient.'

Nelson shook his head. 'Very bad,' he muttered. 'Really very bad.'

'I still think you owe us an apology,' said Cordou. 'It was quite unnecessary to force us to witness something like that. Not at all necessary.'

Michael stared at him. 'With all due respect, monsieur, I disagree. I apologise if I have offended anyone, however I think it is essential everyone in this room understands why I felt compelled to take immediate action. My considered judgement was that more violence was a real possibility if we delayed.'

'But what I am unclear about,' said Helga Brandt, 'is why you did not indicate any of this to us yesterday?'

'Exactly,' snapped Cordou. 'At best, it suggests a lack of respect. At worst, a deliberate attempt to leave us in the dark.'

'I'm sorry if that is the impression you have taken.'

'Indeed it is. And the fact remains that—'

Nelson interrupted. 'Perhaps the most sensible course of action would be for Michael to take us through the sequence of events leading up to this morning's operation. Perhaps it would be a more productive use of our time?'

Nelson Huyk was Michael's closest ally in the Consortium and one of his few, real friends. The two men had first met eleven years ago at the critical European Council of Ministers that had produced the directive setting the ball rolling on the legal protection of biotechnological inventions. Neither man had approved of the stance of their own governments, and had found themselves talking. They'd kept in touch ever since.

In the recent past, they'd worked together from time to time. Michael was even godfather to Nelson's youngest child. Nelson was often exasperated by his friend's inability to trust other people and his tendency to play his cards close to his chest, but he accepted Michael was a driven man and respected his instincts, his intelligence and his commitment.

'I agree,' said Rosa.

'I think that perhaps we would all find a summary helpful,' Bauer concurred. 'Unless, of course, you now do *not* want facts, Pierre . . .'

A couple of people laughed and the tension was broken. Otto was a popular member of the Consortium and the rivalry between the French and German camps was well known. Cordou shifted uncomfortably in his seat, realising he'd boxed himself in.

'Very well,' he conceded. 'But I would like my objections recorded.'

Michael nodded curtly at him.

'Thank you – Rosa, Otto, Nelson – for your support. And I apologise again for not being more open with you before now. But I did not want to waste the Consortium's valuable time on speculation, not until I had enough evidence to back up my suspicions. In the event, the evidence I needed – what was *said* during the attack on the Lightermen this morning – forced my hand more quickly than I expected.'

He looked around the table and saw that he had their complete attention.

'As you know, we have spent a great deal of time and money on monitoring the Lightermen. We have all, I think, at some point been sceptical that there was anything worth monitoring. Isolation has always been considered a fundamental prerequisite for genetic evolution and adaptation. People who have had no or very little contact with the outside world are likely to be a good place to start when looking for super-genes, by which I mean genes with unique possibilities.

'As you are all aware, the Lightermen originated from central Europe. They arrived in Britain about ten years ago and settled in the Unity Pier area of the Marsh Projects. They are a self-contained group, certainly, but in no way can they be considered free from a whole range of outside genetic influences. Despite this, I had information that the Lightermen had been approached by unlicensed bioprospectors at the beginning of the summer and offered a large amount of money in return for blood. They rejected the offer.'

'Who made this approach?' said Cordou. 'This is what you have not told us.'

Michael ignored the interruption. 'At first, I was not sure if the Lightermen were the sole target of the bioprospectors or simply one of several groups within the Marsh Projects. But, two weeks after the first approach, my agents started to report a marked reduction in their numbers. The official explanation was that certain families had had enough of the Marsh Projects and had decided to move on. On the surface, it was a plausible enough explanation – not least because the whole place is a breeding ground for all kinds of diseases and infection – but the psychology seemed wrong. Some go, some stay? I was unconvinced.

'This – coupled with reports of a week-on-week increase

in the number of violent incidents – helped me reach a decision to mount a full-scale surveillance operation.'

'I cannot see why you could not have told us more of this before,' Helga protested.

'There was no doubt that the Lightermen were the targets of intimidation – and the rumours circulating did suggest biopirates were behind it – but there was still no evidence. I had to consider the possibility of it all being a smoke screen for something else – territorial disputes, extortion, drugs – so I decided to increase the number of my agents on the ground to try to come up with something tangible to justify our involvement.

'As you will remember from the films, one of the assailants clearly made reference to the need for them to "cooperate today" during the attack on the Lighterman. It was this explicit link between the timing of the attack and a visit to the Marsh Projects planned by a group called the People's Network, that gave me the impetus to act.'

Michael felt the atmosphere stiffen. Something specific to focus on. A name.

'The People's Network?' repeated Rosa. 'I am not aware of them.'

'They are relative newcomers to the scene and, so far as we know, operate only in this part of London.'

'Who are they?' asked Otto.

'On the surface, they are a charitable group which organises missions to local problem areas to supply food, medicines and advice free of charge. There appears to be no formal membership, but there are regular events at the base near London Bridge, as well as a café and rest space for people passing through.'

'It all sounds laudable,' said Rosa.

'In principle, yes,' Michael agreed. 'However, my suspicions are that the humanitarian and environmental credentials are a front for black-marketeering. Bioprospecting, the acquisition of technological and scientific data, this sort of thing.'

'I see no reason why you should pick this group rather

than any other,' said Cordou. 'There must be hundreds of such groups.'

'During the course of this year, the Network has made several trips to the Marsh Projects. That would not concern us on its own, except for the fact that each visit coincided with an upsurge of other incidents. Vandalism and threats to start with, escalating to suspicions of kidnapping and violence in the last few weeks.'

'Circumstantial,' continued Cordou.

'In a situation of this nature, as you yourself very well know, monsieur, everything is circumstantial in the first instance.'

'Who is behind the Network?' asked Rosa. 'Do you know?'

'A man called Kellen Harris.'

'You have had dealings with him before?' Helga asked.

Michael ignored the question. 'Returning to Monsieur Cordou's comment, I decided to monitor the activities of the Network in the hope of obtaining concrete proof. My agents confirmed that the People's Network was capable both of implementing high-level strategic and organisational initiatives and had the opportunity to do so. What I could not ascertain – and have still not been able to clarify – is how many of those close to Harris are involved in the illegal side of the Network's operations and how many are bona fide members who joined in good faith.'

Michael paused for a moment and took a sip of water from a glass on the table in front of him.

Pierre shuffled in his chair. 'You have not convinced me the Network was responsible for the attack on the old man this morning. The Network or this Mr Harris were not mentioned by name in the attack on the old man.'

'I don't think it is unreasonable to draw the conclusion that the two are connected.'

'In my opinion, it is,' challenged Cordou.

Michael stared at him. 'Then,' he replied in a measured voice, 'I think we must agree to disagree.'

Silence.

'That was helpful background,' said Nelson finally, 'and brings us to what happened during Operation Bayoux.'

Michael was still looking at Cordou, interested in his attempts to rubbish the connection between the Network and events in the Marsh Projects.

'Michael?'

'Thank you, Nelson,' he said, snapping his attention back to the immediate matter in hand. 'My strategy was to steal the blood samples I believed the Network were going to take from the Lightermen. From our surveillance of the Network, we knew they routinely offered vaccinations to communities they visited and my agents already had reported that equipment necessary for the taking and refrigeration of blood was being packed alongside the usual provisions.

'Given the recent threats, I thought it unlikely the Lightermen would cooperate with us over a request for blood – they're no more trusting of official organisations than unofficial ones – and, in any case, there was no time. I assumed Harris's tactic would be to take blood from the more accessible members of the Lightermen community without telling them what it was for.'

'And?' said Otto.

'And everything went according to plan. The Network's operation was disrupted, my agents seized some of the samples and the scientists here in the Ministry are already working on their analysis.'

There was a stir of interest around the table.

'That's excellent,' said Rosa.

Otto nodded. 'When do you expect the first results?'

'It's difficult to give a precise answer,' Michael replied. 'They appreciate the extreme urgency of the situation, but it is conceivable they will not finish all the essential tests before we have concluded our business here. If that is the case – and I hope it won't be – the meeting will need to reconvene tomorrow. Weather permitting.'

Cordou banged his hand down on the table. The spoon fell out of the saucer of his coffee cup.

'That is simply not acceptable.'

'Monsieur Cordou,' Michael relied calmly. 'We all share your impatience. Everyone in this room is as eager to know the results of the tests as you are. But my scientists cannot work miracles.' He paused. 'However, if you – or any of the members around this table – feel unhappy at leaving the samples in the safekeeping of the Ministry overnight, then I'm sure it would be possible to arrange for you to be accommodated here. Until tomorrow morning if necessary.'

Michael was bluffing. The last thing he wanted was to babysit Cordou all night. Preliminary results would in fact be available in a matter of hours, but Michael knew it was essential he had time to analyse the findings before he shared them with the Consortium. If he decided to share them at all.

'There's no question of that,' said Rosa. 'I am prepared to return tomorrow.'

'That is also my opinion,' agreed Otto Bauer. 'It would be absurd to sit here all night. I don't know quite what Monsieur Cordou imagines will happen in the space of twelve hours. No one is likely to break into the Ministry and steal the information away from under our noses.'

There were a few quiet laughs at this comment.

Michael smiled, then threw the ball back to Cordou. 'Pierre?'

'For now, it appears I am outnumbered,' he said. The implication behind his words was clear. He was only biding his time.

'Thank you.'

'But do you have any idea of what you think the scientists might find?' asked Helga.

'None whatsoever,' Michael replied. This, at least, was the truth. 'We will just have to be patient for another few hours. Now, is there any other business?'

Nobody spoke.

'No? Then perhaps we should adjourn and all try to make it back to wherever we are going before the rain starts.'

Everybody immediately looked of the window at the black and angry sky.

'Good idea,' said Nelson.

14

'The point is that they didn't trust us,' said Vicky, opening the fridge to get herself a drink. 'Pure and simple.'

'Bullshit,' replied Lonnie. 'It was just a small group and things got out of hand. You're reading too much into it.'

'Reading too much into it. They had guns, for Christ's sake!'

'I didn't see any guns.'

'What the fuck do you mean. You're not deaf, are you?'

He looked at her with contempt. 'One: I heard *a* gun not guns plural. And two: yes, I heard the shots, but I didn't see any weapons. I don't know why you're getting so hysterical.'

Vicky lost her temper. 'You are such a sexist bastard.'

'Guys, come on,' said Malik. 'We're all frustrated. Let's not take it out on each other.'

Vicky slammed the door of the fridge.

'I suppose a beer's out of the question?' said Lonnie.

'Fuck off.'

Lonnie laughed and hooked his legs over the arm of the chair, so there wasn't room for her to get past.

'Talk about frustrated . . .' he said, as she walked by.

Leah closed her eyes. She hated the way Lonnie and Vicky got at each other all the time and hated the fact that Malik and Jonas always felt the need to intervene, like parents who simply can't accept that their children loathe one another. Most of all, she hated being here at all, just in case anything important got said, when she'd rather be upstairs in her room, resting before she went out. She twisted her plait between her fingers.

'But was the fight premeditated, do you think?' said Malik.

Vicky nodded. 'Definitely, I'd say. Unless the Lightermen are usually armed.'

'Christ,' said Lonnie. 'I keep telling you the Lightermen weren't "armed".'

Jonas was perched on the edge of the sofa, looking apologetic as usual.

'You must have seen something, Lonnie? You were there with Kellen doing the vaccinations.'

Lonnie stubbed out his cigarette, then put the ashtray on the floor, letting it drop the last couple of inches. A dead match bounced out.

'Not really. This group of about seven Lightermen appeared out of nowhere and started throwing accusations about.'

Leah opened her eyes. 'Accusations about what?'

'I thought you'd dropped off,' said Jonas.

'I am tired,' she admitted.

'Is there anything I can get you?'

'That's kind of you, Jonas, but I'm fine thanks.'

'What accusations?' repeated Malik.

'I didn't hear much. Something about an attack, intimidation. Kellen tried to defuse the situation. Next thing I knew, someone had pulled a knife.'

'So you got the impression that it was directed at Kellen in particular?' said Leah. 'Not just anybody who happened to be there?'

Lonnie shrugged, then got up and ambled across to put on some music. Aggressive techno blasted out into the room. Jonas winced.

'Too loud,' shouted Vicky. 'Turn it down.'

Lonnie clicked the mouse, then pulled some beers from the fridge, threw one to Malik, one to Jonas, then wandered back to his seat. The cans popped open with a tiny fizz. It was like being at an awkward party. No one getting on, no one comfortable, everyone waiting for someone else to rescue the evening.

'The thing is,' said Malik after a few minutes. 'The atmosphere was already strange, even before the Lightermen turned up. I got the feeling people were expecting trouble.'

'Exactly,' agreed Jonas. 'First, nobody came. Then when they did, they all seemed nervous.'

Lonnie was rolling a joint, sprinkling the grass in a thin line inside the creased white paper. 'Yeah, at least they're usually grateful.'

'It's not actually supposed to be about you and your feelings,' said Vicky.

'Christ, you piss me off,' he sneered.

'The feeling's mutual, Lonnie, believe me.'

Suddenly Leah couldn't bear it for a second longer.

'Enough!' she shouted at them. 'You're driving me mad.'

Everyone looked at her in amazement. Leah never raised her voice to anyone.

'Yes, pack it in you two,' Malik added quickly.

'I'm sorry,' Vicky looked apologetic. 'I didn't mean to upset you. But it's just such a waste. All that preparation and planning for nothing.'

Leah rubbed her eye, 'I know. And I'm sorry I yelled at you. Forget it. How much of the stuff did we get out?'

'Not that much,' said Malik. 'Some of the medicines and supplies, certainly, but I think most of the inoculation equipment got destroyed in the stampede.'

'I left the food,' said Jonas. 'There didn't seem to be any reason not to.'

'No, that's fine,' said Leah. 'It was more the idea of syringes or drugs left lying about that worried me.'

'We did all we could in the circumstances,' said Malik.

Jonas looked worried. 'Do you think we ought to go back and make sure? Tomorrow or something?'

Lonnie laughed. 'You must be out of your mind. I can't see you getting a friendly reception if you turn up asking for your drugs back. Anyway, kids around there know what to do with a syringe. They'll be grateful for the clean kit . . .'

Leah looked at him. 'That's a particularly unhelpful comment.'

'Just the truth,' he said, lighting his joint. 'Not down to me.'

'What time is it?' asked Vicky, leaning over the back of the sofa from behind. 'Didn't Kellen say he'd be here at seven? It must be after that now.'

Jonas looked at his watch. 'It's twenty past now.'

'Is the cut on his arm all right?'

'Yes,' he continued. 'I dressed it on the boat for him, then cleaned it and gave him a fresh bandage when we got back here.'

'Where is he then?' said Vicky.

'Where d'you think,' said Lonnie. 'Looking after our poor traveller friend.'

Vicky pulled a face. 'Do you have to be such a prick all the time? It doesn't help.'

'What doesn't help?' said Kellen from the doorway.

Vicky and Jonas looked embarrassed, Malik relieved. Leah noticed Lonnie was merely amused. He doesn't care if he was overheard, she realised with a flash thought. He knows Kellen will let it go.

'We were just wondering if Annie was OK,' said Malik.

'She's a bit shocked and she'll probably have a black eye in the morning, but otherwise she's fine. I've talked to her already and she didn't see anything relevant, so she's going to stay upstairs.'

Everyone settled themselves down so they could hear what Kellen had to say. Malik gave his chair up and went to join Vicky. Leah and Jonas stayed put on the sofa. Lonnie twisted his chair around. It looked like a group therapy meeting, everybody watchful and impatient.

'Can we get rid of the music?' said Kellen.

Jonas pressed the control.

'Right. We spent a lot of time and effort on today's visit

to the Projects. Most of our stuff got broken or stolen, some of us got hurt in the process and we're all feeling pretty angry. It's possible the food and blankets might get to the right people, but most of it will end up being sold on. There's nothing we can do about it now, though, so there's no point worrying.'

'What we've not been able to work out,' said Vicky, 'is why the fight started in the first place? And why the atmosphere was so strange. Not just the Lightermen, but everybody.'

Kellen pushed his fingers back through his curly hair, then leaned forward. As if he was about to tell them a secret.

'What you all need to know is that the fight was deliberately started by the Lightermen – nothing we did provoked it – and was intended to both fuck up our reputation in the Projects and disrupt today's expedition. If I had realised how serious the situation was, perhaps I would have made different decisions.'

'Situation?' questioned Malik.

Kellen sat back in his chair again.

'For some time, I've suspected that the Network was being watched. I wasn't certain, but there were all sorts of clues. Questions being asked, people seen hanging about, volunteers being quizzed about what was going on. Not a big deal, but enough to put me on the alert.'

The room was totally silent. Smoke from Lonnie's cigarette twisted up towards the ceiling.

'To tell you the truth, I thought it was journalists to start with. Sniffing around for a story. We all know – anybody who has anything to do with the Network knows – that the official welfare agencies hate us and I certainly wouldn't put it past any of them to put a reporter on to us, to stir things up.'

'Or fabricate something,' said Vicky.

'None of this is new, of course,' Kellen continued. 'This tension between us and them. I've never considered it something we couldn't handle But after what happened today, I've come to the conclusion we're up against something more than scum journalists and a bit of official resentment. I think the fight was engineered by whoever it is who's been watching the Network. Me, in particular. They knew exactly where I was going to be, exactly what I was going to be doing.'

Malik looked confused. 'You can't be saying that the Lightermen are behind this?'

'No, obviously not. What I am saying is the Lightermen are being used by someone else.'

Leah looked at him. 'Do you have any idea who?'

The question hung in the air between them for an instant while Kellen produced a joint from his pocket and lit it. Taking his time.

Finally, he shook his head. 'What I reckon is that we're talking about some massive scam involving the Marsh Projects in some way. Serious money, not just a little bit going missing here and there.'

'I don't understand,' said Vicky.

'OK,' he replied. 'Let me give you an example. After that incredible rainstorm in the middle of July – when the river burst its banks and flooded Unity Pier – a couple of the residents contacted me and asked me to draft a formal letter of complaint to the Agency of Climate and the Environment which—'

'The residents?' Leah interrupted. 'Not the Lightermen?'

'The regular residents. In the letter I spelled out exactly how many homes had been destroyed in the flooding; explained the effects the month-on-month increases in wind speed, temperature and humidity were having, all that sort of stuff.

'But this morning, when I managed to talk to one of the community leaders involved, I heard that nobody from the Agency had come to assess the damage or take readings. In fact, they've not even received an acknowledgement of receipt.'

Vicky looked sceptical. 'That means nothing. It would be a miracle to get any of that lot off their arses in summer.'

'I don't think they'll ever get a reply. I delivered the letter by hand, so I know it got into the building. I'm convinced the letter was destroyed, either before it reached the right department or by someone within the department.'

'I still don't see the point you're making,' said Malik.

'What's the connection between this and what happened today?'

'The point is that somebody does not want any attention paid to the Marsh Projects. They had to get rid of the letter, otherwise there'd be a danger of someone turning up and poking about.'

'I think I see what you're saying,' said Jonas.

'I haven't got a handle on it yet,' continued Kellen. 'It might be that money is disappearing from welfare funds into someone's pockets. It could be that someone is selling power supplies that have already officially been allocated to the Marsh Projects: that is, making money twice on the same electricity, water and gas supplies. I just don't know.'

'But you have no proof?'

'Sweet Leah,' said Kellen softly. 'Always the scientist wanting proof . . .'

'I'm sorry if I'm being stupid here,' said Vicky. 'But I still don't see how this ties in with our reception this morning.'

Kellen passed the joint to her. 'OK. I'm obviously not being clear enough. Rumour has it that the Lightermen are being intimidated. In the past few weeks there have been threats, kidnappings and this morning one of the older Lightermen was badly beaten up.'

'And?' said Vicky.

'And they think the Network is behind it.'

'But that's ridiculous,' exploded Vicky. 'Why could they possibly think that?'

'Easy,' said Lonnie, putting his hands behind his head. 'Someone told them. All it takes is a whisper planted in the right place. Rumours spread like wildfire in there.'

Kellen nodded. 'So it's back to the same question. Who started the rumour?'

Leah sat back and thought while the conversation carried on around her. What game was he playing?

15

Michael was in the kitchen fixing himself a whisky when he heard the sound of the outer door.

He was relieved. There had been casualties in the course of Operation Bayoux and he hadn't been able to find out if Leah was among them. Another Unit agent had reported that he'd seen her running back to the boat with a tall woman with short, dark hair. There'd been blood everywhere, apparently.

'Leah,' he said, charging out into the hall. 'Are you OK?'

'I'm fine,' she replied, wondering why he was so jumpy. Water from her coat was dripping all over the floor, so he disappeared into the bathroom and got her a towel. She eased herself out of her coat and Michael hung it up on the peg, which was too high for her to reach.

'Thanks.'

'Someone saw you covered in blood. It looked as if you had been hurt.'

'It wasn't mine,' she said. 'It had just got all over my clothes as well.'

He smiled. 'Well, that's something. Did you have trouble getting away this evening?'

'There was a post-mortem, which went on for hours, but it was no problem slipping away afterwards. I can't stay long, though. The flooding's already bad. I had to come a very long way round to get here.'

Michael watched her undo her plait and rub the worst of

the rain out. It suddenly struck him he'd never seen her with her hair loose before.

'You look tired,' he said.

Leah glanced at him, surprised by the concern in his voice. 'I am tired,' she said. 'And very wet. But, I'm fine. Did anyone in the Unit get hurt?'

'A few cuts and bruises. Nothing major.'

Michael wandered back into the kitchen to retrieve his glass. The golden liquid slopped against the sides.

'Do you want a drink?'

She shook her head. 'That looks like rather more than a double . . .'

He shrugged. 'Coffee, then?'

'Nothing, thanks. I just want to know how things went at your end, then head straight back to the Pen to sleep. We got some of the blood samples, I presume?'

'Everything went like clockwork. One of the containers of blood was taken and delivered straight to me at the Ministry. I passed it to Professor Stark and her team immediately, then called an emergency meeting of the Consortium for four o'clock.'

'And has she come up with anything yet?'

Michael pulled a piece of paper from his pocket, handed it over without a word, then watched the expression on Leah's face.

'This does mean what I think it means?'

Michael nodded. 'It's early days yet, but it appears that the Lightermen have a genetic resistance to malaria. This is on the basis of Professor Stark's preliminary screening – and she's obviously running more detailed tests now – but she's confident.'

Leah's eyes were shining with excitement.

'Did you expect this, Michael? Truthfully . . .'

'I did think there would be something, but only because of the amount of effort Harris was putting into getting hold of the blood. On a scientific level, I was sceptical. Christ, we all know that unique genes rarely come from non-isolated groups, particularly ones of European rather than Pacific extraction. However, Harris just seemed so convinced that his conviction sort of convinced me. The Emperor's new clothes . . .'

Leah smiled at the expression. She and Michael had had versions of the 'how/what does Kellen know' conversation several times. Once, in passing, she'd casually suggested Michael's faith in Kellen was a classic case of the Emperor's new clothes rather than anything substantial. He'd denied it, but now she found it strangely gratifying to realise he'd tucked the phrase away in his brain. It was always difficult to tell whether or not he was listening to a word she said.

'So this brings us back to the same old point,' she said. 'How Kellen was alerted to the possibilities of the Lightermen genes in the first place. Educated guess?'

'It's got to be more than that. I can't believe he'd go to so much effort on no more than a hunch.'

Leah looked amused. 'As if you don't go on instinct and think about the evidence later.'

Michael frowned. 'That supports what I'm saying,' he said defensively. 'I always build on something, however small or insignificant it might seem. It's all a question of weighing up the odds.'

Leah smiled to herself. He hated to be teased, only slightly less than he hated to be compared to anyone else.

'Getting back to the issue, the question is whether he's working for someone or if he's intending to auction the DNA sample on the black market.'

'Psychologically the latter is more likely,' said Leah. 'He's not someone who likes to be hired. He prefers to be in the driving seat. I think he'll sell to the highest bidder, although that doesn't necessarily mean he knows what property the genes have. Just that there is supposed to be something.'

'Are there adequate research facilities in the Pen to run an analysis?'

'No. Nor, for that matter, anyone capable of doing it.'

'There are laboratories, though?'

'There are,' said Leah. 'However, they're pretty basic and

used pretty much only for manufacturing drugs. Nothing hard. Just Spinners, Special K, Lethe. They're certainly not equipped for separating the blood into its plasma, red cells, white cells – which is the most effective way to proceed with the analysis – and coming up with reliable answers.'

Michael nodded. 'I think the only thing we can do at this point is continue monitoring him and see what he does. Maybe we'll pick up some leads.'

'I agree,' said Leah. 'Getting back to today, how did the Consortium take the news that Operation Bayoux had already taken place?'

'Badly, to start with. But once I'd showed them the footage of the beating given out to the old man, they shut up and listened.'

'The incident last week?' asked Leah. 'There's not been another attack?'

'No, the one you've already seen, although I gave the impression it'd happened this morning, as a way of justifying my decision to act without reference back to the meeting.'

Leah didn't comment. She could see it made sense tactically, but this was the side of Michael she did not like. His cavalier attitude to violence and his willingness to twist the truth.

'Cordou kicked up at the idea of coming back tomorrow to hear the results of the tests on the blood.'

Leah was still thinking, so didn't respond to this. For a moment, they sat in silence, listening to the rain hammering against the window.

'Have you decided how much you're going to tell the Consortium?' she said, after a while.

'I've a meeting scheduled with Professor Stark at nine fifteen tomorrow morning. Once I've heard what she's got to say, I'll make a final decision. At this stage, my instinct is to continue to tell them as little as possible. I'm still convinced one of them is up to something. Using their membership of the Consortium as a cover for illegal biotrading.'

'Cordou?'

'Possibly. He asks a lot of questions. But, then again, I loathe the man, so he's the one I would pick on.'

'What about your Dutch friend?'

'Nelson? I trust him implicitly, so I'll probably fill him in. But not until after the meeting. There won't be time before.'

Leah nodded.

'In any case, even if I'm wrong to mistrust them, there's bound to be somebody who will want to make an immediate statement about our preliminary findings, which would be a disaster and blow our chances of getting Harris. If we go with your gut feeling that he's more likely to be working for himself than someone else, he'll have to guarantee exclusivity to a buyer. He's not a fool. He knows he's only giving someone a head start on their competitors. Once the news is out, it will be a free-for-all to get their own DNA samples.'

'God, forget Kellen for a minute,' said Leah impatiently. 'Surely nobody in the Consortium would be that stupid. They're all professionals. They understand how essential it will be to put safeguards in place *before* even thinking about making a public announcement. Both to guard the research and development and, even more important, to protect the Lightermen.'

'You'd be surprised,' replied Michael darkly. 'Greed is a powerful thing, and I'm not prepared to risk it.'

'I don't imagine the Consortium would support your attitude.'

'I agree. Which is why I'm inclined to tell them nothing at all.'

Leah sighed. 'You're sailing close to the wind, Michael,' she said quietly. 'You have been all along. And now it appears we have a major scientific discovery on our hands, well . . .'

'Don't lecture me,' he said, draining his glass. 'I know what I'm doing.'

Leah looked at him. 'I hope you're right.'

'Don't worry. But tell me, does Harris know a container of blood was taken?'

'I wasn't there, so I'm not one hundred per cent sure, but I doubt it. Too much got destroyed to be able to work out what is missing.'

'So, what did he say?'

Leah gave a wry smile. 'It was a brilliant performance, actually. His explanation for the attack was that someone had put the Lightermen up to it. He said the Lightermen were being intimidated and that he'd long suspected the Network was under surveillance.'

'For what reason?'

'What he claimed – although I have no idea what he actually thinks – is that the Marsh Projects is in the centre of some sort of corruption scandal. By just being there, the Network draws unwelcome attention to the area. The easiest way of getting the Network to stay away, therefore, is to start a rumour that the Network was behind the recent spate of kidnappings and attacks.'

'All very plausible.'

Leah raised her eyebrows. 'And no more than the truth, after all, although he also said he didn't know who was behind it. The interesting thing was how people reacted to what Kellen was saying. Everyone seemed genuinely shocked. I didn't get the impression it was faked.'

'Who was there?'

'Malik, Jonas, Vicky, Lonnie, Kellen, me.'

'Are you saying nobody else knows what's going on?'

'I'm not sure. I don't trust Lonnie, but then it's the same situation as you and Pierre Cordou. Lonnie is a thug, has a problem with women, cares about no one but himself and I'm sure he is more than capable of dishing it out if required. But, then again, if every man I disliked turned out to be a criminal, then I'd be running for cover. On which point, I thought we'd agreed on no guns.'

'It was nothing to do with me,' said Michael, taking her abrupt change of tack in his stride. 'Nobody in the Unit was armed. I made it quite clear our objective was to get the samples and run. Minimum fuss and no casualities.'

'And you didn't supply the Lightermen with anything?'

To her surprise, Michael actually looked hurt. 'I'm surprised you think I'd do that.'

Leah stared at him, trying to work out what was going through his mind. 'I'm sorry,' she said, 'but someone had a gun.'

'Kellen himself?'

'I've never seen him with one,' she replied. 'Anyway, look, is there anything else? If not, I'll get going. I don't want to find myself trapped here by the storm.' She glanced at the window. 'If anything, it sounds like it's getting worse out there.'

Michael shook his head. 'Just the usual. Keep in touch, play it safe and pull out if you think you're in any danger.'

'I'll be fine. Don't worry.'

He hopped down from the counter and walked with her into the hall. Leah put on her boots. Michael handed her down her coat.

'It's not too bad,' she said, feeling the sleeves. 'Almost dry.'

'Just before you go, tell me how the traveller fits in to any of this. Annie Jones. Your report was excellent, by the way.'

'God, I'd forgotten we hadn't talked about Annie yet. She's the one who got clobbered in the face, by the way. Honestly, Michael, I've no idea how – if at all – she fits into anything. I like her a lot. She's bright, funny, inquisitive, good company. Unfortunately, Kellen thinks so to.'

Michael nodded. 'She's attractive, I agree. Are she and Harris . . . ?'

'They're on the verge of starting something, I'd say, although I could be wrong. The thing is that even if Kellen wasn't physically attracted to Annie – which I'm sure he is – he's desperate to learn more about the travelling, so . . . He's got nothing out of Mary Royle. She keeps herself to herself and rarely comes out of her room, except to eat and go for short walks. Kellen worked hard on her to start with, but finally gave up when he realised he wasn't going to get anywhere.'

'What does Royle do up there all day?'

Leah shook her head. 'I've no idea. I guess she's just biding her time.'

'For what?'

'Don't know. And, more's the point, I don't think Kellen knows either. On the odd occasion I have seen Mary, it's been more than clear that she despises Kellen. I guess he's hoping Annie will work out better.'

'Clever lady,' he muttered.

Leah glanced at him.

'Anyway, remind me who knows about the travellers?' he continued.

'The usual crew.'

'And what about Annie? Does she know about Mary?'

'I don't know.'

'But Annie understands what's happened to her?'

'Kellen told her.'

'And she believed him?'

Leah shrugged. 'I'm sorry, I don't know that either. She appears to, in so far as she asks lots of questions about the things she sees. New buildings, things like different foods and stuff like that. But she didn't seem to want to talk seriously about it today. I didn't push her.'

Leah put her hand on the door, then hesitated.

'How do you know Annie is attractive?'

'What do you mean?'

'Just what I said. When did you see her, to know that she is attractive?'

To her surprise, Michael looked at his feet.

'I was at the Pen yesterday morning.'

She stared at him. 'God, I can't believe it,' she exploded. 'What a stupid thing to do. What if you'd been challenged?'

'I wasn't.'

'What the hell's got into you?'

Michael said nothing.

'Look,' said Leah heavily, 'I'm not trying to undermine your authority. But, at the same time, it seems to me that you're increasingly making more and more decisions that could end up jeopardising everything the Unit's trying to achieve. And it's making me nervous.'

He put his hand on her thin shoulder, not wanting them to part on bad terms.

'Don't be nervous,' he said. 'Everything's under control. Get in touch tomorrow and I'll let you know what's happened with Professor Stark and the Consortium.'

Leah reached up and gave his hand a quick squeeze. 'All right,' she conceded. 'But please think about what I've said.'

'Go and get some sleep. And don't get too wet going back.'

'Some chance. Now, you take care. Do you hear me?'

'I hear you,' he said.

Once the door had shut behind her, he went back into the kitchen and poured himself another drink.

16

Outside the Pen the wind was howling, rattling the shutters. Rain splattered against the sides of the building in gusts. Rubbish was hurled high in the air, ricocheting off the roof and walls. The narrow street was a river now, as the water surged over the cobbled stones and plunged into the drains at the bottom of the street.

The eye of the storm was close now. The thunder claps were four minutes apart, then three, then two. Building up like contractions. The Thames was angry, splashing up over to the banks. The trees lining the walkways lunged like tethered horses, as if trying to escape the water massing below them. Once, men and women made sacrifices to propitiate the gods. A thousand years later, people watching from the safety of their lofts and apartments thought only of the financial cost and their insurance policies.

Annie woke from her doze with a jolt, wondering what had disturbed her. She didn't feel cold, hadn't been having a bad dream, and she'd become accustomed to the noise of the storm. Lying safe in bed, it had soothed her at first, then lulled her to sleep.

'Hey,' said Kellen.

Annie turned sideways and saw him sitting in the high-backed chair in the centre of the room. She smiled and rolled on to her side, propping herself up on one elbow so she could see him better.

'Is it usually this bad?' she said. 'The storm, I mean.'

'Usually.'

'The thunder's very close.'

'Yes. Are you scared?'

'No, never. Quite exciting though.'

Kellen smiled. 'This is nothing special. We get much worse.'

Silence.

'Do you want to talk some more about the weather . . .'

Annie grinned. 'No,' she said. 'It's just that you took me by surprise, sitting watching me like that. I didn't hear you come in.'

'Like what?' he asked innocently.

'You know very well what I mean. Just, looking at me in that way.'

'I like looking at you.'

Annie suddenly felt self-conscious. She sat up, swung her feet over the edge of the bed, and started tracing patterns on the wooden floor with her toes to avoid catching his eye.

'I'm glad about that,' she added, after a pause.

'Are you?'

She nodded. 'You know I am.'

'It's always a good thing to make sure,' he said. 'Don't you think?'

'I guess.'

Annie was jittery now, as if her insides were tied up tight like a ball of string. All the time she'd been imagining what it might be like to make love to Kellen. But now he was actually here, she could hardly trust herself to say or do anything. She didn't want to fuck up. More than that, she didn't want him to fuck up either.

She got off the bed and strolled to look at one of the tapestries under the window, as if it was suddenly the most interesting thing in the room to her. It was too dark to see.

'Allow me.'

She heard the strike of a match behind her as Kellen lit the candles, then the hiss of the match as he extinguished it between a finger and thumb seconds later.

'Thank you,' she said.

Her voice sounded squeaky and dry to her. Not normal or relaxed at all.

Kellen barely made a sound as he walked across the room. Annie was aware of every inch of skin on her body, every nerve ending, every muscle. She tried to imagine how it would feel when he put his hands around her waist, when he'd start to explore her body, reaching over her shoulders to stroke her breasts. How he'd pull her body against his and tell her what he was going to do to her. He would seduce her well, she knew that. It was just that she fancied a different sequence of events, one where she did the seducing.

Annie turned to face him, the expression on her face one of amusement and challenge. Kellen stopped still and watched as she began to undo each button of her long, red tunic in front of him. She could see his breathing getting faster, could see him fighting not to let his eyes stray to her breasts, now half-exposed as the material gradually fell open. So many buttons. Annie shook the tunic and felt it land on the ground behind her. Kellen took a step towards her.

'Don't move,' she said.

He smiled. She moved a little closer. She could see the excitement in his eyes now, the anticipation. His breath was hot on her skin. Without taking her eyes from his face, she reached down and took hold of him. Roughly, firmly. He smiled as he hardened against her hand. Still holding his gaze, she pushed his shirt over his shoulders so his arms were pinned to his sides. She began to stroke his chest and his arms and his neck. He closed his eyes.

'You can take these off now,' she said, guiding his hand to her waist. He wriggled out of his shirt, then bent down in front of her. She could feel just the tips of his fingers as he carefully eased her trousers over her hips and thighs and knees. She stepped out of them. Kellen stayed on his knees while she gently kissed his hair, but when he tried to kiss the smooth, flat skin of her abdomen, she pushed his head away.

'I didn't say you could touch.'

Kellen sat back on his heels, smiling.

'Did I?'

'No.'

'Get up now.'

He did as he was told.

'You're over-dressed.'

Without a word, Kellen unbuttoned his flies. Annie knew he wanted her to react to his physical beauty, but she said nothing, did nothing to betray the raw thumping of her blood between her legs. He straightened up, threw his trousers at her feet like a challenge.

Annie took him by surprise. He wasn't expecting her to jump at him and he was knocked off balance. As they fell together to the floor, she felt him grab the back of her neck and pull her face down on to his. He forced her mouth open and ran his tongue over her teeth.

'Is this what you wanted?' she whispered. 'What you've been thinking about?'

She could feel his fingers digging into her flesh. Suddenly, Annie felt she couldn't wait any longer, wanted him inside her. She tried to manoeuvre them into the right position. He wouldn't let her.

'No,' he said, as he felt her struggling. 'Now it's my turn.'

Without warning, he flipped them both over, so she was now lying beneath him on the hard wood. Pinning her down with his legs, he started to bite her breasts, lick them. She clawed at him, but it made no difference.

He suddenly pushed his fingers into her, letting her arch up towards him before snatching them away. Over and over he did the same thing, until Annie thought she was going to burst. Finally, he linked his arms behind her waist, dragged her up from the floor to the bed and pushed up hard inside her.

'Fuck you,' she shouted as she came.

Kellen laughed.

17

Monday 4 August

The storm had blown itself out now. Everything was still.

Kellen was sitting at his computer in the dark, thinking of Annie. He could still smell her on his skin and his hair, as if she had stamped her claim on him. He thought about her exotic eyes and the feel of her short hair between his fingers and her strong legs wrapped round his back. She was only on the other side of the wall. He could go back in there, wake her up . . .

Later, he thought. After all, she wasn't going anywhere.

'Activate.'

Earlier, he had keyed in his report on the day's events in the Marsh Projects. Now what he wanted to do was to add his impressions of how everybody had reacted to his explanation. Vicky had been outraged, Malik keen to make sure he wasn't missing anything, Jonas characteristically quiet, Leah uncharacteristically so. She looked tired and under pressure. Maybe he'd try to have a quiet word with her in the morning. See if there was anything going on he should know about.

Despite the problems, he'd still got what he wanted out of the expedition – blood from the Lightermen. Lonnie had treated it with anti-coagulant straight away and stored it in the secure lab downstairs. Provided it was kept at four degrees centigrade, the blood would be fine for a couple of weeks. He continued to type. Totally old-fashioned, but Kellen found it worked better for this sort of analysis. The sheer physical movement helped him put things in order in his mind more easily than when he was speaking. He liked the sound of the keys tapping and the clear connection between how fast his hands moved and how immediately the text appeared. It always felt as if he was being shown the mechanical workings of his mind.

He lit a joint. The bottom line was that someone had told the Lightermen that the Network was behind the attack on the old man. Was it a guess? Or had his boys left evidence of some kind? Either way, he wasn't thrilled.

After this morning, Kellen was no longer in any doubt that the surveillance that the Network was under was connected to the Lightermen rather than the travellers. It was possible it could be a biotech corporation, one prepared to do a bit of unscrupulous business. It was even possible the Ministry of BioProspecting and Patenting was involved, although unlikely. They were too vulnerable to the slightest allegation of misconduct to be behind something like this. Whatever else, two things were clear. First, that he should shift the Lightermen samples as fast as possible. Second, he should not underestimate his opponent. Whoever he was.

Kellen had just shut down the computer, when a sound outside caught his attention. He looked at the time. Just after one thirty. Late for someone to be coming in. He got up and looked out of the window. One of the streetlights had been smashed in the storm, so it was too dark for him to see much. But he did hear the unmistakable click of the side door. Only a handful of people had keys, so it couldn't be a tramp or stray volunteer looking for a late bed for the night.

He locked the study, then quickly went through the bedroom and out into the corridor. He hesitated for a moment at the top of the stairs, thinking that it might be easier simply to see if any of the bedrooms on the landing were empty. But then it would be hard to explain why he was knocking on people's doors in the middle of the night. Besides, he'd lost track of who was sleeping with whom and there could be perfectly legitimate reasons for someone not being in their own bed.

Kellen crept down the stairs into the hall and looked around, aware that if there was someone, then he was more visible to them, than they were to him. He waited silently. Gave it five minutes, then decided not to waste any more time. He was tired and his mind had been on other things. Perhaps he'd imagined it.

Leah held her breath as she watched Kellen walk back up the stairs, then left into the corridor. Seconds later, she heard his bedroom door open, then close again. But she still didn't move. Gave herself another ten minutes to make sure she was absolutely safe. Only then did she come out of the shadows and run back to her room as quietly as she could. It had been too close for comfort.

In her dream, Annie was standing behind Leah. Slipping her fingers beneath the waistband of Leah's trousers to find wiry hair and folds of wet skin. The sensation was unfamiliar to her sleeping fingers. Like a secret.

Annie imagined herself holding Leah against her. She was so much shorter, that Annie could rest her chin on Leah's head. She put her arms around her and stroked her shoulders and breasts. Leah was so soft. Felt so young. Annie had always imagined her own body felt firm and powerful and strong to a lover, but Leah wasn't like that at all. She felt fragile.

Now she was dreaming that they were sitting naked opposite one another on the bed. Leah's hair was loose, cascading around her serious face like water.

'You've wanted this for a long time . . .' Leah's imaginary voice was husky, 'I can see what you're thinking.'

Leah leaned forward and kissed her. In Kellen's bed, the sleeping Annie rolled over, dizzy at the sensation. She floated weightless in her dream, imagining she could taste wine on Leah's lips and wondering how Leah's stomach and thighs could be so brown when she was always covered up from the sun. Annie put her hands on Leah's hips, pushed her down and buried her face between her legs. She could feel Leah's hands in her hair and Annie pushed deep inside her, feeling the flesh surround her hand like a glove.

'Are you awake?' whispered Kellen.

Annie half stirred. Gradually, Kellen's face came into focus. His green eyes looking down at her in the dark.

'No,' she said, her voice sodden with desire. 'But it's good you're here.'

It was after eight when Annie woke up again. Kellen was already dressed and brushing his hair in front of the mirror.

'Is it late?'

'Hey,' he said, turning around. 'No, it's early. I'm just going to grab some breakfast before I go out. I can get someone to bring you something?'

'No thanks, I'll come down.'

'Yesterday's breakfast was a one-off,' he said, putting the brush back on the chest of drawers. 'Usually we all do our own thing.'

'Who does all the shopping?'

'Everybody, on and off,' he replied. 'Anyway, shops are open all night, so there's never a problem.'

Annie covered herself with the sheet and sat up. 'What are the plans for today?'

Kellen pulled a face. 'I'm afraid I'm going to be out most of the day.'

She was disappointed. She'd hoped they might spend some time together. Go out, maybe get something to eat.

'Can't I come?'

'Sorry, no.'

Annie got out of bed and picked up her clothes from the chair without a word.

'Don't be like that,' said Kellen, giving her a hug. 'You'll find something to do here. I'm sure Leah will be around.

Or Vicky. Malik's running the coffee stall. You could help him out.'

'What coffee stall?'

'Over in the corner of the hall. We give out free drinks, a bit of food.'

'Drugs more like,' she said. 'According to Leah.'

'You puritan,' he said. 'Anyway, we sell the grass . . .'

'I can think of things I'd rather be doing,' she said, slipping her hand between his thighs.

He laughed. 'I'll remind you of that later.'

The normal early morning bustle greeted them as they walked into the kitchen. The clatter of cutlery and plates and spoons, the smell of hot bread, coffee and oranges.

Kellen helped himself to a few bits and pieces, then leaned over and kissed the back of her neck.

'I've got to run. See you later.'

Annie took some food and settled herself in between Jonas and Lonnie. 'Are most of these people staying here at the moment?' she asked, looking around the room.

'Most of this lot came yesterday and were too gutted to go home,' sneered Lonnie. 'Look at them. They all look so fucking miserable . . .'

Annie and Jonas conducted their entire conversation against the backdrop of sarcastic comments from Lonnie. She tried to take no notice, even though his observations were often accurate. People's hairstyles, their eating habits, he found something to criticise in everyone. As time went on, Annie got the definite feeling that he was doing it as much to annoy Jonas as to amuse her.

Suddenly, Lonnie leaned right across Annie. 'Shouldn't you be going now, Jonas? Haven't you got a job to go to?'

'Oh, what do you do?' she asked, sensing how tense Jonas was getting.

'I'm working at the Coma Hospital at the moment, just around the corner from here. It's very convenient.'

'Coma Hospital? What's that, exactly?'

Lonnie laughed. 'What do you think?'

She shuddered. The thought of rows of coma victims lying side by side waiting to be switched off turned her stomach. It was somehow just too inhuman.

'There are a few general hospitals left nowadays in the suburbs,' Jonas explained. 'But within the Peripherique, everything is specialist care. If you're having a baby you go to the Maternity Hospital, if you've got flu you go to the Flu Hospital.'

'At least you don't have to put up with any shit from the patients,' said Lonnie.

'For Christ's sake,' snapped Jonas.

Lonnie held up his hands, as if he was surrendering. 'Joke. Just joking.'

'Not a very nice one,' Annie said.

'Good jokes rarely are,' he replied. 'But don't worry. I'm just going.'

Lonnie got up, leaving his dirty plates on the table, then slapped Jonas hard on the back as he walked past him.

'Just you try to keep your hands off her, man . . .'

Annie and Jonas sat in silence until Lonnie had left the room.

'Lovely man,' said Annie. 'What an arsehole. Is he always like that?'

Jonas nodded. 'He particularly dislikes me for some reason. Never misses an opportunity to have a go. And he and Vicky are always at each other's throats.'

'Why does anybody put up with him?'

'He and Kellen are close. I can't work it out myself, but that's how it is.'

Annie fleetingly wondered why men she fancied always turned out to have wankers for friends.

'I'm afraid I've got to go as well,' Jonas continued. 'I'm sorry to leave you on your own.'

'Don't worry. I'm fine here.'

'Nice talking with you.'

'Yes, you too.'

Annie watched him clear his plates, then head out of the

room. Feeling a bit abandoned and sorry for herself, she got up and poured herself another cup of coffee. She already felt at a loose end and it was only just after nine o'clock in the morning. It was like being on holiday when all your friends are at school. You think it's going to be fun, but you end up bored out of your mind.

She was balancing a spoon on her fingers when Leah appeared. The dream, which she'd completely forgotten until now, suddenly came back to her.

'Hello,' said Leah, kissing her on the cheeks. 'What's up?'

'What do you mean?'

'You've gone all red.'

Annie's hands flew to her face. Her skin was burning.

'Nothing,' she mumbled. 'Anyway, what about you? Look at those bags under your eyes.'

'I didn't get much sleep last night,' Leah admitted.

Annie waited while she got some coffee. 'So, what are your plans today?'

'Nothing much,' said Leah.

'You haven't got a job to go to?'

'I do the odd day of consultancy here and there, but nothing today.'

'Fantastic. Would you like to do something then?'

'Sure,' said Leah, cutting her apple. 'I've one or two things I have to finish first—'

Annie's face fell.

Leah laughed. 'It won't take long, I promise. Say, twelve o'clock. Then I'm completely at your disposal for the rest of the day.'

'Brilliant,' she said, as another part of the dream suddenly came to mind.

'You've gone red again,' said Leah, as she popped a piece of fruit into her mouth.

18

Michael was down in the maze of secluded corridors in the lower basement of the Ministry of BioProspecting and Patenting, which surrounded the laboratories and test areas.

His shoes clipped precisely on the tiles as he walked. It was so quiet he could almost hear his heart beating above the faint hum of the air-conditioning. He straightened his jacket and looked at his watch: 09:14:22. Less than an hour until the meeting with the Consortium partners. More time wasted explaining and justifying and jumping through hoops. He hated it. Being questioned, being called to account. But he had no choice. Without the Consortium, there was no money for the Unit. And without the Unit he wouldn't even get close to achieving what he wanted.

He headed towards the door marked 'Code Area 4 – Restricted Access', put his hand on the fingerprint recognition panel on the security door and was admitted through to a smaller lobby.

There were six laboratories, three on each side. Michael walked to the last door on the left and repeated the access procedures. He was impatient, kept pressing his hand on the panel, as if it would work faster if he bullied it.

Professor Marie Stark, a small woman with her brown hair cut into a bob, was standing next to the long chrome workbench. They'd already spent half an hour talking on the phone at eight o'clock. A perceptive, decisive and clear-thinking woman, he had no hesitation in choosing her to head up the team working on the Lightermen samples.

Her two junior colleagues, Dr Habib and Dr Masopeh, were with her. From the glint of adrenaline and exhaustion in their eyes, he realised they had also spent the night in the lab running tests and double-checking their results. The question was, could Michael bring them onside?

'Good morning, gentlemen,' he said. 'Marie.'

Professor Stark smiled. 'I've brought Nabeel and Joseph up to date on our earlier discussions, stressing the need for their absolute discretion.'

'Thank you. As Professor Stark has explained, we have found ourselves in an unusually sensitive and difficult position. The implications of the Lightermen DNA possessing a resistance to malaria are enormous. Obviously, we will have to set up field tests, run controls and commit considerable resources into research and analysis. But if these preliminary findings are verified, this could be one of the most significant medical discoveries this century.'

Michael looked at them and was reminded of himself at their age. Enthusiastic, full of zeal, desperate to make a difference to the world. Fifteen years ago he had been in New Zealand and was one of the few independent signatories to the Mataatua Declaration which called for a global moratorium on any further commercialisation of traditional plants, medicines and human genetic materials until indigenous people and the international community had set appropriate protection mechanisms in place.

All of it had been predicated based on the crucial relevance of genetic isolation. Now, if the Lightermen analysis held good, then everything they had achieved would have to be fought for all over again. Any vulnerable group, anywhere in the world – not just isolated peoples – could be at risk from aggressive gene harvesting. And by the time some of the checks and measures designed to protect the South were extended to people of the North, the damage would have been done. The patents already filed, the money in private pockets.

Dr Masopeh cut into Michael's train of thought. 'Sir?'

'I'm sorry. As I was saying, the scientific significance of this is something we need to absorb and think about, aside from issues connected to the Lightermen DNA itself. I suspect we will all look back on this and see it as one of the most significant nights of our careers.'

He was aware of Professor Stark nodding.

'In any other circumstances, I would not consider with-holding information from my partners. However, I don't think we have a choice here. Any leak or public announcement would not only be premature but would almost certainly jeopardise much of what we hope to achieve.'

Michael's intention was to create a sense of drama and of history-in-the-making and put pressure on the two young men to feel a sense of loyalty and responsibility to something larger than the Ministry. His calculation was that the more important they felt, the more likely it was that they would play along.

'I will be honest with you, gentlemen. The Lightermen samples were obtained by unorthodox means. With the exception of the members of the Consortium itself, nobody outside of this room knows we have the blood. It must stay that way.'

'Go on, sir,' said Dr Habib.

'I do not wish to compromise your integrity in any way. And I am not asking you to conceal or distort information. However, I do not want you to reveal what you have discovered about the Lightermen samples to anyone. Confirm there is something, convey a sense of excitement, but keep the facts to yourselves for the time being.'

He paused to give them the chance to speak. Neither of them did.

'As I said, I hope you will not feel compromised by this. I am confident Professor Stark chose wisely.'

'I understand the situation is delicate,' said Dr Habib

finally, meeting Michael's gaze. 'And I am happy to help in any way I can.'

'Dr Masopeh?'

'It presents no problem for me either, sir.'

'Thank you,' said Michael. 'I appreciate your support.'

Professor Stark also looked relieved as she turned to Michael. 'The report is already up on Terminal 6,' she said. 'Dr Masopeh, Dr Habib and I will take a few minutes now to run through things. We'll be in Suite A if you need us.'

'Thank you, Marie.'

'If not before, then we'll see you in the meeting at ten fifteen.'

Michael waited until she'd left the room. Just one more phase to go, then he'd be free to carry on his investigations without someone always looking over his shoulder or demanding explanations. He went over to the computer, adjusted the height of the chair to suit his longer legs, then sat down. He'd got that prickling behind his eyes again that threatened a migraine. He rubbed the back of his neck to release some of the tension at the tip of his spine. Every now and again, he wished there was someone to do it for him.

Michael was a driven man. He knew it, everyone around him knew it. He had no personal life, no attachments and had devoted his adult life to fighting the biotech barons as a way of running from the anger inside him. Like many men committed to a cause, Michael cared about people only in the abstract. Not in the particular. Even Leah did not realise how few emotional resources he had, how little anybody mattered to him. That his concern and dedication were fuelled by a wish to obliterate memory, not a passion to make things better.

Michael sat at the terminal jigging his legs up and down, his head buzzing. He was nearly there. Soon, he'd have enough evidence to expose Kellen and it would be over.

The atmosphere in the Conference Chamber was tense. Dr Guitierez, Nelson Huyk and Otto Bauer were already seated, their body language making clear both their discomfort and their lack of unity with the others. Cordou was standing with his back to the window with Helga Brandt.

Michael took his place at the head of the table. 'Shall we begin?'

For a moment, Cordou did not move. Then he slowly walked to his usual seat and made a big performance of sitting down. Brandt followed him.

'Monsieur,' he said, at last. 'We have been talking. And, I regret to say, we are extremely unhappy.'

'We?' said Michael.

'Some of the members of this Consortium, who feel – like I do – you are in danger of forgetting we are joint partners in this venture.'

Michael looked at him with an expressionless face.

'No one denies your people have taken risks to obtain the samples,' Cordou continued, 'and no one denies the hard work you have done and no one disputes the success of Operation Bayoux, despite our reservations about the timing and absence of prior approval. However, you fail to acknowledge it is our money that funds it all. We have paid for the information your scientists possess.'

'Pierre,' Michael said. 'I am at a loss as to why you are making these comments at this particular point in time. You made us all very well aware of your opinions yesterday, but I was under the impression you accepted the situation even though you didn't like it. Was I mistaken? Or has something happened between then and now to alter your attitude?'

Michael could sense the embarrassment around the table. Rosa shuffling in her chair, Otto drumming his fingers on the table impatiently, wanting the confrontation to be over, Nelson sympathetic. He made a quick assessment of the situation. Was it possible Cordou had seen the unedited report on the Lightermen samples and was firing a shot across Michael's bows? He didn't see how, unless one of Stark's boys had talked. He made a note to re-check the psychoprofile records of Habib and Masopeh, on the remote possibility there was some connection to Cordou he'd missed. But he doubted there would be.

Michael dredged his memory, trying to account for every minute between the end of yesterday's meeting and ten o'clock this morning. There was simply no way Cordou could have got access to Code 4 areas or the laboratories themselves, but his cockiness was worrying. It certainly gave the impression he knew something.

'No,' replied Cordou slowly, after a long pause. 'I just wanted to make sure we understand one another.'

'In that case,' said Michael, 'you can consider your point made. Shall we move on?'

Bauer looked pointedly at Cordou. 'Please do,' he said.

'Thank you. As you know, I assigned one of my top scientists, Professor Marie Stark, to the Lightermen material as soon as it came into our possession. She and her colleagues Dr Habib and Dr Masopeh, have worked through the night in order to have something to show you this morning. I have invited them for ten fifteen to present their findings in person. Does anyone wish to raise any other points before they arrive?'

'Do you know what is in their report?' said Otto.

'Just the bare bones.'

'But it is good? What we hoped for?'

'The initial signs are extremely promising,' he replied. 'But it's early days yet.'

Otto nodded.

For the next few minutes, Michael let them sit, allowing the silence to reassert his authority. Nobody said anything. There was an occasional shuffle of papers, someone clearing their throat. Finally, he pressed the concealed button on the arm of his chair. There was an immediate knock at the door.

'At last,' muttered Rosa Guitierez.

Michael stood up.

'This will be Professor Stark now,' he said.

19

Annie was bored, bored, bored.

She knew it was pathetic, since she only had to kill a couple of hours. Leah had said she'd be ready to go by midday and she clearly wasn't a person who made promises she couldn't keep. But Annie simply could not think of one single thing to do to pass the time. It was no fun listening to music alone, even if she'd got to grips with the sound system. Besides, it wasn't her music. She supposed she could read something, but she wasn't a great book person. She'd always preferred magazines she could dip in and out of as the mood took her, letting the colours wash over her without too much thought. It wasn't that she was lazy, so much as she found it hard to sit still for long. Every school report had remarked on her short attention span and the way she constantly flitted from one thing to another. Commented that it seemed as if she was always looking for an adventure.

Her inability to settle this morning was entirely Kellen's fault, though. Annie recognised the signs well enough. The disembodied feeling, the drifting around in a daze, the endless replaying of conversations and gestures. All the usual warnings that she was falling for someone. They'd known each other for less than forty-eight hours, but she was already obsessed.

Annie thought of herself as independent, rather than as someone scared of being tied down. And because she was physically satisfied with the way she was – unlike virtually every other woman she knew — it was easy to ignore any doubts that occasionally pushed themselves to the surface. She was OK with taking what the outside world had to offer and leaving her inner world to fend for itself. Didn't see the point of worrying about who she was or where she was going.

So, she would have laughed if someone accused her of waiting to be swept off her feet. But even though she couldn't see it herself, the fact remained that a loss of self-motivation and emotional direction happened every time. New relationship, new sex, same old pattern of behaviour. Lust and romance turned her into a woman waiting. Kellen had taken over her mind.

Annie kicked her shoes off and lay down on Kellen's bed, the sheets still crumpled from their love-making earlier. She put her hands behind her head, closed her eyes and thought about what they might do tonight.

In a small room hidden away at the top of the warehouse, Mary Royle was wondering if it was possible she had been mistaken.

She had been living in the Pen for three months, eating the Network's food, accepting its shelter, but otherwise keeping herself to herself and rarely exchanging a word with anybody. The advantage of being sixty-three was that people let you alone and accepted behaviour they would consider rude in someone younger. She wasn't interested in the Network or what it did. She wanted nothing to do with any of them. After the initial excitement and effort, they had given up on her too.

On Friday 2 May 1997, Mary had set off for work at the usual time. She'd followed the same route as always, done nothing different, seen nothing different. Up Abbey Street, through St Saviour's Estate into Tanner Street, right into Tower Bridge Road, then zigzagged through the backstreets to Crucifix Lane itself. The only difference was that she never arrived.

After the initial shock of finding herself eleven years into the future, Mary accepted what appeared to have taken place with relative ease. She didn't know how or why it had happened, nor why she had been chosen rather than anyone else. But she had seen and heard too much in her life that defied logic to discount the idea of alternative worlds coexisting alongside her own. Mary wasn't religious, she didn't live intimidated by visions of hell below or heaven above, but she did consider all things were ordained. That human life was just one small element of a pattern so brilliant, so complex and so resilient, that it was beyond most human understanding. Her philosophy was to always balance knowledge with imagination.

Secure in her belief that there must be a reason for her journey, Mary had set about trying to understand and make sense of her experience. Why 2008? Was the year significant? Or could it just as well have been 2007 or 2009? The strange mark that had appeared on her head was the obvious place to start. A vertical line, with two smaller lines like stubby arms, she recognised it was a letter from the secret Celtic language of Ogham, although she couldn't identify the precise one. Sitting behind the till day after day in her friend's shop, surrounded by charts and books about ancient belief systems, Mary had learned a little about lots of things, Celtic mythology in particular. Easily the most popular subject with customers, she was regularly asked for her advice on which book to buy. Over time, she'd ended up flicking through most of them at some point.

Mary had plundered her memory for information. Under the Celtic system, everything was believed to exist on three levels. The physical, the mental and the spiritual. In Ogham, the physical level was the notch on the stone or twig. The mental was the word or letter of the alphabet itself. And the spiritual was all the associations it had when used as part of a system of spiritual or magical development. Until she was sure how to interpret anything she discovered, Mary therefore understood how important it was not to discount even the tiniest scrap of knowledge, however irrelevant it seemed.

At the beginning of June, four weeks after she had arrived, Mary left the Pen for a few hours for the first and only time. Slipping out in the middle of the day, she'd found the nearest bookshop and spent hours scouring the shelves for familiar-looking spines. When she returned, it was with the information she needed scribbled on several pieces of paper. Now she had reminded herself of the names of the letters in the Ogham alphabet and discovered the letter on her head was *Duir*, which represented the seventh month of the Celtic year. In other words, the month of May.

Mary realised that Kellen must have seen her go out, because he renewed his efforts to get her to talk to him. It was during these attempts to charm her that he had revealed there had been an earlier traveller. A man who had come through at the beginning of February, but who had been too badly burned to survive. Mary assumed he was so graphic as an attempt to shock her into confiding in him. It hadn't worked. She told him nothing.

After he'd gone, Mary looked up the letter Kellen had described on the man's head. It was *Saille*, the letter representing February, the fourth month of the Celtic year. Mary tried to work out if there could be a connection between her and the man who had died. But she knew so little about him, not even how old he was, and it was impossible. Next, she looked for a connection between the months themselves. Were they part of a pattern of any sort?

Reading through her notes, she noticed that two of the four Celtic Fire Festivals took place in February and May. Marking the turning of the seasons – as well as being a religious celebration in its own right – she knew each festival lasted three days. The day before the first of the month, the first day itself, then the day after. November, February, May and August. It would make sense for the passage between one world and another to be open at times of such spiritual significance. She had come through on the second of May. According to Kellen, the other traveller had come through at the beginning of February.

Perhaps it had been the first or second? What's more, fire had claimed him..

Now, on the fourth of August 2008 Mary sat in her chair and looked at the four letters written on the sheet in front of her. Everything seemed to fit so perfectly. She was convinced she was right. By her reckoning the door should have been open for the three days of the August Fire Festival of *Lugnassadh*. So where, then, was the third traveller? Had the journey claimed them as it had claimed the first?

All Mary could do was wait. And hope.

20

The Lido was busy. Regulars, day-trippers, office workers on their lunch break, students on holiday, Annie couldn't tell.

The enormous floating structure was moored on the south-side of the river, between Deptford Creek and Washington Steps, upstream of the Greenwich Heritage Village and Cruise Terminal. Huge spotlamps stood at the four corners, like the hooded eyes of an insect. At night, Leah said their white beams shone over the wooden decks and splayed across most of the width of the river too. The atmosphere was relaxed, filled with the sounds of swimming and occasional blasts from liners preparing to sail from the twenty-metre cruising docks. Music blared out over the top of the noise of kids splashing and squealing, the yelled orders for beer and coffee from the poolside bar.

A yellow and white striped awning ran all the way around the poolside, giving limited shade from the hot early afternoon sun and a bit of protection from the strong wind. Annie and Leah had spread their towels in the corner of the deck furthest from the turnstile and now sat under large-brimmed hats protecting the backs of their necks. Both were wearing T-shirts and shorts and Annie had a swimming costume on underneath, having been marched into a shop and kitted out by Leah.

'After this, we're going to be tourists,' said Leah. 'See the sights, wear ourselves out and stop in thousands of places for ice cream.'

'I'm not really into cathedrals and all that stuff . . .'

'I'm not offering you cathedrals. I'm offering you pit-stops to give you a sense of what London is like.'

'Such as?'

'Shops, obviously.'

Annie grinned. 'That sounds more like it.'

'And a few places like this – recreational complexes, as they're unpleasantly termed – that make the city bearable. Maybe we'll go to the Barrier and I'll introduce you to my friend Syd, who works there.'

Wriggling her toes, she lay back on her towel. Annie wasn't remotely interested in the Barrier, but she was intrigued to meet a friend of Leah's. She was so private that Annie had wondered if she had any sort of social life at all.

'Don't take this the wrong way,' she said, 'but I don't really see you as the type to be hanging around pools all day.'

Leah smiled. 'I'm not. I'm hopeless at switching off. In any case, I don't much like being in a crowd.'

It was the hottest part of the day and the noise level was definitely increasing. Annie listened to the water slapping against the rim of the pool as people dived in. Teenage boys showed off to their girlfriends, shoving each other and shouting in their half-male voices.

'So,' said Annie after a while. 'Tell me something about yourself.'

'Like what?'

'Anything.'

'There's nothing much to tell. Worked hard at school, worked hard at university, worked hard to get my doctorate, came out the other side with a few letters after my name. That's about it.'

Annie laughed. 'Well, tell me something about your work, then. I don't even really understand what it is you do exactly?'

'It's too complicated to explain.'

'Well, what about relationships? Stuff like that.'

Leah sighed. 'Look, it's too hot to go into my life history. We'll talk about it some other time.'

Annie propped herself up on her elbow and looked at Leah, who was sitting bolt upright. It was the second time she'd dodged perfectly straightforward questions about her personal life. Funny, given they were getting on so well.

'I didn't mean to pry,' she said.

'You're not. I'm just not very good at those conversations, that's all.'

Annie jerked her head towards the pool. 'So, are you going to come in?'

'No.'

'Don't you like swimming?'

'Not really,' answered Leah.

'Not even when you were a kid?'

'Just go and swim, Annie. I'll see you in a while.'

An hour later, they were on the top deck of a Bateau Mouche heading towards the Barrier. Annie felt exhilarated by the wind and the spray.

'This is so much better than yesterday,' she said. 'I can see millions of things from up here. It's weird, but all the cars seem the same colour.'

'They are the same colour,' explained Leah. 'Well, range of colours. Emergency services are white, official cars are black and taxis red. No private cars are allowed inside the Peripherique.'

'That's incredible. They were always trying to ban cars from city centres, but nobody ever thought they'd do it.'

'It's made a big difference. Everybody gets about on buses, overgrounds or the Lightway.'

'What about the tube?'

'That too, but it floods so frequently that it's not operating half the time. Anybody with a bit of cash has their own helicopter or boat.'

'Cannes sur Thames . . .'

Leah smiled. 'Absolutely. Needless to say, having your own pier is a real status symbol. The bigger, the better.'

'I'm biting my tongue here,' giggled Annie. 'I will *not* make the obvious joke about boys and their toys.'

As they sailed downriver, Annie started thinking about her first walk along the river path with Kellen and about their conversation on the boat yesterday morning. Already, these things were landmarks in their relationship. Without him beside her she felt a greater sense of displacement, as if he blotted out everything else. Now, without him as a barrier, she could see how much London had moved on. It wasn't the place she knew. It wasn't only down to the artificial-looking reeds or the bright blue water, the new buildings or the insects or the birds shrieking on the river. It was the city itself. It had a different spirit.

'Are you all right?' asked Leah. 'You've gone very quiet.'

'Just thinking.'

'About anything in particular?'

'It's just hit me that this isn't my home. Your London, I mean. I know it sounds strange, but I hadn't really taken that in before. It's kind of like being on holiday somewhere when you're not quite sure of the local customs. Yesterday with Kellen, I didn't feel like such a . . .'

'Guest?' suggested Leah.

'I was going to say alien,' Annie replied. 'But, yes, guest is right.'

Leah had been finding Annie's apparent lack of interest in what had happened to her frustrating. For two days, she'd wanted to ask Annie questions. How had she physically got here? What did she feel about it? Did she believe it, even? But because as she'd said to Michael the night before, she knew her best tactic was patience, she had to bide her time and tread carefully. Not push her too far or too fast. Let Annie introduce the subject when she was ready.

'Well,' Leah said. 'I have a theory. Maybe you feel odd because things aren't actually different enough. I mean, when did it all start happening?'

Annie looked at her with interest. '1997. Saturday the second of August.'

'Right. So the bottom line is that you've only come forward eleven years. Not much at all.'

Annie was puzzled. 'I don't understand the point you're making?'

'What I'm trying to say is that if you had gone forward fifty years, for example, everything would be completely different. It wouldn't be able to slip your mind, even for a minute. But because we're not so far ahead, not even a generation away, it's easier to forget, think that nothing's changed and that it can't be happening to you. Then, suddenly, something hits you and you remember again. Do you see what I mean?'

'I think so,' Annie replied dubiously.

'The other point is that from what I can remember of the last few years of the twentieth century, everybody always talked about the year 2000 as if it was this impossible date. As if the whole world would be transformed as the last chimes of Big Ben died away on the first of January 2000. Space stations, men in silver suits, computers in charge . . .'

Annie laughed.

'Obviously, I'm exaggerating,' said Leah. 'But you see what I'm saying? Everybody thought the Future – with a capital F – would arrive with the next millennium. That it would look unrecognisably different from what had gone before. But of course it was just another day, following on from the day before and the day before that. History is now. You don't necessarily feel it while it's happening.'

Annie was frowning. 'You've totally lost me.'

'OK, try this. Imagine if someone had come up to you when you were fifteen and asked you to describe the world ten years ahead. You might have come up with some great ideas, but essentially it would have been the world you knew. You wouldn't have expected things to change beyond all recognition in such a short period of time.'

Blankness.

'Annie, it's simple,' Leah insisted. 'The date 2008 makes

you think of something out of a science fiction movie. And because it's more normal than you would expect, you forget about it and then feel even more displaced when you do remember.'

Annie draped her arm around Leah's shoulder and gave her a hug. 'If you say so,' she said.

Leah grinned. 'It was just a thought . . .'

'And I'm sure it was a very good thought, it's just I'm too thick to understand it!'

There was silence for a moment.

'How old were you at the millennium?' Annie suddenly asked.

'Twenty-two.'

Annie shrieked. 'That's how old I am now. And all this time I've been letting you boss me about, thinking you were older, when actually I've got three years on you. Mind you, it's weird. Thinking how your body is eight years older than mine as we stand here now, even though you're actually younger . . .'

She broke off, suddenly realising that if Leah was twenty-two eight years ago, then Kellen was only . . .

'No, it doesn't bear thinking about.'

Leah misunderstood. 'Then don't.'

'I won't. I'll think of something else. Like how did you spend that once-in-a-millennium New Year's Eve? Having the time of your life, I hope.'

'I can't remember. I don't expect I did anything special.'

Annie looked sceptical.

'Honestly,' said Leah. 'I really can't remember at all.'

21

Leah hadn't been back to the Barrier since resigning in April.
On the few occasions she'd seen Syd since then, they'd always
chosen somewhere to meet in town. Neutral territory.

It felt strange to be here. She had forgotten how striking
it was. Several months of scorching sun had taken their toll on
the grass, which was now brown and worn away around the
edges. But the trees and rushes planted to separate the banks
from the Barrier Complex were glorious, covered by leaves
of green and red and silver, leaping and rustling in the wind.
Leah had always loved the sound they made. Like a whisper
echoing around the buildings and across the blue water.

There were insects everywhere, worse than Leah remembered. She and Annie were forced to flap their hands madly
in front of their faces to keep them from getting flies in
their mouths. Leah told Annie to be prepared for a blast
of wind when they got to the walkway that led to the
staff entrance. Known as Hurricane Alley, whatever direction
the wind was blowing, you'd turn the corner and be hit
in the face by the ferocious blast. Winter or summer, it
made no difference. Only the temperature changed. It was
icy from November to March, lukewarm from April to
June and hot enough to take your breath away from July
to September.

'What about October?' said Annie, shouting over the
noise.

'Bearable,' replied Leah pressing her hand on the entry panel.

The door clicked open and they walked in, Annie trying to keep her nosiness in check.

'Hey, stranger,' called a middle-aged black woman, hurtling down the stairs. 'How're you doing?'

Annie watched as Leah and Syd embraced, feeling a bit like a spare part.

'Mm,' said Leah. 'You smell nice. New?'

'New significant other. With a better sense of smell than some I could mention . . .'

Leah smiled. 'Syd, I'd like you to meet a friend of mine. Annie Jones.'

'Pleased to meet you,' said Syd, holding out her hand.

'Hi.'

'What are you guys doing here, anyway?'

'Just showing Annie around. I thought we might tag on to one of the tours.'

'No problem,' replied Syd. 'There's one starting upstairs in about five minutes. If you sneak up the back way, you can slip in. Ralph's doing it.'

Leah raised her eyebrows.

'I've got to get back, so I'll see you up there. Don't rush off afterwards, though. There's something I want to show you.'

'That sounds ominous.'

'Yep,' said Syd. 'Anyway, enjoy.'

Annie and Leah stood watching her bound back up, two at a time.

'Are you ready for that?' said Leah, pointing at the stairs.

'Exactly how many stairs are there?' asked Annie suspiciously.

'I can't remember.'

'You never fucking well remember anything . . .'

Leah laughed.

*   *   *

The tour was just starting by the time they got up there. Ralph was in the process of introducing himself. Annie could see Syd in the background, tapping away at a keyboard and taking no notice of what was going on around her.

'In a few minutes, I will be giving you a brief history of the building of the Barrier and explain a little bit about how things work here,' droned Ralph. 'Then we will have a tour of the Barrier itself, before visiting the Guest Centre, where you can purchase informational material about both the Barrier itself and the work of the Agency of Climate and the Environment, which is also based on this site. After that, I expect everyone will be in need of refreshment. Our final port of call, therefore, is our excellent restaurant overlooking the River Thames.'

'Shit,' Annie said. 'He's like something out of the ark. Why haven't they computerised him?'

Leah ignored her.

'Visitors have only been allowed into this part of the complex in the past year,' he intoned. 'As those of you brave enough to take the stairs will have realised, we are ten storeys up. On a clear day, we can see as far as Kent to the east and the spires of Westminster to the west. More importantly, we also have an uninterrupted view of the entire Barrier. If you'd like to come this way . . .'

The group obediently followed Ralph to the windows.

'We can take photos?' said a young Brazilian, a camera around his neck.

'Please do,' he replied, 'although we do have some wonderful posters, cards and bookmarks in our Guest Centre downstairs.'

'It's excruciating,' Annie hissed in Leah's ear.

'It gets worse,' she said. 'But listen. You might learn something.'

'Ever since the Romans established the city of Londinium on the banks of the River Thames, our great capital has been liable to sudden and devastating flooding. It is a little known fact, but King Canute's famous encounter with the tides actually took place here, not at the seaside.'

Syd started to hum the 'Death March', very faintly, but loud enough for the two lads at the front of the group to hear. They smirked, then giggled when Syd caught their eye and winked. Ralph pretended not to notice. Annie could feel the hysteria bubbling up inside her. She bit the inside of her mouth, looked at her feet and tried not to lose it.

'The earliest record of a flood in London is listed in the Anglo-Saxon Chronicle of 1099. In 1236 there was another terrible flood, when it was possible to row boats in Westminster Hall. And, in December 1663, the great Samuel Pepys wrote in his diary, of a flood that had submerged all of Whitehall under water. One of the worst incidents of modern times was in 1953 when over 300 people were drowned.'

From the boys' reaction, it was clear that 1953 was as remote to them as 1663.

Ralph ploughed on. 'It was obvious that something had to be done to avert a major catastrophe. As early as 1907, a permanent barrage was proposed at Gravesend. However, because a barrage is in position all the time, it fundamentally alters water flow and tides, so the idea was rejected.

'It was the closure of London's docks which helped a decision to be reached,' he continued. 'Because the number of ships passing upriver of Woolwich was greatly reduced, it was possible to design a Barrier with openings no wider than the openings of Tower Bridge. Namely, 61 metres.'

'Do you know all this?' Annie whispered.

Leah nodded. The combination of the sun blasting through the windows, lack of sleep and too many people in too small a space was making her drowsy. She could just curl up and go to sleep right here on the floor, were it not for the fact that she didn't trust either Annie or Syd to behave themselves properly.

Ralph was reaching his climax. 'The Barrier took eight years to build and cost £500 million, equivalent to over £1 billion today. There were four openings of 61 metres, two of

31.5 metres and three subsidiary non-navigational openings. To complete the flood protection scheme, new walling was constructed east of the Barrier, and two major and nine minor floodgates were built. And it was opened by Her gracious Majesty Queen Elizabeth the Second on Tuesday the eighth of May 1984.'

He paused, to allow the full effect of his words to sink in, then waved his hand flamboyantly behind him. 'Now this,' he said, 'is the central computer. That top line of lights is the switchgear for each of the gates. As you can see, each has its own situation indicator light so that we can see at a glance the exact position of each gate and sill. When the Barrier was built, this equipment was some of the most technologically advanced in the world. Since then, many engineering projects – both here and abroad – have made huge advances on the systems we have here. Nonetheless the Barrier was designed to protect London from flooding until at least the year 2030 and shows every sign of fulfilling its role splendidly.'

'Yeah, right' muttered Syd under her breath.

'The consequences of a major flood today would be catastrophic. Over 1.5 million people would be at risk. The London Underground, rail and Lightway systems would be irreparably damaged. All gas and electricity supplies would cease to function and there would be no telephone or cable lines. The entire water supply would be polluted . . .'

Annie started to pay more attention to what Ralph was saying. It sounded a bit apocalyptic, but at least it was interesting.

'However, thanks to our Flood Protection Systems,' Ralph continued, 'it is not a scenario we are likely to see in our lifetime.'

'Well, that's good,' drawled an American. 'Wouldn't like to think we was in any danger, right here in London . . .'

Ralph smiled. 'With the recent river stabilisation pro-gramme and alterations to the waterside environment as a whole, many of the causes of flooding in the past have been greatly diminished. The action of surge tides, however, does remain a potential threat.'

'What are surge tides?' Annie heard herself ask.

'Surge tides originate off the coast of Canada, where the warm Gulf Stream meets the cold Labrador Current. Predictions that the Gulf Stream would become less influential have turned out to be incorrect and it is still the case that, within these zones, the sea is raised approximately 300 millimetres over an area of roughly 1,610 kilometres diameter. It doesn't sound much, but this hump of water can do great damage as it moves across the Atlantic, at speeds of anywhere between 80 and 100 kilometres an hour. From time to time, the associated northerly winds can force the depression down the North Sea which, in turn, sends millions of tons of extra water up the Thames.'

The kids at the front were impressed. 'How d'you know one is on its way?'

Leah hoped there were no scientists or meteorologists in the group who'd challenge the facts. She'd heard Ralph caught out a couple of times in the past and she couldn't be bothered to step in and pick up the pieces today.

'The Primary Control Centre receives weather forecasts and sea tide level information from several different sources. From the local and national meteorological offices, from weather ships in the Atlantic, from rigs in the North Sea, recording stations on Stornoway in the Outer Hebrides and from the East Coast Tidal Warning System. Forecasts of tide levels in the North Sea for thirty-six hour periods are made and updated every twelve hours.'

Not bad, thought Leah. He'd obviously been practising.

'The decision to shut the Barrier is taken by the Duty Barrier Controller. Today's Controller is Dr Sydelle Freer.'

Syd stood up, gave a quirky bow, winked at Annie, then sat down again without a word. The impression given was that she was a wholly inappropriate person to be in charge.

'Thank you,' he said. 'Once a flood warning alert has been received, we notify the Port of London navigation service, who in turn warn shipping and pier operators in the area by radio. On the Barrier piers themselves, navigation signals are changed to indicate closure and special signboards up and downriver are illuminated. The operating sequence and speed of the gates was designed to cause minimum interference to the normal flow of the river, although procedures have obviously been modified in the past twenty-four years since the Barrier was opened. First, the three falling radial gates on the north bank and single gate on the south are shut and the main gates are raised from the outside in. None of the gates will be opened again until water levels up and downriver have been checked to ensure they are equal. If they are not, there would be a slight risk of precipitating a minor tidal wave – or tsunami – in either direction.'

'Why have procedures been modified?' asked Annie.

Leah looked at her, surprised at her sudden interest.

'The effectiveness of flood defences is measured by estimating how often the water is likely to just flow over onto the land,' he replied. 'When the Barrier was constructed, high water levels – with added wave action – were estimated only likely once in every 1,500 years. At that point, sea levels were also not expected to rise more than about 30 centimetres per one hundred years.'

'Have these estimates turned out to be wrong?'

'Not entirely accurate,' Ralph admitted. 'Due to global climate change, sea levels are rising faster than originally anticipated. Thermal expansion of oceans, the melting of glaciers and polar ice, the greenhouse effect, all play their part. In addition to this, land levels are also sinking faster than expected, particularly in the south-east of England.

'So, as a result of the accelerated rate of environmental change, the decision was taken several years ago to permanently raise the level of the Barrier gates. No work was necessary on the six main gates, but the remaining four were modified by fixing extra steelwork to the top. The programme of raising flood defences downstream is also well underway, although not yet complete. They were not considered such a pressing priority and, in the unlikely event of flooding, the consequences would not be particularly severe. Some water might be driven over by wind and waves and, under the pressure of exceptionally high levels, it is possible there would be minor leaking and some localised flooding. But it would not be on the scale of anything that might occur in the London river area itself.'

'How many times do you close the Barrier?' asked the American.

'In recent years, the average has been in the region of fifteen to eighteen closures annually.'

Ralph looked at the group, ready for another question. This time, no hands went up.

'Right,' he said, moving towards the door. 'If there's nothing more, then perhaps we can move on to the next stage.'

There was a smattering of polite applause, then everybody trooped out behind him. Leah and Annie stood back to let everyone pass.

The moment the door was shut, Syd got up and ambled over. 'What a load of bullshit. He didn't mention that nasty little rainstorm that flooded Gallions Reach again. How many times is that in the past three months? Three? Four? Or all those nasty swamps.'

'Swamps are not good for tourism,' said Leah. 'Not an effective selling tool.'

'You've got it.'

'How bad is it now?'

'Put it like this. Someone's got to do something, and fast. Because if they don't, any day now we're going to be hit by a flood of such force that it will make Ralph's doomsday commentary sound like a bedtime story.'

'You're exaggerating. Surely.'

Syd leaned forward and kissed the top of Leah's head.

'You better believe it, girl. It's nearer than you think.'

They arrived back at the Pen just after five o'clock, the skin on their faces and hands burnt by the wind and sun despite their protective measures.

Annie had spent most of the journey back from the Barrier asking the same questions over and over again, like a child who can't believe the grown-ups are being so stupid. What did Syd mean? If she was right, why was nobody doing anything about it? Why did people fuck with nature in the first place? At first, Leah had tried to answer each question seriously, until she realised Annie was enjoying her outrange at the same time as being rattled by Syd's worst-case scenario. The image of London submerged under thousands of tonnes of water scared her.

Leah gave no indication this was the stuff of her recurrent nightmares too, just limited her responses to yes and no. As soon as they'd got inside the Pen, she'd given Annie a quick kiss, then disappeared to her room. Completely drained mentally.

Annie immediately went up to Kellen's room to see if he was there, but he wasn't and everything looked untouched. Exactly the same as when Annie had left it hours earlier to go out with Leah. She was tempted to stay put and wait for him, but she didn't want to leap all over him like an eager puppy the second he walked in through the door. Equally, she didn't want to give him the impression she'd been sitting waiting all day like the little woman. In the end, she decided to go downstairs and hang out. She might at least find someone to talk to.

Leah had bought her a couple of guidebooks to London. Annie thought she might as well read them – or at least pretend to read them – so she settled down and got stuck in.

She'd already got through the first (with the help of a large amount of unmeltable chocolate with zero calories) and was on to the second, which appeared to have been written with Agatha Christie fans in mind. It was a real throwback museum piece, with archaic vocabulary, cream teas and cheeky cockneys the major themes. Annie assumed it was intended to be reassuring to visitors who associated London with high levels of violence and biting insects. It was funny to start with, but she soon got bored and, by the time Lonnie made an appearance, she was in desperate need of company.

'Hi,' said Annie enthusiastically, forgetting about his behaviour at breakfast.

Lonnie walked straight to the fridge and got a beer. 'Do you want anything?'

'A beer would be great,' she replied. 'Thanks.'

'No problem.' He slammed the door, then dropped the cold can into her lap as he walked past her chair to collapse on the sofa. He was tight-lipped and looked as if he was in a foul mood.

'Not a good day?' she said.

'No,' he replied curtly.

Annie waited for him to ask her in return, but he didn't appear to be interested. He just opened his can and started drinking.

'I had a really good one,' she said after a moment. 'Leah took me all over the place. To the shops, the Lido, down to the Barrier. It was great.'

'Sounds pretty tedious to me.'

This irritated the hell out of Annie. She'd never liked cynics and affected ennui. It seemed like such a waste of time. 'Well, it wasn't,' she said.

Lonnie laughed. 'If you say so.'

They sat in silence. Lonnie was apparently oblivious to the cranky atmosphere. Annie was trying to think of something to get a conversation going. He wasn't her favourite person in the Network, but he was the only person she'd got to talk to.

'I wanted to put some music on earlier. But I couldn't work it out. Don't you have a CD player or something?'

'Shit, no. That's all well past its sell-by-date.'

'Well, what is there? I had a look around, but couldn't find anything.'

Lonnie jerked his head towards the PC. 'That.'

'But that's a computer.'

'It's all MP3 files now. Nobody buys music. You just download it.'

Annie looked blank.

'Mpeg-1 Layer 3 compression files,' he said in a bored voice. 'People turn CDs into high-quality MP3 computer sound files, then swap them. Either on Zip disks and newly-burnt CDs or via music groups and FTP over the Internet. Easy. You get any track you want, from anywhere in the world, free of charge.'

'The record companies can't like it . . .'

Lonnie took a ready-rolled spliff out of his pocket. 'Who gives a fuck,' he said, lighting up. 'The industry's been trying to stop it for years. People just dumped their static sites, started moving them around, used overseas file servers and messaging services like ICQ to find out where they were. If they've got the equipment and know-how, musicians can sell their stuff direct to fans via digital cash. Record labels are on the way out.' Lonnie looked at Annie. 'You don't have a clue what I'm talking about, do you?'

'Not entirely,' she said.

He laughed. Annie couldn't work out if he was deliberately trying to sound unpleasant or if it was just how it came out.

'Want some of this?' he offered, holding out the joint. 'It might help clear things up.'

As Annie took it Lonnie brushed his hand against her leg. There was something about it that made her think it was deliberate. She glared at him, but he was now lying on his back with his eyes closed. Annie let it go. But the same thing happened when she gave the joint back a couple of minutes later. This time, his hand was just too high for it to be an accident.

'Do you mind,' she said loudly, moving out of his reach.

He opened his eyes. 'Mind?' he repeated.

Annie suddenly realised he was a bit drunk. The way he was drawing his words out, the slight edge in everything he came out with. She kicked herself for not noticing it earlier.

'So,' he said, 'are you having a good time with Kellen? More fun than playing tourist with Leah . . .'

Annie stood up. 'I think I'd better go. Before you say something you regret. I'll see you.' She walked past him to the door and was completely taken by surprise when he suddenly grabbed hold of her wrist.

'Don't rush off,' he said. 'We're having a nice chat.'

'Let go,' she demanded.

He tightened his grip. 'What's the hurry?'

Annie was furious. She could feel his fingers digging into her skin. 'Let go of me,' she repeated. 'I mean it, Lonnie.'

'There's no need to be like that.'

She tried to yank her arm away. 'This isn't funny.'

'Come and sit with me,' he said, pulling her towards him. 'I won't bite.'

'Lonnie, let go. This is getting beyond a joke.'

He gave a sudden tug and Annie lost her balance. She fell forward on top of him and realised for the first time that the situation was serious. Everybody knows how quickly things can get out of hand, but nobody ever believes it will happen to them. Instinct had told her he was bad news, but because he was a friend of Kellen's, she'd made the mistake of giving him the benefit of the doubt.

'For Christ's sake,' she shouted as he tried to kiss her. 'What the fuck do you think you're doing?'

His tongue was hot and wet and tasted of beer. Annie lashed out with her free hand, struggling to get back on her feet.

'Bitch,' he muttered as her fist connected with his ear.

She managed to get free and collided with Vicky on her way in. Annie stopped dead in her tracks, her face flushed, breathing heavily.

'Are you all right? What's going on?' demanded Vicky.

'Ask Lonnie.'

Vicky fixed him with a look. 'Well?'

Lonnie smiled at them both, as if nothing had happened. 'Just talking . . .'

Annie straightened her clothes. 'He made a pass at me, that's what happened.'

'As if I would.'

'You bastard,' said Annie.

'You're all the same, aren't you,' he added, tapping his head. 'Always imagining things. Just can't help overreacting.'

'How fucking dare you!' yelled Vicky, on Annie's behalf.

'Leave it,' Annie said. 'He's not worth it.'

'Have a nice evening, ladies,' he said as they left. 'Sweet dreams.'

Vicky and Annie managed to salvage the evening, by settling down in a bar around the corner and slagging Lonnie off.

It was the first night for weeks that the evening had not been interrupted by a storm and London was making the most of it. Office workers sat at tables outside, talking over their day and comparing holidays taken or to come. Jackets were off, arms were bare, safe in the shelter of the UV zappers which killed all the bugs. Women kicked off their sandals to cool their feet. Strains of jazz and blues and salsa mingled together in the air as the sun cast its dying rays against the yellow brickwork and glass of the riverside developments.

By the time they returned to the Pen, and gone their separate ways, it was nine o'clock. It was now nearly twenty to ten, Kellen was still not back and Annie was fed up. She seemed to have spent the whole day waiting, each arrangement interrupted by a return to the room, just in case. Now in the streets below, the night staff were turning up to take over from the day shift. Her excitement at the thought of seeing Kellen was all worn out. Instead, she was pissed off. With him, for not making it clear he'd be away for so long, and with herself for minding so much. The longer she sat in the chair staring at the door, the more irritated she got.

At last, she heard the sound of footsteps and voices in the corridor. They stopped outside the door, then after a couple more minutes, the door opened and Kellen was standing there.

'Hey,' he said. 'It's so great you're here. I was worried you might have given up on me and gone out.'

'I'm done with going out for one day,' she said tetchily.

Within seconds, he was across the room with his arms around her.

'Are you OK?' he asked, straightening up. 'You seem, I don't know, a little tense?'

'Sorry,' she replied, taking his hand and pulling him on to her lap. 'I'm fine. Who were you talking to out there?'

'Lonnie,' he said, leaning over to kiss her again. 'Why?'

Annie froze and put her hand out to stop him.

'He didn't tell you what happened earlier, did he?'

Kellen looked blank. 'No? What?'

Annie hesitated. If she explained, it would make it sound like a bigger deal than it was. After all, the last thing she wanted was Kellen storming off to confront Lonnie. Anyway, she didn't want it between them.

'Nothing,' she said. 'Forget it.'

'Forget what? Look, Annie. Tell me.'

She was kicking herself for mentioning it at all. 'It's nothing really. Just that Lonnie made a pass at me earlier and wouldn't take no for an answer.'

'What?' he said roughly.

Annie was gratified by his reaction. 'If Vicky hadn't come in when she did it might have got a bit nasty.'

'I can't believe it,' he said.

The misunderstanding persisted.

'I'm fine about it. Really. It's no big deal.'

'It sounds so out of character,' he said. 'You don't think you maybe just got the wrong end of the stick. I'm sure Lonnie wouldn't do anything to upset you like that.'

One look at Kellen's face told her he was serious. Annie was livid and shoved him so hard that he fell off her lap and on to the floor.

'Hey,' he said. 'I didn't mean—' He tried to put his arms around her, but she pushed him away.

'Don't,' she shouted. 'I can't believe what you just said.'

'Jesus, I'm sorry,' said Kellen. 'I'm really sorry. It's not that I don't believe you, it's just that it sounds so . . .'

'So what?' she snapped. 'Impossible? Just because he's a friend of yours? Is that it?'

'No, you're twisting my words. That's not what I meant at all. Really.' He cautiously put his hand on her shoulder. 'Look, please don't be angry with me. I'll talk to Lonnie, if you want me to. But don't take it out on me.'

'You just don't get it, do you? I don't *want* you to talk to Lonnie, for fuck's sake. And I'm not taking it out on you. It's your reaction that stinks.'

He edged a little closer. 'I'm sorry. I wasn't thinking.'

Annie took no notice. 'I don't need you to go in there and sort it out, man to man. That's not the point.'

'OK, OK,' he whispered. 'I won't do anything you don't want me to. Just don't be angry.'

Later, as they lay side by side looking up at the ceiling, Annie thought about what had happened. Kellen's black curls were tickling her arm. He lay completely still, one hand resting on her hip, the other by his side. After all the talking, the love-making, the whispering of secrets in the dark, there was silence. Annie felt curiously detached. As if she wasn't really there at all.

'My arm's gone to sleep,' she said, easing it out from under his neck. 'Your head's too heavy.'

'I'll get a new head.'

She smiled.

'Kellen?' she added, after a while. 'How old are you?'

'Does it matter?' he said.

'No. I was just wondering.'

'I'm twenty-eight. Born February the twenty-second, 1980.'

'Shit, I knew it. That makes you five years younger than me.'

'Hey,' said Kellen. 'That's fantastic. I've always wanted to sleep with an older woman.'

Annie propped herself up on her elbow. 'That means, in 1997 you were only seventeen.'

'But it's not 1997.'

'But if we were meeting in real life, I'd be thirty-three. An old woman . . .'

His hand moved up to her breast.

'You don't feel like an old woman from where I'm sitting,' he said.

'What if . . . ?'

Kellen put a finger to her lips. 'Don't talk about it any more,' he said. 'OK?'

She shifted position. Pulled the sheet up to her chin.

'Cold?'

'A little,' she admitted. 'You know, something else I was wondering?'

'Mmm?'

'How come you've got this warehouse. It must be worth millions.'

'Easily,' he agreed. 'Not that I've ever had it valued.'

'Is it yours? I mean, do you actually own it?'

'Yes, as it happens. My father bought up loads of property around here, years before the area got fashionable. He always said west London was washed-up and over-developed, so snapped this place up, along with lots of stuff like it, when I was a kid. This was one of the places he didn't get around to developing and selling on before he died, so it came to me.'

'Don't you have any brothers and sisters?'

'I do have a brother, as it happens,' said Kellen. 'But I haven't seen him for over fifteen years. He disappeared somewhere in the Pacific. New Zealand, Australia, somewhere in that part of the world.'

'You never hear from him? Nothing at all?'

Kellen shook his head.

'And he didn't inherit anything from your dad?'

'They never got on. I never really got to the bottom of what had gone on between them.'

'You must have seen him at your Dad's funeral, though?'

'The lawyers sorted things out. He didn't come, I didn't get involved.'

'Doesn't it bother you?'

'No,' said Kellen. 'Families tie you down. Better to choose who you spend time with rather than have people dumped on you.'

She paused, testing the water. 'I guess some people see the Network as a family . . .'

'No way,' he said. 'I don't feel responsible for anyone here and I sure as hell don't expect them to feel responsible for me.'

'I can see their point, though,' she said. 'It is quite like a family in some ways. Lots of people coming and going. People looking out for each other. I think it's pretty good, actually.'

Kellen leaned over and kissed her forehead. 'Well, I'm pleased you feel at home.'

'I do,' she said seriously. 'I've sometimes missed not having a real family. Only sometimes, you understand.'

He began to run his hand up and down her arm. Annie snuggled closer to him, feeling very loved and very safe. Her eyes started to close.

'Perhaps,' he said. 'It's why you're here.'

'Mmm,' she murmured, no longer listening.

'Perhaps you're here because there was nothing to hold you back. You're a free spirit.'

23

Tuesday 5 August

Annie's dreams were full of monsters. She was wandering through long, white tunnels, full of doors that led nowhere. Putting out her hands to no one. Images from her childhood faded into memories of the present, that should have been her future.

She woke up with her heart thudding and the sheet knotted around her. Kellen was fast asleep next to her, his black curls tumbling on the pillow like a vine. She watched the rise and fall of his chest and reached out to touch him, willing him to wake and keep her company. But he didn't move. The feeling reminded Annie of all those lonely nights she'd spent with Dan, lying in the bed they'd shared. It was the first time she'd thought of him for days, she realised. Had she always known – or was it just with the benefit of hindsight – that she was more alone when she was with him than when they were apart?

She tried to snuggle around Kellen, hoping the heat of his body would warm her up. But the coldness was all on the inside and her mind was buzzing too much to let her go back to sleep. Perhaps she'd go and get a drink from downstairs. Trying not to disturb Kellen, she climbed out of bed and pulled on a T-shirt and pair of his baggy trousers that were hanging over the back of the chair. A perfect fit, long in the leg, wide on the waist. She fumbled on the table for a candle and the matches, knowing that it would be dark in the hall. Leah had explained that all the lights were turned off in the communal areas as soon as it got dark, so as not to attract bugs.

She tiptoed out and along the corridor in her bare feet towards the top of the stairs, then had a change of heart. Suddenly she didn't fancy the idea of going down there.

Annie peered along the corridor that ran on straight ahead and wondered where it went. So far as she could see in the dim light of the candle, it looked the same as the hallway leading to Kellen's room. Panelling on the walls, wooden floorboards, a few tapestries. But, at the end, there was an archway.

She had no idea what the time was, but she thought it was unlikely she'd bump into anyone at this time. Everything was quiet. She walked slowly and carefully through the arch and found herself on a small landing with three closed doors leading off it. Presumably bedrooms. There were no lights showing.

She stopped and considered what to do next. She could hardly knock and barge in. She'd sound ridiculous explaining why she was snooping around in the middle of the night. Besides, one of the rooms might turn out to be Lonnie's and then she'd really be in trouble. She still was livid about what he'd done. Then again, she wasn't ready to go back to bed yet.

Annie tapped on the first door, just loud enough to be heard by anyone inside. She waited. No answer. Carefully, she pushed down the latch and found it wasn't locked. She opened the door a fraction of an inch and cautiously stuck her head into the room. Light was coming in through the window at the top revealing it to be a rather messy bedroom. She could hear the sound of sleeping from the double bed and could see a figure under the sheet, but couldn't make out who it was from this distance. There was a wooden chest of drawers with a few bottles and brushes on it, a table, tapestries on the walls – although nowhere near as elaborate as those in Kellen's room – or the shared spaces downstairs – and clothes and books all over the floor. She could just make out a tower of underwear balanced precariously on a chair. Vicky's room?

She shut the door carefully and moved on to the next. There was clearly someone in there too, but because the shutters were closed it was too dark inside for her to see anything.

The third door was locked. Annie was quite surprised. People tended to wander in and out of all the rooms at the Pen. In fact, the only locked door she'd come across was Kellen's private study and he'd explained that was only because of the need to keep the Network records confidential.

'Get a grip,' she muttered to herself, wondering what the hell she thought she was up to, ambling around in the dark, spying on people and reading things into the simple matter of a locked bedroom door.

Annie was just about to give up the adventure, when she noticed another opening at the far end of the landing. She went to look, holding her candle high to get as much light as possible. Disappearing into the black was a narrow flight of stairs. She hesitated for a moment, then tentatively put her foot on the bottom step and started to climb. It was very steep and she could feel the dust between her toes, as if the staircase was rarely used.

She started to count, finding the low sound of her voice comforting. At thirty, she found herself looking at a door, no more than five feet high. It had the same sort of old-fashioned latch as the rooms below, just smaller. Annie had a prickling feeling on the back of her neck. She could sense there was someone in there. The question was, what now? It was incredibly late and there was no way she could have found herself up there by accident. On the other hand, if she turned and walked down again, the person inside the room might hear and come to investigate. And it would be even more embarrassing to be caught skulking.

'Who is it? Is there someone there?'

Annie jumped, taken by surprise by the voice.

The woman repeated her question. She sounded bad-tempered. 'I said, is somebody there?'

'Shit,' Annie whispered, trying to summon up the courage to answer. 'Shit, shit, shit . . .'

The door was suddenly flung open and Annie found herself looking up at a tall woman with short grey hair and unwavering eyes. Her arms were crossed.

'And you are?'

'Annie,' she said quickly. 'I didn't . . . I mean. I didn't mean to disturb you.'

The woman sized her up. Annie had to fight the urge to stand straight, wipe her hands, salute. She felt like she was on parade.

'Thank God,' the woman said suddenly. 'Come in.'

Annie was so surprised by the change of tone and the mellowing of her expression, that she did what she was told without even thinking about it.

'Don't just hover in the doorway,' she said. 'Come and sit down where I can see you properly.'

Annie ducked under the frame, shut the door behind her and followed the woman into the room.

'You can have that one.'

Feeling rather awkward, Annie perched on the edge of one of the armchairs.

The woman nodded at the candle. 'You don't need that now,' she said.

Annie looked down and immediately blew out the flame. 'Sorry.'

'I'm Mary Royle.'

Annie was sure she'd heard the name before, although she couldn't quite place it.

'Annie Jones,' she replied, shaking hands.

Mary sat down in the chair opposite and stared at her. 'You have no idea how relieved I am to see you.'

'You are?'

'I was expecting you several days ago. In fact, I'd almost given up on you altogether.'

Annie suddenly felt anxious. As usual, she'd charged into something without thinking about the consequences. And here she was sitting with a strange woman in the middle of the night, miles away from anyone else. She knew they'd never met before, even though Mary was behaving as if they knew each other.

'I'm sorry,' Annie said. 'I think perhaps you're confusing me with somebody else. I don't think we've . . .'

Mary smiled. 'We haven't met. I'm sorry, this must be very confusing for you. When I said I'd been expecting you, I didn't mean you personally. Just someone.'

'I'm afraid I still don't . . .'

Mary beckoned her over. 'Come here.'

Ill at ease, Annie got to her feet. It would have been rude not to, but she felt uncomfortable. Surely Leah or Kellen would have warned her if they had a Mrs Rochester tucked away in the attic? On the other hand . . .

'There,' said Mary.

Annie followed the line of her finger and saw the small, black symbol on the side of Mary's head. She stepped back, as if she'd been burned. 'It's like mine,' she said. 'Well, almost.'

'They're different letters of the same alphabet.'

Annie looked at her in amazement. 'Are you saying you know what it means?'

'Not exactly. I recognise the letters and what they stand for. I'm not sure what they mean, in our context. It's a symbolic not a literal alphabet, you see.'

Annie shook her head.

'You will,' answered Mary. 'Neither, incidentally, does the boy downstairs. He's finding it all very frustrating.'

'Do you mean Kellen?'

'Yes.'

'He wants to know what the symbols mean?'

'Yes.'

'And he thinks you know, but won't tell him?'

Mary nodded.

'Why not? Don't you like him?'

'Liking doesn't come into it,' she replied. 'Although, as it happens, I don't. He's a little too eager.'

Annie looked defiant. 'I like him.'

Mary looked at her. 'I see.'

'Why do you stay here then, if you don't like him?'

'It's as good a place as any. More to the point, there's nowhere else to go. He, at least, understands the situation. Most people would not believe us. We're like illegal aliens, you and me. No papers, no money. We don't officially exist.'

Annie held up her hand. 'Hold on a minute. I feel completely out of my depth in this whole conversation. I don't know what's going on any more. What is this "we" and "our" you keep talking about?'

'I'm sorry,' said Mary with surprise. 'I assumed you were thinking along the same lines as me, having seen the mark on my head too. You do understand what has happened to us, don't you? That we are both travellers?'

Annie paused. 'I'd not been letting myself think about it,' she said finally. 'At least, I've thought about certain things — how some stuff looked different, the fact that Leah's actually younger than me, how the future's not as different as I'd have imagined — but not about how I got here.' She looked at Mary. 'Does that sound stupid to you?'

Mary's response was to get up, fetch two glasses, a corkscrew and a bottle of wine from the sideboard and put it all on the table between the two armchairs.

'Will red do?'

Annie still looked dazed. 'Fine. Anything.'

Mary poured two glasses and handed one to Annie. 'Now, tell me,' she said, 'how long was it before you were able to accept what had happened to you?'

'I don't know. It was more that I could find no logical alternative explanation. At first, I thought it was all a trick. You know, to make me think I'd travelled forward in time.

It's all so fucking impossible. But, then I couldn't see how it could be an illusion. The buildings, the heat . . .'

Mary sipped her wine. 'Go on.'

'Then I thought I must be dreaming, I suppose. Or having some sort of hallucination after hitting my head.'

'When did you hit your head?'

'On Saturday morning,' she replied. 'I'd come out of this club. It was really early and I was trying to avoid going back to my flat. This weird fog came out of nowhere and, to cut a long story short, I ended up banging my head on the wall in Crucifix Lane and knocking myself out.'

'And when you woke up everything had changed?'

'Exactly.'

'Saturday,' muttered Mary. 'That would be the second of August. Perfect. That's what I'd expected.'

'I'm sorry?'

Mary waved her hand dismissively. 'Don't worry about it for the time being. Tell me instead what year you're from.'

'1997.'

'And how do you feel physically? Apart from your cuts and bruises?'

'No, these are nothing to do with the accident. I went out with the Network on Sunday and got hit in the face by some bastard.'

Mary raised her eyebrows. 'Clearly a dangerous business.'

'But, Mary, here you are, calmly sitting here telling me we're both "travellers" – that's what you called us, isn't it? – as if it's the most normal thing in the world. I mean, what did *you* think? Did you believe it was possible that you'd travelled forward in time?'

'Yes,' she said.

'Just like that?'

'There seemed no point in not believing. My main concern – both then and now – is how to get back.'

'Back to where?'

'Same as you. Crucifix Lane. 1997. Except I came through in May, three months before you.'

Annie took another large gulp of her wine. 'I still can't really believe it. I keep pinching myself and thinking that any minute now I'll wake up.'

'But you don't strike me as the sort of person who'd dream up a story about travelling through time to the future.'

'I know,' agreed Annie.

Mary got up again and went in search of a paper and pencil. 'For the time being, let's forget about what you can or cannot accept, and concentrate on the letters.'

Unconsciously, Annie put her fingers to her head.

Mary smiled. 'Tell me this. Did you notice any letters on the wall when you fell?'

Annie nearly dropped her wine at this. 'How did you know?'

'I saw them too,' answered Mary.

'I thought I must've imagined them. I was convinced I'd seen these lines carved into the bricks under the railway arch just before I passed out. They were really clear in my mind. When I came round, I looked for them. I looked really hard but there was nothing there.'

Mary nodded. 'I think the letters are only on our side,' she said. 'Like some sort of one-way sign or key to the door that leads from one time to another.'

'Just between 1997 and 2008?' Annie asked. 'Or between any periods of time?'

'That I don't know. The logical assumption would be the former, given we are both here.'

Annie watched as Mary wrote on the paper.

'Concentrate hard now. How many letters do you think you saw?'

Annie thought for a moment. 'Three, I think,' she said slowly. 'Although there could have been more. I only saw them for a fraction of a second.'

'Each different? Or was one letter repeated more than once?'

'Different, I think.'

Mary pushed the sketch across the table. 'Is this what you saw?'

Annie leaned forward and looked at the sheet in front of her.

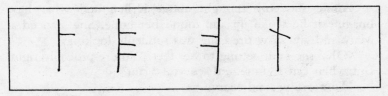

'That, that and that,' she said, pointing at the last three. 'Not the first one.'

Mary sat back in her chair. 'Very interesting.'

'But what does it all mean?' said Annie with frustration. 'I'm more confused now than ever . . .'

'I must have your word that anything I tell you will stay between us and these four walls?'

Annie looked surprised. 'That sounds very heavy,' she said.

'I mean it, Annie. I do not want you to repeat anything to the people downstairs.'

'Am I allowed to say we've met? Or is that a secret too?'

'That is up to you,' said Mary. 'Provided you don't think that will make things awkward for you, I don't see why not.'

'I don't understand why you don't trust Kellen. He's really wonderful. There are lots of great people down there, actually. Leah, for one. Vicky's nice too.'

'Annie, I'm not asking you to agree with me. I'm delighted that you feel comfortable with them. However, I would prefer to keep my thoughts and opinions private.'

Annie shrugged. 'If you say so.'

'So we understand one another?' said Mary firmly, topping up their glasses.

'I suppose so. Although I still think you're being suspicious for no reason.'

'We'll see. Anyway, it's late. Perhaps now I know you're here, safe and sound, I feel perfectly happy to wait until the morning. In any case, you should probably be getting back. You'll be missed.'

Annie suddenly thought about Kellen and what he'd imagine if he woke up and found her gone. She glanced at Mary and saw how tired she was suddenly looking.

'OK,' she said, getting to her feet. 'You're probably right. But when can I come and see you again?'

'Tomorrow,' said Mary.

'What time?'

'Whenever,' she answered. 'I'm always here. Don't forget your candle.'

'I won't.'

On impulse, Annie gave her a quick peck on the cheek, then went to the door. 'I'll see you then.'

'Yes,' Mary replied. 'And Annie?'

Annie paused.

'I'm very glad you're here.'

Annie smiled, then turned and walked down the stairs.

24

Wednesday 6 August

Annie lay in bed as Kellen quietly dressed and brushed his hair in the gentle pink morning light. The shutters were open. He didn't realise she was watching him.

She shut her eyes as he kissed her, then he left, closing the door carefully behind him. The silence surged back after he'd gone. Annie snuggled back under the sheets to catch up on some sleep. She felt, for the first time in her life, that she was involved in something good. A real relationship where plans were made and decisions taken with affection and consideration. She and Dan had spent a lot of their relationship arguing. At least, she had argued. He'd tended to withdraw and pretend that nothing was happening, leaving her to carry the burden of what was going wrong between them. She couldn't remember him ever kissing her goodbye when he left for work and meaning it.

When Annie woke again several hours later, it was with the heavy feeling of having slept for too long. From the shifting shadows in the room, the sun was already quite high. Maybe it was as late as ten o'clock?

Because she wasn't particularly hungry – and couldn't face the possibility of dealing with Lonnie over breakfast – she decided she might as well go straight up to Mary. Shifting her lazy limbs into gear, she rubbed a cold flannel over her face and tried to flatten her hair, which was sticking up in tufts all over her head. She quickly got dressed – in a mixture of clothes pinched from Kellen and bought for her by Leah – then headed out the door with all the questions she wanted to ask buzzing in her head like flies.

Annie could see the imprint of her own night footprints in the dust on each step as she climbed the stairs. Twenty-eight, twenty-nine, thirty. As she knocked, she hoped it was OK. Although Mary had said to come whenever, often people didn't really mean what they said.

'Who is it?'

'It's me.'

'How nice,' said Mary, as she opened the door.

'I'm not too early, am I?'

'Good lord, no. Come in and have some coffee. I was just making a pot.'

'That would be great. I've not had anything this morning so far.'

Annie sat in her armchair and waited as Mary got things ready and brought them over to the table.

'So, where's your boy this morning?'

Annie helped herself to a biscuit. 'I wish you wouldn't call him that. It sounds condescending.'

'I'll try to remember,' Mary said wryly.

'Anyway, in answer to your question, he's gone out and won't be back until this evening.'

'Did you tell him about your adventure?'

'There wasn't time,' she said, then caught sight of Mary's expression. 'Don't read anything into it. I *will* tell him we've met, as soon as I get the chance . . .'

Mary smiled, as Annie avoided her eye, helping herself to coffee – milk and two sugars – before settling back in the chair with her feet tucked up under her. 'I've got so many things I want to ask,' she said.

'Fire away.'

'Where to begin?'

'Anywhere,' Mary replied. 'It doesn't matter if there's no particular order and we go round in circles.'

'OK. But I warn you, my mind tends to jump all over

the place. I'll probably end up confusing you as well as myself.'

'I think I'll manage,' said Mary with amusement. 'Just start and we'll see how we get on.'

'The first thing is what were you doing in Crucifix Lane in the first place? And how did it all happen for you? Was it early in the morning, like me? Did you hit your head? All that kind of stuff.'

'I was there because I work in the little bookshop on the corner of Crucifix Lane and Bermondsey Street.'

'I know it. It sells all that New Age stuff.'

'It's called Astrocat, in fact, and it belongs to a friend. I help out from time to time when her regular staff fail to turn up.'

'I wouldn't have thought it was your sort of thing at all. You don't look the dangly-earring type.'

Mary raised her eyebrows. 'Whatever do you imagine goes on there?' she said. 'It's a bookshop specialising in books about divination, ancient religions, alternative philosophies and so forth. It's not some tent at a funfair, for goodness' sake.'

'But you don't believe in any of that stuff, surely? I mean, only deeply tragic people who can't cope with real life fall for all that horoscope and crystal ball business.'

'I think you're lumping rather a lot of different things together,' said Mary mildly. 'Many things we believe and take for granted are actually rooted in systems hundreds or even thousands of years old. Faith has a habit of reinventing itself.'

Despite Annie's sceptical expression, Mary smiled. 'Let's not get sidetracked. To answer your question, I was on my way to work as usual. I've gone over the sequence of events that morning many times since then, but I cannot remember one single thing that was unusual. I took the same route as always, it was about the same time, between half past nine and ten. The weather wasn't exceptional in any way. No mysterious fog, like you experienced. It was, to all intents and purposes, a completely unremarkable Friday morning.'

'But *something* must have happened?' said Annie.

'I was just walking into Crucifix Lane itself, when I noticed a piece of paper on the ground. There's always lots of rubbish in there blown in by the wind and traffic, as you know, so ordinarily it wouldn't have caught my eye. But this looked very clean and white and I thought it might be important. A letter or document that someone had dropped by mistake. You didn't see anything like that?'

Annie shook her head.

'As I bent down to pick it up, I noticed some odd scratches on the wall. Two symbols or letters that seemed vaguely familiar to me, although I didn't recognise them.'

'Just two? Not three, like I saw?'

'Only two. The two middle ones I showed you last night.'

'But, why—'

Mary held up her hand. 'Hold your horses. Wait until I finish this bit of the story, then you can ask questions.'

'My grandad always used to say that "Hold your horses". I'd completely forgotten that.'

'Used to?'

Annie dropped her shoulders. 'He's gone a bit funny in the head. Not really with it any more.'

'I'm sorry,' said Mary gently. 'It's so awful when that happens. What about your parents?'

'There's only me. My mum disappeared when I was a baby and Grandad brought me up.'

'And your father?'

'A one-night stand. My grandad never told me anything about him. Well, more to the point, I don't think he actually knew anything about him, other than that he was from Hong Kong. By all accounts, my mother was a bit vague.'

'You don't have any brothers or sisters?'

Annie shook her head.

Mary leaned over to top up their coffee. 'This is all quite interesting,' she said. 'Like you, I have no family to speak of. Both my parents died during the war when I was very young. My father was one of the first to enlist and, as it happens, one of the first to be killed. My mother was in our house when it took a direct hit. We lived in Woolwich, close to the Arsenal, so I'd been evacuated to the country. There was awful damage along this part of the river, all the way from here out to the sea.'

'That's awful.'

'At the end of the war, I was sent to live with my unmarried aunt in East Anglia. It wasn't too bad. When I grew up, I did what was expected of me. Got married, moved around with my husband's work, nothing fancy. He died ten years ago, just a year after my aunt, in fact. A few years later, a friend offered me a room in her house in London and so, finally, at the tender age of fifty-three, I started to live my life.'

'Don't you have any children? I thought everybody did in those days.'

'My husband was keen. Saw being childless as some sort of comment on his virility. I was never interested in being a mother and given the fact he was both a drunk and rather too free with his belt, I saw no reason to inflict him as a father on anybody.'

'Shit,' muttered Annie.

Mary simply smiled. 'It was a long time ago,' she said quietly. 'Nothing remains.'

'They don't sound like the sort of memories that go away . . .'

'As you get older, you'll find that even the worst memories get less painful in time. The reason I brought this up was that it appears to be a similarity between us.'

Annie nodded. 'Yes, I see.'

'But we can think about it later. For now, let's continue with Crucifix Lane.'

Annie nodded.

'When I looked, I could see it was a sheet of music. I went to pick it up, but somehow a gust of wind sent it out of my reach. I didn't run after it and didn't really think any more of it. Just carried on down the road towards the bookshop, except—'

Annie finished the sentence for her. 'It wasn't there.'

'Precisely.'

'That is exactly what happened to me. I didn't take it in, at first. Just kept thinking the knock on my head was making everything look a bit funny. You know, normal except different.'

For a moment the two women sat in silence, both remembering. Trying to picture themselves in Crucifix Lane, reliving the experience.

'You know one thing,' Annie added. 'I didn't see any music, but I did hear some. Just before the accident, I heard this amazing singing, although I couldn't work out where it was coming from then. When I came round, I heard it again and followed it. That's how I ended up in the Pen. So perhaps music is important in some way or another?'

'Very possibly. So could being female.'

'How's that?'

'Do you know there was an earlier traveller? Did Kellen tell you?'

Annie looked surprised.

'No? A man tried to come through at the beginning of February.'

'What do you mean by "tried"? What happened to him?'

'It was very unpleasant. Kellen claims to have a film that shows a man appearing from nowhere in the middle of Crucifix Lane. He was on fire. Burning to death, in fact.'

'No!' exclaimed Annie. 'But how come Kellen told you all this? You don't talk to anyone.'

'This was at the beginning. He told me about the traveller and the mark on his head, hoping for something in exchange.'

'But you didn't tell him anything?'

'I didn't, no.'

'But why would that happen to him and not us? Just his bad luck?'

Mary folded her arms across her chest. 'I've been thinking

about this for some time. There are all sorts of things that could affect or influence what happened. And I certainly don't rule out the possibility that there's something about all three of us that made us susceptible to being . . . sucked forward in time. But, in the end, I think it's more likely that the key to our experience is rooted in something connected to – or driven by – the Celtic calendar. That it is the timing that matters most.'

Mary's voice was serious now. Annie shivered and, for the first time, understood she was involved in something so extraordinary, that it would change everything. If only she could understand. What Leah had said on the boat suddenly came into her mind. 'History is now'.

At the time, Annie hadn't grasped what she was saying. Now, perhaps Leah's words were starting to make sense.

25

It was very humid. Mary got up and closed the shutters to keep the sun from the room. Annie sat completely still, aware of Mary moving around her. She made no effort to help.

The chink of glasses and ice in a jug of water jolted her back to the present. Mary poured, Annie drank it down in one go, then held out her glass for more.

'You look tired,' Mary said. 'Are you sure you wouldn't prefer to have a lie down?'

Annie shook her head vigorously. 'I want to hear everything you've worked out. Everything that's got you to where you are now.'

Mary smiled. 'You forget that I've had nothing to do but think. A great many ideas have come and gone.'

'I still want to know,' she said.

'My basic assumption – although I had no idea if it would turn out to be valid or not – was that the door between our time and this was open on specific, predetermined occasions. The question was if there was a detectable pattern? I started with the Ogham alphabet, given the presence of this mark on my head, the problem being that it was an archaic and symbolic alphabet. It wasn't intended for use on a day-to-day basis, but was instead both a ritualistic form of address and a way to express complex ideas and beliefs on many different levels. I won't swamp you with the details, but broadly speaking, there are twenty letters and five compounds, each of which takes the form of a series of notches or lines – known as *flesc* – spaced along a central stem-line.'

'How do we know about it?' Annie asked. 'Were there sacred books or something?'

'No, it wasn't a written language. About three hundred Ogham-inscribed standing stones were discovered, mostly in Ireland, a few in Wales – all in areas originally inhabited by Irish tribes – and a handful in England, Scotland and the Isle of Man.'

'Were they gravestones?'

'No one really knows, although since no human remains were ever found near or under any of the stones, it's unlikely they were burial sites. The important thing is to remember that the letters are symbolic. They don't mean anything, in the accepted sense of the word. They have to be interpreted.'

Annie looked admiringly at Mary. 'Christ, I don't know how you kept all this up. I would have given up miles back.'

Mary smiled. 'One advantage of age, is mental stamina.'

'I'll remember that when my time comes,' said Annie.

'The Celtic year starts at sunset on October the thirty-first. There are thirteen months, rather than twelve, the final one being the last three days of October alone. It's important to remember that everything in the Celtic tradition works on three levels – the physical, the mental and the spiritual – otherwise it will be hard to make any sense of any of this.'

'You're telling me . . .'

'It's also important to bear in mind that each month has an Ogham character and group of characteristics associated with it. So, for example, November is represented by the Ogham letter *Beith* and by the birch tree. Its colour was white, signifying purity and unity and, as befits its position at the beginning of the year, the number associated with it is the number one. As with us, the new year was considered a time for settling and reckoning. A time for discarding redundant ideas and starting again. February—'

Annie interrupted again. 'Hang on. What's happened to December and January?'

Mary looked at her. 'Well, think about it. The next traveller came through in February, the fourth month.'

'Of course,' said Annie. 'Sorry.'

'I decided to see what, if any, significant dates of the Celtic calendar involved both February and May, focusing on the solstices, the equinoxes, the Fire Festivals and any other times when divine forces were considered to be more readily accessible to people. What I discovered – and this is the key piece of information – was that there were four Fire Festivals in the year. *Samain, Brigantia, Beltane* and *Lugnassadh.*'

'And they were?'

'The first, fourth, seventh and tenth months of the year,' said Mary. 'That is, on our calendar—'

'Don't tell me. November, February, May and August.'

'Correct.'

Annie could barely keep still in her chair. 'Incredible.'

'I couldn't be sure, of course, with just two experiences to go on. But the Fire Festivals seems as likely an explanation as any other, particularly given the unpleasant death of the first traveller. That is why I had been expecting you – or someone – to come through at the beginning of August.'

'It's amazing,' repeated Annie.

'Of course it leaves many questions unanswered. Not least of all why you and I are perfectly unscathed. Two of the Festivals are male, two female, so that didn't seem to be relevant. Because we both came through on the second of the month, it did cross my mind that, if the path is indeed open for the duration of each Festival, perhaps it's only safe to travel through the day after the Festival. Not on either the eve or the actual day.'

'Because the heat or power or whatever is simply too intense?' suggested Annie.

'Something like that,' Mary replied. 'Although again it could be a coincidence. In any case, we don't know the exact date the man came through.'

'Is there anything relevant in the month. I mean, some association or another that might help?'

'Not that I can think of.'

'Well, what about you?'

'The letter *Duir* represents May. The colours associated with it are black or dark brown and the number is seven. I can't remember the bird Ogham, but the tree is the oak, which was one of the most important trees in Celtic tradition.'

'And me?'

'*Muin* represents August, the tenth month. Your colours are variegated tones and there are links with the gift of prophecy. Again, I can't remember the associated bird, but the tree is the vine. The first of August was also the Harvest Festival. That,' said Mary, 'is as far as I've got to.'

'It's miles. I think you're a total genius.'

Mary smiled. 'No, not a genius. Just persistent.'

Annie's mind was spinning. She didn't think she'd ever tried to take in so much information in one go. Cupping her glass in her hands, she pushed herself back in the armchair and swilled the water round and round. The motion was soothing and helped her to think.

'What I don't understand,' she mused after a while, 'is why Kellen hasn't found all this out for himself. I mean, it can't be that difficult.'

'I'm sure he knows the basics,' said Mary. 'All he needs to do is press a button on his computer to summon up any fact he wants. But the skill is in the interpretation. With something such as the Ogham, there is no such thing as information.'

'Speaking of Kellen, why do you stay up here and not go out? I mean, I know you don't like him and feel uncomfortable with the others, but surely you could go and visit places? Do something, at least.'

'You misunderstand my objection to the people here. With the exception of Kellen, who I don't trust, I have nothing against any of them. But I do not want to engage with their world in any way whatsoever. I don't want to observe it and I don't want to find myself interested or implicated.'

'But why?' insisted Annie. 'I don't understand. Is it such a big deal?'

'I think so, yes. The point is, Annie, that neither you nor I should be here at all, however, we are here. In my opinion, our primary responsibility is to ensure we do not influence the pattern of history.'

'I don't understand what you mean.'

'Well, take this as an example. This morning, as you leave this place, if you saw a child drowning in the Thames, and you were the only person on the riverbank, would you dive in and save him?'

'Obviously.'

'But if you had not been pulled forward to 2008, the child would have died.'

Annie frowned. 'That's good I saved him then, surely. Look, it's no different from seeing the same thing happen in 1997. You'd still have to choose to act or not to act.'

'That's true. But we are written into the fabric of our own time. Perhaps that child was supposed to drown.'

'You sound so fatalistic. As if you think everything is preordained and we have no choice but to go along with what life has in store for us.'

'What about if the child grows up to kill or destroy? Then what would you feel about your intervention . . . ?'

Annie was silenced by this idea, unpleasantly aware at what poor intellectual shape she was in.

'There are also the personal consequences to consider,' continued Mary.

'What do you mean?'

'If you were seriously hurt, would you carry that injury back to 1997 or would it exist only in this present? Or what if you became pregnant? Could you give birth to a child ten years before it had even been conceived?'

Annie was now looking quite pale. Mary felt a pang of affection.

'You're young, Annie,' she said gently. 'It's harder for you. You have less patience, feel you are missing more. I can't tell you how to behave. I don't have all the answers. What I can say, however, it that these are questions you must ask of yourself. My way of coping is to behave as if I were not here. Concentrate my attention on getting home. You must find your own way.'

Annie thought about why it was she felt so differently to Mary. It couldn't just be that she and Mary were different generations, saw things through different eyes. If pushed, she would have said that she didn't know what she was going to say, until she heard the words coming out of her own mouth.

'The thing is, I'm not sure I want to go back.'

26

Thursday 11 September

It was still hot, but now there was the unmistakable smell of autumn in the air at dawn and at dusk. Half-remembered memories of bonfires and damp leaves and excitement. Children ready to go back to school, parents lost their tempers in shoe shops. Everywhere the scent of polish and freshly-ironed cotton and the return of routine.

Most mornings, Annie woke to a brilliant blue sky, stretched taut like silk over the city. Most afternoons, the clouds came down and turned the world grey. At night, a heavy rain fell and woke London again to streets of glistening silver in the low sun.

Annie had settled in. All the things that had seemed strange at first, were now second nature. Like Dorothy in the Emerald City, she became less confident about ever getting home, even if she decided that that was what she wanted. From time to time, she had pangs of homesickness and, increasingly, her grandad was on her mind. But mostly she was completely happy.

She concentrated on living, rather than hiding away like Mary. She taught herself to think of this London as home. It was where she'd be living – probably – in eleven years' time, maybe even in these streets. Perhaps she'd be a successful, professional woman. A mother, even. She was here just a little too early, that was all. Right place, wrong time.

Annie was proud of herself for adjusting so quickly, how

she was used to the lack of cars and the continual strumming from helicopters and boats on the river, she'd got to grips with the new currency and spent it without thinking, she learned about palmtops and nanotransistors and computers that recognised your voice, and hotels built underwater in the Pacific Ocean where the view from the dining room was the coral beneath the sea. She got a kick out of recognising the faces and voices of politicians and personalities on the television, internet and display screens which dominated most public places. Some of them were just older versions of people whose faces she already knew. It was amusing to see who had lasted the course and who had not, who had aged well, and who had slipped between the cracks.

The thing Annie found most peculiar was the way she had become reliant on the people around her, both emotionally and financially. Whereas the old Annie revelled in her 'I'm-looking-after-number-one' credentials, the new Annie felt good about the idea that other people were watching out for her. She wasn't a one-woman show any longer.

Leah, Mary and Kellen gave her life its backbone. The others were there, more or less as circumstances dictated. Her friendship with Jonas and Malik developed mostly over coffee at breakfast and hanging out last thing at night. She was especially fond of Jonas, his gentleness, lack of self-confidence and his conscientious manner. Often, they ended up running the coffee bar in the main hall together for most of the day. When it was quiet, they confided their hopes, their dreams, for the future.

Annie felt less comfortable with Vicky, possibly because of the aftermath of the incident with Lonnie, when they'd told each other too much, too soon. Annie always felt a little awkward, like she was being sized up. As for Lonnie, Annie hadn't forgotten what he'd tried to do. But as time went by, her anger faded. For the sake of everyone else, it was easier to draw a mental line under the whole thing, rather than let it poison the atmosphere. Annie managed to work alongside him without engaging with him in any way, although she did make certain she was never on her own with him. From the expression in his eyes, Annie knew he'd not forgotten either.

The truth was, she had been accepted into their group like any other new girlfriend. At first they welcomed her, then they got used to having her around. In the end, they grew to like her for herself.

Annie usually spent the afternoons with Mary. She saved up tit-bits of the day to share with her and made an effort to find things to amuse her. Since their initial conversations, Mary kept her opinions about their situation to herself. Annie didn't mind so much. She had visions of working everything out herself, then bursting in and stunning Mary with the brilliance of the theory she'd come up with. Instead, they reminisced about the past and discussed what they wanted from the future. They talked of friends and music, what made them laugh. Annie found she could confide her feelings about her grandad, in a way she would never had dreamed of before. Not even to herself. What he meant to her, how much he'd tried to do for her and how she had taken most of it for granted. But if anyone had suggested to Annie that Mary had become a mother figure to her, she would have bitten their head off.

Every now and again, in the peaceful moments, Annie would think of something she was supposed to have been doing and wonder if her own time had moved on in parallel. She imagined what the V97 Festival at Chelmsford in August might have been like. How she should have been dancing to Blur, Kula Shaker and Reef with her friends. Had they gone without her? Missed her? Been pissed off at the lack of message?

These were the days when Annie understood why Mary believed they had no choice but to go back. That she could no more avoid her present than she could run from her past. When she was feeling particularly disjointed, she would press Mary to tell her what she was really feeling. Was she scared? Did she feel she was in limbo? Why was it wrong to be so much happier here? Mary's answer was always the same. Wait and see.

Her relationship with Leah was very different. Unlike most girls, Annie had never really had a best friend before. A group, sure, but no one special. She knew she was partly attracted by the fact that she couldn't figure Leah out at all. She was so serious – although she had a dry sense of humour when she could be bothered – intensely private and appeared to have no interest in sex or relationships whatsoever. Annie got the feeling that half of Leah's mind was always elsewhere and, despite their growing intimacy, Leah was hard to pin down. Usually, she was friendly and, when Kellen was away, sometimes they'd talk all night and end up falling asleep on Leah's bed. Other times, though, Leah was almost secretive about where she was going or where she'd been. Once or twice, Annie had the feeling that Leah was on the verge of revealing something important. But at the last minute, she would draw back and the shutters would come down again, leaving Annie trying to work out what was going on.

But they had fun and Annie felt more comfortable with Leah than with anyone she'd ever known. Leah took her shopping, they went to movies and sat drinking iced tea in the cool shadows down by the river before evening fell and the bugs came out, talking about every subject under the sun. Annie would smile as she watched her friend twisting her long plait in her fingers, her serious little face animated as she explained some theory or another.

The one person Annie never discussed with either Mary or Leah was Kellen himself. She was too experienced to risk it. Her teenage years had been blighted by rows with friends over lovers. Too often, she'd been in the no-win situation of being stuck in the middle as friends and boyfriends competed for her attention and tried to undermine one another. Besides, Annie wasn't altogether sure of Leah's past relationship with Kellen. She suspected they might have had something going at one point, but she didn't want to have it confirmed. And as for Mary? She knew what Mary thought about Kellen and did not want to fall out with her over him either.

From time to time, though, Annie did feel claustrophobic. The constant stream of people coming and going in the Pen, the sense of being in a goldfish bowl and on public display. When it got too much, she took to her old habit of walking the streets. Seeking out the old skeleton beneath the new skin of the city.

One of her favourite places was St Mary Magdalene churchyard around the back of Bermondsey Street, with its ornate, gabled fountain standing in the centre. Annie had spent many hours here when she was younger, sitting on the uncomfortable green benches and trying to avoid the men clutching beer in plastic bags who invaded the park in summer. Now, the gravel paths had been replaced with cool pink and white tiles that were like an ice rink when it rained. The strange obelisk in the corner was still there, but with clutches of geraniums rather than pansies growing around its base. Continental flowers.

Bermondsey Street itself had been transformed. Gone were most of the quaint little antiques shops, the sorts of ramshackle concerns that had been handed on from generation to genera-tion. Instead, the street was filled with loft conversions and delicatessens, and the only signs of decay now were the flood stains along the bottom of the walls. Annie could see the paint marks where efforts had been made to repair the damage. Even the church itself had been converted into luxury apartments, the old crooked black light above the original door one of the few features to have survived its metamorphosis. Bermondsey Exchange, Newton's Row, Morocco Lofts, all single units designed for single people with money to burn. It was hard to imagine Charles Dickens leaning out of one of these windows and yelling at children in the street below to be quiet. Nobody was ever about. Modern versions of CCTV and entry systems had replaced people as the guardians of the neighbourhood.

The strangest thing was how compromised Annie felt by the enormous gulf between the wealth and prosperity of the city within the Peripherique and the conditions in which people were forced to exist outside. She looked at the prices in the realtors' windows and discovered it was impossible for anybody who was not significantly wealthy to live in London any more, as Leah had told her. The aspirational middle classes lived in the urban suburbs and spent a great deal of time defending their reasons for being there, as if it was a question of morality rather than bank balance. Further out, the suburbs were as grim to the north and south as they were in the Marsh Projects in the east. Anybody who didn't have the right ID or enough money in their pockets, simply wasn't allowed into the Peripherique. Security guards were everywhere, protecting the sensibilities of the tourists and residents from human eyesores. The tramps and down-and-outs and disabled who'd once made their homes in St Mary Magdalene churchyard had all been evicted. Out of sight, out of mind.

The old Annie would not have cared, she'd have shrugged her shoulders and said it wasn't either her fault or her problem. The new Annie not only minded, but also felt guilty at having so much, when others had nothing. It was as if she'd grown up overnight. She started to dislike her old self, remembering, with regret and embarrassment things she'd done and said which now made her cringe. As the weeks went by, the mental list of people she wanted to apologise to – if she ever had the chance – got longer and longer. Top of the list was her own name.

Annie knew she was being hard on herself, but once she had started to revise her view of the world, she simply couldn't stop. All the things that she'd thought satisfying and fulfilling before – casual friendships, clubs and cinemas, spending her days preparing for her nights – now seemed trivial and superficial. She wanted Mary and Leah to think well of her. And Kellen to stay in love with her.

Kellen. His beauty still stole her breath away. His pale skin and green eyes and black curls. Her heart still beat faster when he walked into the room. Annie felt as if they were reflections in the same glass, a perfect match. She was physically and emotionally obsessed. Totally obsessed. Sex was fantastic – imaginative and adventurous – and, at first, she had experienced a sense of everything being possible. She would have thrown herself off a cliff if he'd asked her to.

He was very changeable, though. There were nights when he surrounded her with affection and promises, made her feel she was the centre of his world. Other times, like Leah, he was distant and preoccupied. She admired him and respected how hard he worked to make things better for other people, but found it hard to reconcile his sensitivity with his need for control. She knew herself well enough to acknowledge that it was precisely because she did not know where she stood, that he was so attractive to her. At the same time, she didn't like to acknowledge she knew very little more about what made him tick than she had on the second of August, when she'd come to the Pen, listened to him speak and fallen in love with his voice.

But, like all lovers, Annie lived in the present. Unwelcome thoughts, she pushed from her mind.

27

As they swept east along the line of the Thames, Michael leaned his head back against the seat to reduce the juddering effects of the helicopter. He'd have a couple of hours of it before they reached Paris. The sound of the blades drilled through his head, making him nauseous and dizzy.

The business with Cordou had limped on for a few days after the last meeting of the Consortium on the fourth of August. The Frenchman had remained in London after everyone else had gone home, continuing to demand daily updates on the Lightermen samples. His contention was that it strained credibility for Ministry scientists to claim that there were medical possibilities in the Lightermen DNA but yet they could not say precisely what the possibilities might be. He contacted individuals at the Ministry, tried to intimidate them into admitting Michael was withholding evidence.

Cordou was right to be sceptical. But he was a businessman not a scientist and, in the face of such adamant statements from Professor Stark and her colleagues, he started to doubt his conviction. Perhaps his advice was inaccurate? He was no longer sure.

Throughout, Michael's tactics were straightforward. He denied the accusations outright and otherwise stayed silent, leaving Cordou with two choices: to resign from the partnership or accept Michael's word. He'd chosen the latter option, but Michael was under no illusion that it was anything other than a temporary ceasefire.

Within days of Cordou leaving London, there was word that he had started to dig around in Michael's past. Looking for dirt to use against him. Up until this point, Michael had tried to keep the continuing hostilities between themselves. Now, he'd had no hesitation in informing the Consortium of Cordou's behaviour and had flown to Paris in mid-August to confront him in person. Six hours later, after an acrimonious but intensely satisfying meeting, Michael had a copy of Cordou's letter of resignation in his hand.

After the pressure of Operation Bayoux and the showdown with Cordou, Michael found it difficult to cope with the lack of action. The weather continued to get hotter and more humid. Record temperatures, sudden and devastating rainstorms, as if the intention was to test Michael's endurance.

His assumption had been that Harris would want to get rid of the Lightermen stock immediately, so Michael set up the Unit to work round the clock in Weston Street, monitoring all likely Internet sites and following other leads. A week passed. Ten days. Two weeks. Nothing. Gradually, Michael became convinced they had missed the notification. Leah, on the other hand, was convinced Kellen would play it safe. Since he knew the Network was under surveillance, he'd keep his head down. Watch and wait. He'd let the dust settle before taking any action. Unlike some of the Unit members – who privately thought they should widen their net to look at other possible perpetrators – Leah didn't doubt Kellen was behind it. She just felt she knew him well enough to know he'd not take unnecessary risks for no tangible benefit.

She advised patience and tried to convince Michael that Kellen was flaunting his leisure. Spending a lot of time with Annie, being seen around the Pen. For Leah he was putting too much effort into giving the impression of taking things easy.

But Michael had no patience. Waiting was torture to him. He could not sit, passive, just in case Harris made a move. He had a knot in his chest so tight that on some days he thought he was having a heart attack. His skin was even paler then usual, he was drinking too much and he could barely sleep or eat. The food seemed to stick in his throat, then lie like an alien presence inside his stomach. He was buzzing with nervous energy, constantly jigging his legs as he sat at the computer, endlessly drumming his fingers on his desk.

Michael knew Leah worried about him. More than once when they'd been working alone together, she'd gently pressed him to tell her what was going on with him. Tried to pull him out of the dark place he inhabited. Surely, the hard part was over? They'd obtained the blood samples and were running their tests; they'd confirmed that it was Harris and the Network behind the intimidation of the Lightermen; they'd acquired evidence of him taking blood without authorisation. All that remained was finding proof that would stand up in court. They were nearly there. They just had to keep calm and wait, hoping Kellen had not already made arrangements to get rid of the material without their knowledge. In fact, even if he had already sold the Lightermen stock, the Unit had nonetheless achieved their primary objectives of verifying the unique properties of the Lightermen DNA and beginning to put in place safeguards to protect their genetic property from biopirates. It would be the icing on the cake to nail Kellen, but not it was essential. Operation Bayoux had easily achieved what they'd hoped for already.

Once, as they were talking, Leah put her hand on Michael's arm and told him he should feel proud. Not understanding how so much stronger than love is revenge. Michael looked at her serious face and wanted so much to reassure her. But he could not find the words to explain that getting Kellen was the only thing that would save him from himself. How his dreams were full of water. How he could still remember the sensation of falling forward, then being trapped under the surface of the river with the taste of mud and slime in his throat. How he could still see the distorted hands of rescuers reaching down for him, his father's irritation and look of triumph on the face of his brother. He could not explain how, when he woke in a cold sweat in the early hours of the morning, it was with the possessive touch of the already-drowned on his legs and feet. Claiming him as one of their own. Michael had been twelve when the accident had happened. He was thirty-two now. Twenty years ago. But he did not believe the river had forgotten him.

The drinking, the temper outbursts and the long periods of dark silence continued.

Finally, the deadlock was broken.

On Wednesday 10 September a coded communication was posted on the Internet, alerting potential customers to the availability of certain genetic materials and worded in such a way that only those already involved in previous negotiations could possibly interpret the instructions. Immediately, they had tried to trace the advertisement, hoping to link it directly back to the Network. Predictably, the identity of the originator was protected by a high-security Mixmaster system and, after many abortive attempts to break it, Michael admitted defeat and stopped wasting the Unit's time. It had been a long shot anyway. They'd have to rely on following the lead to the buyer, instead of the seller.

Just as Michael's instinct had all along told him that Harris was the seller, he was now equally convinced Cordou was the buyer. So far as he was concerned, Kellen's reason for making a general market notification was solely to push up the price Cordou would have to pay. Not because he was planning a general auction.

It had been relatively easy to deduce Cordou was acquiring illegal samples. With the co-operation of the Office Français des Biotechnologies, Cordou had been under surveillance from the moment he had resigned from the Consortium on 11 August. The OFB suspected Cordou had been involved in black market trading. They too were sniffing for hard evidence.

It was a risk to concentrate all his resources on the belief that Harris and Cordou were the key players. Michael knew that. If he turned out to be wrong, by the time they realised their mistake, any chance of discovering who was responsible would be long gone. The samples would have been traded without leaving a trace.

But the gamble had paid off. The day before the OFB reported that a large sum of money, destined for London via an offshore account in the Channel Islands, had left Cordou's bank in Boulevard Henri IV. The French team tracked it successfully up until the point it arrived in Britain. Then the trail went dead and the Unit could find no trace of it. Michael's temper had finally got the better of him and he'd lost it. Ignoring Leah's attempts to mollify him, he threatened everybody, yelling that if they failed to identify the recipient or whereabouts of the cash within twenty-four hours, then they could all consider themselves out of a job. No excuses. Just fucking well sort it out.

Two hours ago, the key piece of information had come through. Cordou had arranged a meeting in Paris at midday on Friday 12 September. Tomorrow. Michael glanced at his watch, shaking because of the motion of the helicopter. They were due to pick up Nelson Huyk and his son in Lille at six o'clock, then fly on to Paris to be at their hotel in the Bastille by nine to meet with their counterparts of the Office Français des Biotechnologies.

Even now, Michael couldn't let himself believe his moment had finally come. He'd been this close to Harris before and had lost him, through a mixture of arrogance and indecision.

Michael was not superstitious, yet there was a voice in his head warning him not to let his guard down. Not to tempt fate. It could all still fall apart in his hands.

'Are you OK?' asked Leah, shouting over the noise. 'You don't look so good.'

'Don't like these things.'

'I'm surprised you're not used to them by now.'

Michael shook his head and kept his eyes closed. Anything to take his mind off the journey.

While his conscious mind had been gridlocked by whisky and anxiety, his subconscious mind had been casually dropping pieces of another jigsaw into place. All the edges neat. A perfect fit. Michael had always believed the appearance of the travellers must be important, but he'd never considered it relevant to his pressing day-to-day concerns with the Unit and at the Ministry.

He couldn't account for the fact it had taken him so long to see what had been staring him in the face all along. Namely, that if it was possible to travel forward in time, then maybe it was possible to travel back. Obvious. It was so obvious. And the possibilities were endless. With the benefit of hindsight, they could take better decisions in certain knowledge of the consequences. They could take different decisions in the past to safeguard the future. All those plants mindlessly wiped out before medical science realised how essential they were. Now, it was too late. But ten years ago, how many of them were still around then. Half? Nearly all?

The idea crossed Michael's mind that he shouldn't fuck with history, but he dismissed it. History was already fucking with them. If not him, then certainly Mary Royle and Annie Jones and the poor bastard who'd ended up in the City Morgue. The fact remained, that if he could only persuade one of them to make a return journey, then perhaps he could use them as a courier to bring back things from the past to the present. Perhaps, in time, he would even find a way of travelling through time himself?

The only thing that tarnished Michael's excitement was the knowledge that Kellen had almost certainly been one step ahead. The attention he'd shown to both Mary and Annie made sense now. He wasn't just interested in the principle of travelling in the abstract, but as a specific way of manipulating events to increase his own power.

Michael glanced through the window at the bank of

clouds chasing them down. The wind had been so strong earlier that the pilot hadn't thought they'd been able to get up at all. This morning's Worldwide Weather Navigator had run a story about how the climate was collapsing faster than even the worst-case scenarios had predicted. Apparently, two more dormant European volcanoes were now waking up, one close enough to Rome to make evacuation a serious option. He tried to imagine a world of nuclear winters and burning summers. Everything ruled by flood and fire exactly as it had been thousands of years ago. Was this how it would end? Back where it had all started?

The helicopter suddenly swerved sharply to the right and headed due south, down over the Kent suburbs. Michael thought of the river hundreds of feet below and closed his eyes again. Tried to shut the water out of his mind.

28

Friday 12 September

Michael stepped out of his small hotel in rue Castex and breathed in the hot Parisian morning.

Nelson Huyk and his son, Piet, were staying at Bar Rémy in rue de Charonne, just around the corner from rue de Lappe, where the Cordou rendezvous was to take place. The four of them had arranged to meet there at nine. Suddenly, Michael heard the squeak of the glass door on the steps behind him. He looked at his watch: 08:37:01. Perfect timing.

'Morning,' he said. 'Did you sleep well?'

Leah smiled. 'Yes, thanks. How about you?'

Michael nodded. 'Fine. Shall we get going?'

They headed down the street, then turned left and walked towards Place de la Bastille, with its lunatic traffic and chaos of pedestrian crossings leading dangerously from one junction to the next. The market on Boulevard Beaumarchais was full. Fruits and vegetables, honey and cheese and olives, all bussed in at four o'clock from the country. Old Portuguese women in black wandered slowly between the stalls with huge woven baskets. The flower seller on the corner was offering bunches of delphiniums and lilies, watched by a group of young Algerian men perched on the railings smoking cigarettes. Little children, their brothers and sisters already at school, clutched *pains au lait* tight in their fists as they were pushed along in their all-terrain buggies. Little had changed from when Michael had spent time here ten years ago. More run down, perhaps.

Suffering the effects of its recent notorious past, but otherwise much the same.

They arrived at Bar Rémy at five to nine. The concierge was clearly expecting them and showed them straight through to the tiny tiled dining room where Nelson and Piet were waiting. The only other people having breakfast were a noisy German family, getting their money's worth as they ploughed their way through a mountain of baguette, butter and jam with fixed concentration. The twin boys were arguing and kicking each other under the table, ignored by their parents. Huyk and Leah exchanged glances.

None of them said much as they waited for their breakfast to arrive. Tension and the need for discretion had taken away their appetite for polite conversation and every detail of today's plan had already been hammered through the night before. Passing comments about the weather in London and Amsterdam, the imminent European elections, the chances of Britain ever hosting the Football World Cup in their lifetime, were topics all briefly raised and dropped.

'*Merci, Madame*,' said Leah, as the wife of the concierge found room on the small table for their coffee and croissants.

'*Je vous en prie.*'

They ate quickly and in silence. Finally, Michael looked at his watch.

'It's time to go,' he said.

Most of the salsa bars and clubs in rue de Lappe were not yet open. Piles of rubbish and boxes stacked high on the pavements bore witness to a late and successful night. The curtains of the windows on the floors above were still drawn.

Michael went into the café opposite Le Bleu Nuit and took up his position at the counter, facing the door. His hat was pulled low on his head, covering his hair and eyes. From his pocket, he produced a copy of *Le Monde* and pretended to read. He was aware of Nelson browsing in the window of the music shop next door. Leah and Piet, the two Cordou would not recognise, were already ensconced inside Le Bleu Nuit. They couldn't be seen from the street, but the angle of the glass gave them a good view of everyone who came in.

At ten forty-five, Pierre arrived and took a table out of earshot, in the corner on the opposite side of the bar to Piet and Leah.

'I'm going to try to get closer,' Piet whispered immediately. 'You stay here.'

He slid along the bench and disappeared to the bathroom. When he emerged a few minutes later, he headed for the table behind Cordou instead and sat down with his back to him. After another couple of minutes, he called the waiter over and pointed to the empty glass in front of him on the table as if it were his.

'*Encore une fois.*'

'*Panaché?*'

Piet nodded, then sat back and watched the minutes ticking by on the digital clock flashing over the bar. He could feel Cordou's impatience, the way he was fidgeting and shifting and looking up at the slightest movement.

At five past eleven, a man appeared at Cordou's table and handed him an envelope. Cordou ripped it open and read the note inside. He was clearly not pleased.

The man clearly wanted an answer. '*Monsieur?*'

'*Oui,*' growled Cordou abruptly. '*J'arrive.*'

Piet didn't have time to think. He tossed some money on the table and followed the two men out. They walked fast, threading their way through the maze of small streets, across Boulevard Beaumarchais and into rue des Tournelles. Piet didn't look back to see if anyone was with him, just kept his eyes on Cordou and the man with him. He had been shown photos of Harris, but couldn't tell at this distance if it was him or not.

The all-weather ice rink in La Place des Vosges was crowded. Tourists leaned on the railings and looked enviously at the skaters below. Schoolchildren in matching green scarves and hats were filling in worksheets on their clipboards, copying down information about *La Patinoire de l'an 2000*, while their teacher fanned herself with her hat. At the far end, bravura performers swerved in and out on sharp one-line boards, smacking into the sides of the rink when they ran out of space, spraying showers of artificial ice into the faces of those watching.

Piet ran to the barrier, breathing heavily and cast his eyes around the square. All the men looked the same in their lightweight suits and pale hats.

'Have we lost them?' said Michael at his shoulder.

'They're here somewhere,' he replied.

'Do you know where they're going?'

'No. The man appeared and gave Cordou a letter. Then they left together. Neither of them said anything.'

'And is it Harris?'

'I couldn't tell,' Piet replied. 'I didn't get a good enough look at him. Are the others with you?'

'Your father was at the far end of the street when you came out, so he should be just behind me. I'm not sure about—'

'There,' shouted Piet. 'At the top.'

Michael followed the line of his hand and caught a glimpse of Cordou's back disappearing through the gate leading from the ice rink to the gardens beyond.

'You take the left-hand side,' he yelled. 'I'll take the right. We ought to be able to pick them up in rue des Francs Bourgeois.'

'Right.'

The two men separated and ran swiftly along the sides of the rink and into the park beyond. Cordou and his companion were in their sights now. Michael slowed down. There was no sense in being seen, not until the transaction was actually taking place. He indicated to Piet and Nelson to pull back also. Nelson stuck his thumb up to show he'd got the message.

Despite the heat the gardens were even more crowded than the rink. Lunchtime picnics and performance artists were clumped in the shade under the trees. Families were milling around the water sculptures on the grass, listening to the music.

Michael could hear the scrunch of the gravel under his feet and feel the lines of sweat seeping down his cheeks into the collar of his shirt. He'd not expected Harris to conduct his business with Cordou in the bar itself, but he was surprised that they were going so far elsewhere.

At the main gate the two men suddenly stopped. Taken by surprise Michael dropped down and pretended to tie his shoelaces. From beneath the brim of his hat he saw their faces clearly for a second. Their voices were lost in the noise of the street and he tried to read their lips. Then almost at once they took three steps out of the gate, climbed straight into a waiting taxi and were lost from sight.

Piet leaped after them and pushed his way through the gate, but was too late. He stood on the pavement with his hands on his hips. After a few moments, he turned and walked back into the park.

'Shit.'

Michael took off his hat and pushed his fingers through his hair.

'It's not your fault, Piet.'

'Do you think they saw us?'

'They'd already taken precautions.'

'You don't think Harris spotted us in rue de Lappe?' asked Nelson. 'And changed his plans as a result?'

'I don't think so, but it's possible,' replied Michael. 'In any case, it wasn't Harris.'

'Then who was it?'

'I don't know. I didn't recognise him.'

'One of Harris's men?'

'Yes,' said Michael. 'Unless I'm wrong about everything.'

Nelson clapped him on the shoulder. 'Whenever have you been wrong, my friend?' he said kindly. 'Things have just not gone our way quite yet.'

By the time they got back to rue de Lappe, the streets were filling up with students and proprietors opening their bars and clubs for the afternoon session. The rhythms of North Africa and South America spilled out on to the street, mixing with the smells of hot and spicy cooking.

Michael and Nelson waited outside while Piet went in to the bar to look for Leah.

'No sign of her,' he said, coming out a couple of minutes later. 'I asked, but nobody noticed her leave. It's too busy in there now.'

'What do you want to do now, Michael?' asked Nelson.

'Go back to the hotel. We agreed to meet there if we got separated.'

'And Harris?'

'We'll find him. He's here, I'm sure of it.'

Nelson raised his eyebrows. 'Yes, but where?'

'I was thinking more of Cordou. He's got to come back to his office or home sometime. We can pick him up easily.'

'And say what? Accuse him of accepting a lift from a stranger?'

Despite his anger at losing Cordou, Michael smiled briefly. 'We can put a bit of pressure on. If he has closed some sort of deal with Harris, he'll be on edge. However he's been briefed to deal with the situation, he won't be a hundred per cent sure about how much we know. It won't take much to persuade him to cooperate . . .'

Nelson nodded.

'In the meantime, can you contact the French office immediately, get them up to speed on what's happened and ask them to arrange cover of Cordou's home and office?'

'Right.'

'And maybe I'll try and figure out where Harris might be.'

Nelson looked quizzically at his friend. 'I don't rate your chances of finding him in a city of six million people. Or have you something in mind?'

Michael didn't answer. 'Unless anything happens before then, we'll meet again at six at Bar Rémy. OK?'

'Are you not walking back now?'

He shook his head. 'Soon. You go on.'

Michael watched the two men until they were out of sight, then turned and disappeared in the opposite direction.

29

A couple of hours later, Michael was back in rue Castex, having failed to achieve what he wanted. He found Leah lying in her room with the curtains drawn and a cold compress over her eye.

'What the hell happened?' he asked.

'I'm fine. It's not as bad as it looks. Did you get Cordou?'

'No,' said Michael. 'What happened to you?'

'I'm not sure, to tell you the truth.'

Michael could feel the veins in his neck jumping. 'For Christ's sake, woman,' he said. 'Tell me!'

'All right, all right. Calm down.'

He walked over and sat down on the chair next to the bed. Rubbed his eyes. 'Sorry. It's been a long day.'

'It's only three o'clock . . .'

'I know that,' he said.

'I've been sitting here for hours wondering where the hell you'd all got to. What happened after Piet left the bar?'

'The short version is we tailed them across half of Paris, then lost them. I'll fill you in later. But I really do need to know what's been going on.'

'Fine. Don't shout at me, Michael.'

'I'm sorry.'

'Stop me if I'm repeating stuff Piet's already told you. I didn't notice anything unusual in the bar. Nobody looking as if they were paying special attention to us. Then Cordou arrived and Piet moved to another table to get a better look. My back was to them, so I could see virtually nothing. It would have been too obvious if I'd turned around.'

'Hold on,' interrupted Michael. 'Did you get a good look at the man with the letter?'

'Not then. I caught sight of his reflection in the mirror behind the bar as they were leaving.'

'Did you recognise him?'

'I'm just coming to that. I got up and tried to follow them too, but I was longer getting out of the bar because the waiter dropped a tray of drinks in front of the door at precisely that moment. There was glass everywhere and there was lots of shouting, everyone in everyone else's way trying to clear it up.'

'Coincidence?'

'It's possible it was deliberate, I suppose. The point is that by the time I did get on to the street, they were nowhere in sight. Incidentally, where were you? I didn't see you at all.'

'I was already up with Piet,' Michael said. 'Nelson was at the wrong end when Cordou came out.'

'Yes, I saw him,' said Leah. 'I started off not thinking about much else than keeping him in my sights, when three men stepped out of a doorway in front of me.'

'In rue de Lappe?'

'No. Another of those small roads around the back of Place de la Bastille. Didn't notice the name. At first, I just thought it was one of those things. You know how narrow those pavements are. But when I tried to go around, they blocked my way.'

'Nationality?'

'Don't know. They spoke in French. I asked them to move. Not aggressively. One of them asked for money and, rather than just handing it over, I hesitated and he hit me. Hence this on my face. It was so sudden, I completely lost my balance and slipped off the pavement. He held me down, while the others went through my pockets.'

'Did they get anything?'

'Just money. As a precaution, I'd left all identification here.'

'Good,' said Michael thoughtfully. 'Then what?'

'Nothing. They ran off. I got up and came back here.'

'You've got that tone in your voice,' said Michael, 'that suggests there is something more.'

'It might be nothing, but when I was down, I heard one of them say: "*voilà de ton copain*".'

'What the hell does that mean?'

'Roughly speaking, it translates as "that's from your friend".'

'And you think this was some sort of warning?'

'I don't know. It might be a straightforward mugging. Nothing more to it than that. On the other hand, it could be that someone did recognise one of us – you, me or Nelson – and decided to let us know by getting me.'

For a few minutes, they sat in silence and weighed up the situation. Michael got a bottle of water from the table.

'Glasses?' he said.

'Above the basin.'

He disappeared into the bathroom.

'Here you go,' he said, handing her a drink.

'Thank you.'

'How do you feel now?'

'Fine. A bit shaken, but fine.'

'So, what about the man in the café?'

'He's called Lonnie Bell and he's Kellen's closest associate in the Network. He's the person I've mentioned I've been suspicious about. If anyone is in on what Kellen's doing, then it's him. But it's not much in the way of evidence linking the samples back to Kellen,' said Leah. 'Lonnie could come up with a perfectly legitimate reason for being with Cordou.'

Michael nodded. 'It was stupid of me to expect Harris would make an appearance in person, but he's always struck me as the sort of man who'd want to be in at the kill. Obviously, though, it was far more likely he'd send someone else to hand over the goods. The cash is already in the bank, after all.'

'The money's been tracked home then?'

'I'll rephrase that. Cordou has paid someone, and I'm *assuming* that someone is Kellen. We've not actually managed to locate the money yet.'

'So where are Cordou and Lonnie?'

Michael shrugged. 'They had a car waiting on the far side of La Place des Vosges. I presume Lonnie has taken Cordou somewhere private to close the deal and hand over the samples.'

'So we're going to try to pick Cordou up later?'

'Exactly. The OFB have his apartment and office covered. They'll be in touch as soon as they have anything to report.'

'He'd be a fool to come back.'

'He is a fool,' said Michael. 'And arrogant with it.'

'So what's the plan now?'

'We wait. I've arranged to meet Nelson and his son at their hotel at six o'clock. At that point, depending on what – if anything – I discover in the course of the next few hours, I'll come to a decision about whether we should stay another day or go back to London.'

Leah suddenly felt overwhelmed with exhaustion. 'If there's nothing more you need me for at the moment,' she said, 'then I think I'll take a rest for a couple of hours.'

'Sure,' he replied. 'I'll let you know if anything comes up.'

Michael opened the door, then hesitated. 'If you are right that it wasn't an ordinary mugging, then it might be too dangerous for you to go back to the Pen, Leah. You'll be too vulnerable.'

'But then, as you said, perhaps I'm overreacting.'

'I don't want to take any risks.'

Leah smiled at him, touched by the concern in his voice. 'I'll be fine. We're so close to cracking it, Michael. If I disappear now, then Kellen's going to put two and two together. We'll lose him.'

'I thought you were the one telling me that getting Kellen wasn't the thing that mattered . . .'

'I don't think it is. What I care about is preventing the Lightermen from being exploited, but—'

'But what?'

'It is what matters to you.'

Michael didn't trust himself to answer.

'So, obviously I'm not going to pull out now,' she continued, 'because that would jeopardise everything you – personally – have been working towards.'

He looked at her with gratitude, noticing the affection and concern in her eyes. 'Thank you,' he said. 'I don't deserve your loyalty.'

'And if you ever want to talk . . .'

He shook his head. 'I'm sorry,' he whispered.

She gave a resigned smile. 'I know,' she said. 'But you know where I am, if you change your mind.'

He nodded. 'The slightest hint of trouble, and I'm pulling you out. Is that clear?'

She laughed. 'Absolutely clear. Now, get out of here and let me have my rest.'

Michael spent the next hour in his room talking to London, learning little of any significance. Kellen Harris had not been seen in or around the Pen all day; the money had still not been traced; the posting on the Internet site had not been revised; and Lonnie Bell did not exist. At least, not according to the ID checks his people were running. Michael wasn't surprised. He assumed it would be a pseudonym. It would just take a little longer to discover the man's identity, but they'd get there in the end.

At four-fifteen, he took a call from the Office Français des Biotechnologies to say they'd picked up Cordou at his office in Boulevard Henri IV and were taking him to their headquarters. Michael scribbled a note for Leah saying he'd meet her at Bar Rémy as soon as he'd finished, gave it to the concierge at the desk, then left.

By the time Michael had made his way half way across Paris, they had been working on Cordou for nearly an hour. The French agent met him inside the main door and introduced himself as Yves Noubel. En route to the interrogation cell where Cordou was being held, he briefed Michael on the sequence of events leading up to the arrest.

'Any progress so far?'

'A little,' Noubel answered, in his heavily accented English. 'At first he denied it all. He didn't know anything. He didn't know a Monsieur Bell. But when we suggested we had recorded their meeting and knew merchandise had changed hands, he was less confident. Shouted more, but less confident about it. With a bit of persuasion, he finally admitted he had bought some DNA samples, but claimed he did not know they were stolen. He stuck to his story that he never knew what Bell was called nor who he was working for.'

'How was contact made in the first place? Did he say?'

'A message telling him to be at *Le Bleu Nuit* at eleven o'clock this morning. That's all.'

Noubel led Michael through a series of reinforced security doors, then down a flight of concrete stairs to the basement. There were no windows and the only lighting was from dim bulbs set into the low ceilings. Nobody had bothered with the plants or water dispensers or other human touches which characterised the public reception upstairs.

'Has he mentioned Kellen Harris or the Network at all?' Michael asked.

'Not yet,' Noubel replied. 'But if there is something to tell, he will say it. He is not a brave man.'

Michael followed him into a small observation area. On the other side of the one-way glass, he could see Cordou strapped into a chair. His head was hanging down and there were wires running up the inside of his lower arms. From this distance, they looked like thick, black veins.

'My people are going through Cordou's office and we will confiscate anything that could be evidence. The important thing now is to get a confession about his deal with Harris. It is so much bigger than the other biopirating activities we know about, that if we can make this one stick,

we've got a good chance of making all allegations good
in court.'

Michael nodded. Behind the glass, Cordou screamed.

'Do you want to question him yourself, Monsieur?'

'No. Just keep me informed and let me know when he
gives us what we want.'

'Of course,' he said, then added. 'If he continues to deny
knowledge of the Network, how far should we go?'

Michael took another look at Cordou, then turned back
to Noubel.

'As far as necessary,' he said.

It was just before seven o'clock and Leah, Nelson and Piet
were sitting in the dining room of the Bar Rémy, which
the concierge had opened up for them specially. The tables
were already laid for the following morning's breakfast. Knives,
plates, napkins, packets of sugar cubes in the saucers and round
cartons of jam with garish pictures of fruit. They had been
waiting for over an hour.

At last, a figure appeared on the other side of the frosted
glass door and pulled it back with a swift tug.

'Michael,' said Leah, leaping up in relief. 'We were
beginning to wonder what had happened to you.'

Nelson shook his hand. 'Did he talk?'

'Not enough,' replied Michael, 'but he will.'

Nelson nodded. 'What sort of shape was he in?'

'So-so.'

Leah and Piet listened to this exchange in silence, not sure
what was going on.

Nelson pushed a drink across the table to Michael. 'Any
sign of Bell?'

'No, which is hardly surprising. He'll be back in London
by now, I should imagine. Cordou claims the handover took
place close to the Place des Vosges and lasted no more than a
matter of minutes.'

'You seem very confident Cordou will tell us what we want

to know,' said Leah. 'Wouldn't his wisest course of action be to keep quiet?'

'That's not an option,' Michael replied.

Leah stared at him, hoping she was reading the wrong message between the lines.

'Why not?' she insisted.

'I—'

His phone rang, echoing loudly in the tiled room. Michael answered it and listened. The others tried to work out what was being said from his monosyllabic answers.

'Thank you,' he said finally. 'Yes. I'll let you know it's arrived safely as soon as I get back to London.'

He snapped the mouthpiece shut.

'We've got him,' he said. 'Cordou's admitted knowing Harris and has come up with dates and times linking himself and Bell directly back to Harris.'

Nelson slapped his friend on the back. 'Congratulations,' he said. 'You don't think there will be problems over the question of using evidence acquired under duress?'

'Unlikely,' said Michael. 'Who can Cordou complain to without incriminating himself even further. In any case, there is nothing to implicate the Consortium in any of this. So far as Cordou is concerned, this is purely a domestic matter. It's the OFB who picked him up and the OFB who will prosecute him.'

Nelson nodded. 'True. And they are sending you a copy of the confession transcript?'

'It should be waiting for me by the time we get back to England.'

Nelson smiled and leaned back in his chair. 'So, we have enough to expose Harris. I presume the articles of attorney protecting the Lightermen have been drawn up?'

'The lawyers will deliver the documents to the Ministry for signature tomorrow morning. Now, so far as the Consortium is concerned, I think the first priority is to call a full meeting for as soon as everyone can make it. I will explain Cordou's absence and inform everyone of the results of the genetic screening with a view to formulating a declaration. We should aim to make a public announcement by the beginning of October at the latest.'

'Very good,' he said.

Nelson was in such a good mood, that he didn't notice the atmosphere had turned sour. Piet was kicking his heel against the leg of his chair in a temper, over and over again. Leah was winding her plait around her fingers. Michael suddenly realised she was deliberately avoiding catching his eye.

Nelson drained his glass and put it back on the table with a bang. 'So,' he said, turning to Leah. 'You must be relieved it's over, after all your hard work. You must be proud of what you've achieved.'

'Oh yes,' she said sarcastically. 'Very proud indeed.'

Michael looked away.

30

Saturday 13 September

Over eight hours had passed since Leah and Michael had left Paris. She'd said as little as possible on the journey back and had shot off the moment they'd landed. Now, she was back in the Pen, sitting in the dark on her bed.

She thought about all those times she'd excused Michael's brusqueness, his lack of emotion. She knew he had a darkness inside him, but had always thought it would be less dominating when the pressure was off. And that perhaps, when they were no longer caught up in such an intense spiral of work, there might be a chance of real friendship growing between them.

From the start, Leah knew he played by his own rules and did not always act within the law. That she could accept. The law was not always right. But until now, she had never doubted he was fundamentally both a good man and a moral one. She had never allowed herself to believe that he would use violence to get what he wanted. Condone it, maybe. But not actually initiate it or resort to it himself. How naïve.

A noise in the hall outside attracted her attention. Leah immediately sat up.

'Who is it?'

'It's me,' hissed Annie.

'Annie, it's two o'clock in the morning. Can't it wait?'

'Please . . .'

The last thing Leah wanted was company, but she knew

Annie wouldn't take no for an answer. She got off the bed and unlocked the door.

'Come in then.'

'I didn't mean to wake you,' said Annie, trying to look contrite.

'You didn't. I was awake anyway.'

'Why are you sitting in the dark?'

'There's a candle on the chest of drawers. Light it, if you want.'

Annie sorted it out, then sat down and took a good look at Leah's face. Her eyes were puffy and her cheek appeared to be bruised.

'Have you been crying?'

'No.'

'But your eyes are all red.'

'I don't want to talk about it.'

'And what's happened to—'

Leah shocked them both by shouting.

'Leave it, Annie! I said I didn't want to talk about it!'

Annie drew back as if she'd been slapped. 'OK, OK,' she said. 'Don't bite my head off.'

'Look, I'm sorry. I'm just a bit on edge tonight.'

'Do you want to talk about it?'

Leah shook her head. Annie let it go.

'So, when did you get back?'

'About midnight.'

Annie crossed her legs and tucked her bare feet under her. 'Where've you been? You've been away for days.'

'A slight exaggeration,' Leah replied. 'Anyway, you haven't come here at this time of night to talk about what I've been up to. Tell me what's happened.'

Given the weird state Leah was in, Annie felt a bit guilty about pouring out her woes. But she did feel in desperate need of a bit of support and comfort.

'I just really feel like I need some company.'

'In the middle of the night?' said Leah, guessing what was coming next.

Annie looked at her feet. 'I've just had a terrible row with Kellen.'

'What about?'

'Well, that's why I'm so freaked out, in a way. I'm not sure what it was about. It just blew up out of nowhere.'

'Why don't you start at the beginning,' said Leah. She obviously wasn't going to get rid of Annie for a while.

'We hadn't seen much of each other today, which was OK. But he has been away a lot recently, so I suggested we should grab a bit of time together early evening. We were just getting started when there was a knock at the door. Kellen went outside for a moment, then charged back in with a face like thunder, disappeared into his study and slammed the door. Without a word to me.'

Now Leah was listening. 'What time was this?'

'A little after seven o'clock,' she replied. 'Why?'

Leah thought about it. About the time that Michael had taken the call in Bar Rémy.

'No reason. I was just wondering.'

'He didn't come out for over an hour and, obviously, I was completely pissed off. But when I said something, he just went for me. Started shouting, making mean comments. It was just so unlike him. It was as if he was deliberately trying to be hurtful.'

'What sort of comments?'

'That I was totally self-obsessed, that I never thought of anybody else but myself. Accused me of not being open or honest with him. Of only being interested in him for sex.'

'What did you say?'

'I told him to fuck off,' said Annie. 'He'd left me sitting there like an idiot for hours, then suddenly it's my fault.'

Despite everything, Leah laughed. 'How did he react to that?'

'He freaked out.'

'What? Shouting at you?'

'No, the opposite. He went all silent on me, which I really can't stand. I kept at him until finally, he came out with a speech about how he felt we were moving apart, that he felt he was competing for my attention with you and Mary all the time and how it made him feel bad. That I trusted Mary more than him, blah, blah, blah.'

'The manipulative . . .' muttered Leah.

'I still didn't really get what was going on.'

'Trusted Mary more about what?'

Annie hesitated. 'What?' She looked at her feet.

'What?' repeated Leah.

'I don't know how much to tell you,' said Annie after a while.

'What do you mean?'

'You know what I mean,' she replied. 'We've been down this road before. Sometimes I look at you and I feel like everything I'm saying is being stored up and reported back.'

'Reported back to who?'

'To Kellen,' she said loudly. 'Who the fuck do you think I'm talking about?'

Leah looked at her, then realised why Annie was so volatile all of a sudden.

'What have you taken?' she said.

'I just had a couple of spinners earlier to relax me. Why are you asking me that?'

'You're totally paranoid.'

'No I'm not.'

'You shouldn't take so many.'

'I only do it when I'm with Kellen.'

The tension that had been building between them finally reached breaking point. Leah grabbed hold of Annie's arm and shouted at her. 'And Kellen's mostly stoned out of his head. Grass, spinners, whiz, you name it. He's not in this world half of the time. Why do you have to copy him? Don't you have a mind of your own?'

'Don't be so fucking ridiculous,' Annie shouted back.

'Well how come it's OK for you to accuse me of talking about you to Kellen behind your back? Why would I do that?'

'Because you're jealous.'

Leah was so staggered by this comment that she laughed. 'You can't honestly believe I'm interested in him?'

Annie immediately felt both embarrassed and angry that Leah was taking the piss. 'Well, I got the impression you were interested in someone,' she said. 'Is that such a strange idea?'

Leah reached out and took Annie's hands. Conciliatory. 'Yes, if you're talking about Kellen,' she said. 'Believe me. I would not sleep with Kellen if he was the last man left on earth.'

'You just seem so close a lot of the time.'

'Kellen gives the impression of being close to everyone,' Leah said dismissively. 'You can't read anything into that.'

For no reason she could fathom, Annie suddenly had the overwhelming urge to kiss her. 'Why are we arguing?' she said, touching Leah's cheek.

Leah stared at her. 'I don't know,' she replied, after a pause.

All the recriminations they had hurled at one another seemed to hang suspended in the air between them. Both women were motionless, realising they had reached some sort of line. They could either go on in the heat of the moment. Or back away and pretend that nothing had happened.

Annie leaned forward and put her hands firmly on Leah's shoulders.

'Are you sure about this?' she said quietly.

Leah nodded.

Very gently, Annie curled her fingers around the back of Leah's neck, threading them under her hair, and kissed her. Careful and delicate, not greedy. Annie was shocked by the intensity of her own response. The immediate surge of desire, the rush in her head as the blood hit her brain. She closed her eyes and leaned across Leah to snuff out the candle with her fingers. Now, the only light was the orange glow from the streetlamp outside, filtering through the thin material that hung in front of the small window.

Annie felt Leah's hands circle her waist, pulling her deeper into the kiss. Then Annie felt her shirt – Kellen's shirt that she'd grabbed when she'd run out of the room – being eased off her shoulders. The night air felt warm on her back.

She opened her eyes and slipped down the thin straps of Leah's white vest, then rolled the material down over her breasts and stomach until it was gathered like a belt around her waist. She was tiny, her ribs and shoulder blades jutting out like the bones of an underfed child. Annie leaned forward and let her tongue skim the pale blue skin of her breasts. Leah caught her breath as she took first one nipple, then the other, into her mouth. Traced out patterns with her breath, like circles in water. Annie felt dizzy and heavy, as if she was going to fall.

Annie slipped her arm behind Leah to take her weight and climbed into the bed beside her. And, never taking her eyes from Leah's face, slipped her hand into the space between her thighs. Smiled at the wetness.

Very slowly and rhythmically, she started to move her fingers in and out. Leah lay back on the bed, stretched her arms above her head and opened her legs to give Annie more room. Annie ran her tongue over Leah's abdomen and hips, lightly biting her and all the time continuing to push higher and higher. Leah suddenly reached down, grabbed Annie's short hair and pulled her up until their mouths collided.

Little by little, the room stopped spinning. Annie opened her eyes and stared up at the shadows on the ceiling, waiting for her pulse to return to normal. She felt as if she was recovering from a race. She could feel Leah lying flat on her back in the bed beside her, her toes only touching half-way down Annie's long legs.

Annie tilted her head on its side to look at her. 'That was—'

Leah laid her finger on Annie's mouth. 'Don't say anything,' she said.

'I never thought—'

'Nor me,' whispered Leah.

★ ★ ★

In the morning, both women felt a little awkward. Neither of them were sure how they should behave. Pretend nothing had happened? Pick out curtains? It was uncharted territory for Annie. She'd never been unfaithful in a relationship before.

'Should we talk about this?'

Leah stopped putting on her shoes. She looked very pale and tired. 'Probably,' she said. 'Do you want to?'

'I don't know. Maybe . . .'

Leah broke the tension by laughing. 'You should see your face. You look so, well, stunned.'

Annie giggled. 'There seems to be a bit of role reversal going on here. You're the one who's supposed to be serious. I'm the relaxed, take-it-as-it-comes character.'

'It's not such a big deal,' replied Leah. 'I'm glad it happened. But, if you just want to forget all about it, then that's OK.'

'Not a big deal,' exclaimed Annie. 'I don't go around jumping into bed with my friends every minute of the day. Particularly not female friends.'

'I don't see why it should make any difference. Not really. Anybody can be attracted to anybody else.'

Annie looked at her suspiciously. 'You can't really mean that.'

Leah shrugged.

'Hold on a minute. Are you telling me last night wasn't the first time for you? I mean, with a woman.'

'Of course it wasn't.'

'You've never mentioned anybody.'

'I don't like talking about my personal life.'

'But there's no one at the moment?'

She shook her head.

'Neither a man nor a woman?'

'Look, Annie. Stop panicking. We're friends and we're going to stay friends. What happened last night doesn't alter that. You're very keen on Kellen. You've told me a million times what you feel about him. Last night was just one of those things. For what it's worth, I suspect it happened partly because you were trying to get back at him.'

Annie looked appalled. 'I don't see that at all,' she said. 'Anyway, if that's the case, then what about you? Who are you trying to get back at?'

Leah sighed. 'No one. Look, it was just a thought. I'm only trying to make you feel better.'

'But what should I say to Kellen?' said Annie, thumping down on the bed.

'Whatever you want. It's pretty straightforward. Either you tell him the truth or you don't.'

'How can I tell him the truth?' she wailed.

'I don't think he'd be as bothered by it as you think,' Leah replied.

'What do you mean?'

'Same as I was saying earlier. Kellen's into sex. He's had lots of partners.'

'What, men as well as women?'

'A few.'

Annie crossed her legs under her and thought about what Leah had just said.

'It doesn't make any difference to how I feel,' she said, after a while. 'I still think it would be the wrong thing to do.'

'Then tell him the truth.'

'I can't do that.'

'Then don't tell him the truth,' said Leah impatiently. 'Just say we were talking and you fell asleep.'

'But that would be lying.'

'Right. So we're right back where we started. You can either tell the truth or lie. We'd worked that out five minutes ago. Just decide.'

Leah looked over at Annie and immediately felt guilty. She seemed genuinely distressed. 'I'm sorry,' she said. 'I didn't mean to bully you. I know you want things to work out.'

Annie wasn't listening. 'I'm really into him, Leah.'

Leah put her arm around her waist. 'I know.'

'And I don't want to lose him. But if I don't tell him, then it's always going to be there in the background. Poisoning things. I feel like I owe him the truth.'

'I honestly don't think he'd back off because of this,' said Leah. 'It'd be different if it was another man, but a woman . . . Knowing Kellen, the idea will probably turn him on.'

Annie wasn't listening. 'I'll tell him later,' she said. 'Maybe not straight away.'

'Whatever,' said Leah, finishing getting dressed. 'Just make sure I know what I'm supposed to say too. Now, come on. Let's go and get some breakfast.'

'OK,' said Annie, already feeling in a better mood. 'Have you got some trousers or something I can borrow?'

Leah laughed. 'You must be joking. I've got nothing that would fit you.'

'I'll have to go back to my room, then,' she said. 'I'll meet you down there. Unless, of course, Kellen's waiting for me and we make up . . .'

They stopped at the top of the stairs, Leah about to go down to breakfast, Annie to go back to her room.

'By the way,' Annie said. 'You never did say what happened to your face? It's a hell of a bruise you've got there.'

Immediately, everything that had been pushed out of Leah's head by the interlude with Annie, came flooding back. Paris, Cordou, the mugging, Michael. Most of all Michael.

'I had an argument with a door,' she said, avoiding Annie's eye. 'Walked into it in the dark when I got back last night. It's not so bad.'

'Well, it looks fucking awful. In fact, you look pretty awful this morning. You seem really stressed out.'

'I'm just tired,' she said. 'And I've got a couple of things to sort out.' She stood on tiptoe to give Annie a kiss on the cheek. 'Good luck with Kellen,' she said. 'I'll see you later.'

Then before Annie had the chance to say anything else, Leah turned and scarpered down the stairs.

31

'I'm glad you called,' said Syd. 'I was going to get in touch anyway.'

'Of course you were.'

'I was. Honest to God.'

Leah released herself from the bear hug. Syd took a good look at her. 'You're not looking so hot, babe. Trouble?'

'Where to begin?'

'Tell me.'

'Hang on a minute,' Leah protested. 'Why are we getting the lift? You promised me breakfast.'

'We'll grab something in a moment. There's something I have to show you first.'

Leah glanced at her. She sounded serious, not like the usual wise-cracking Syd who joked her way through everything. 'What's up?'

'You'll see,' she replied, banging the call button on the wall again.

'Thought you hated these things,' Leah said. 'You always used to take the stairs.'

'Yeah, well.'

The lift arrived and the doors opened with a swoosh to let them in.

'About time,' muttered Syd. 'So, anyway. What's happening with you?'

'It's all going wrong,' said Leah. 'And I don't know what to do about it.'

Syd had never seen Leah flustered. She looked at her pale face, the bags under her eyes and the bruise on her cheek. 'Did someone do that to you?' she said. 'Because if they—'

'No. It's nothing like that,' interrupted Leah. 'I was mugged a couple of days ago, which was horrible, but it's not as bad as it looks. As I told Annie earlier.'

'Yeah, Annie. How is she? She seemed nice when you brought her here that time.'

'She is nice. Although I made a bit of a mistake last night . . .'

'Go on,' said Syd.

'We ended up sleeping together. Neither of us meant it to happen. Well, not to start with. I was feeling bad, she was feeling bad. One thing led to another.'

'That doesn't sound so terrible,' said Syd.

'It is. First, because she's serious about Kellen. Second, because I'm feeling completely confused about everything. Third, because I think it will change things between us at exactly the point when I need her to trust me.'

Syd looked at her. 'Take a step back, babe,' she said firmly. 'Now. Did you enjoy it?'

'Yes. Yes I did.'

'Right, so you don't have to feel bad on that account.'

'I guess not.'

'And did Annie enjoy it? Was she embarrassed or angry with you this morning?'

'Not really, no. We dealt with it pretty well under the circumstances. I was deliberately casual. Her main concern was that she'd been unfaithful to Kellen, not the fact that she'd been to bed with me.'

'Right, so you don't have to feel bad on her account.'

'Not in that way, I suppose,' agreed Leah.

Syd looked at her. 'Right. So Annie's not the problem. What's really going on here?'

To her astonishment, Leah burst into tears.

*   *   *

Twenty minutes later, the two women were still sitting on the floor in the lobby outside the Primary Control Centre.

'You feeling all right now?' said Syd. 'The answer better be yes, because I've run out of tissues.'

Leah sniffed. 'I'm really sorry to burden you with all of this. I just didn't know what to do.'

'Don't apologise. I can't believe you've been carrying all this on your own for so long. But you know, you've got to talk to Michael before you do anything else.'

'I can't face it.'

'You have to, Leah. It sounds as if the Unit's been doing important work. Shit, I'm not excusing him using violence to get what he wants. But at the same time, it doesn't automatically make Michael a bad person. There might have been no alternative.'

'But that's the point,' said Leah. 'First, there's always an alternative. But second, I feel that if he's capable of it, then he's not the man I thought I knew.'

'You always knew he was capable of it,' said Syd kindly. 'You just didn't want to admit it to yourself.'

Leah nodded, knowing she was right.

'Just go and see him. Talk it out.'

She got up. 'I'm OK now. Let's get on with whatever you've got to show me.'

'Good,' said Syd.

She put her hand on the recognition panel, waited for them to be granted access, then headed straight for the central computer. Leah followed. Immediately, she looked at the line of red switchgear lights to see the exact position of each gate and sill of the Barrier.

'Why are these shut?' she asked, pointing at the position lights for the three falling radial gates on the north bank and single gate on the south. 'Everything looks calm. A bit windy, perhaps, but pretty good on the scale of things.'

'They're permanently closed now,' said Syd.

Leah looked at her in surprise. 'All four of them?'

'Yeah.'

'As of when?'

'As of that series of storms at the beginning of August.'

'Sounds a bit drastic,' said Leah. 'Who made that decision?'

Syd snorted. 'They didn't want to, believe me, but they weren't left with much choice in the end. The downstream flood defences are next to useless now. There's been a permanent increase in average wind speed – or at least that's what it's looking like – and the rise in water levels over the past six months has resulted in extensive leaking.'

'There was always a problem downriver. It's never bothered anyone that much before.'

'No,' agreed Syd. 'But it should have done.'

'What precisely is the problem?'

Syd took a seat in front of the Barrier Model console. A set of windows flashed open on screen, data collected from meteorological offices and sites from North America to the Baltic. Readings were taken and the Model was updated every twenty-four hours, although Syd had been arguing for months that readings should be increased to a minimum of every twelve hours, with sixty-minute updates from the 'wet spots'. Another battle she had not managed to win. Leah watched the dateline flash for its statutory five seconds: 09.13.2008. Then in an instant the hundreds of figures appeared, colour-coded for ease of analysis.

'This takes me back,' she said. 'Although I can't say I've missed it . . .'

Syd ignored the interruption. 'This group of figures here,' she said, pointing to the top right-hand corner, 'is the actual incidence of surge tides as against, here, the forecast for September.'

Leah was staggered. 'The numbers are all over the place. What happened here? An inexperienced forecaster?'

'That's my data, Leah. Based on your formulas. So, no. The figures aren't wrong. There was a similar discrepancy in August, though not so extreme.'

'Is this to do with the low pressure zones off Canada?'

'The trouble definitely starts with the Gulf Stream and

Labrador Current. For some months now, we've been getting information that there have been sizeable changes in tidal patterns up there. When the divergence in temperature between the two is particularly large, sea levels within the zone are now being pushed up approximately 450 mm per 1,610 kilometres diameter area.'

'My God, that's up 150 mm on the old control average.'

'Right. The other change is that these monster humps of water now move across the Atlantic at average speeds of 110 kilometres an hour. Did you hear me say "average"? There have been a couple of occasions in the last month when they've moved as fast as 120 kilometres per hour.'

'Hence the decision to shut the radial gates,' said Leah. 'And dare I ask the million dollar question of how effective the measure has been?'

'The usual crap's going on, of course,' said Syd. 'The bastards in charge are refusing to accept things are as bad as we say they are. They did agree to curtail the visitors' tour, but more to avoid embarrassment than out of concern for the public's safety. Total arseholes.'

'How many times have you had to raise the Barrier this year? January through September.'

Syd hit another button and a new window was superimposed on the figures on the screen.

Leah quickly scanned the graph. 'Twenty-three times!' she said. 'I don't believe it.'

'This is only the half of it,' said Syd. 'It wasn't even the reason I got you up here, although it's a pretty black outlook. But come look at this.'

She walked over to the corner of the room to a small video terminal Leah had never seen before.

'What's this?'

'My new toy,' said Syd proudly. 'It uploads video stills from 160 digital cameras covering the whole flood defence system.'

'Wow!'

Syd smiled. 'Yeah. It is wonderful. Each camera takes a shot every three seconds. I decide what I want to keep, want I want to throw out, and the whole process starts all over again. Brilliant. Anyway, take a look at this.' Syd flicked a switch and the screen came to life. Leah recognised one of the narrow streets that lead up from Unity Pier.

'The Marsh Projects,' said Leah.

Syd nodded. 'Now, take a look at this.'

Leah looked at the screen and concentrated as the images changed. It was like watching the shutter open and close on an old-fashioned camera. She could see the streets, houses, puddles on the ground, more houses. The same shot over and over again. After five minutes, she was starting to get bored.

'What am I supposed to be noticing here? Help me out.'

'I'll fast forward a bit. OK. This is three hours later.'

Leah looked at the next sequence of shots. The same houses, the same street, the only difference was that the water was fractionally higher.

'Hang on a minute,' she said. 'I thought you said this was three hours later. These stills can't have been taken from the same camera in the space of a few hours. Even without enlarging the frame, I can see the water is covering the bottom step now. It was slightly under it when the film started.'

'Three hours, eleven minutes, eight seconds between the first shots and this lot.'

Leah stared at her. 'You're telling me that water has risen 3 mm in the space of thirty-five minutes. And it's not even raining. That's ridiculous.'

'Not if there's a slow leak.'

Leah walked over to the huge windows and looked out over the Barrier, gleaming silver and white in the sun. The water was peaceful and flocks of crakes and kites were following the small tugs making the journey from the southside to the northside. Everything like a picture postcard. All under control.

She jerked her head back towards the screen. 'When was this filmed?'

Syd got up and came to join her. 'Today.'

'This is live?' exclaimed Leah.

Syd shook her head. 'Today, as in about six o'clock this

morning. Not today, as in right now. Christ, babe, how live do you want it . . .'

'Show me what it looks like now.'

Syd tapped on the keyboard and a new frame appeared. The two women looked at it in silence.

'What do you want me to do?' said Leah, after a moment's hesitation.

Syd gave her a quick hug. 'I knew you'd come through,' she said. 'I feel bad asking you to do this, in the light of what you were telling me earlier, but I can't think of anyone else who might have the power to do anything. I need you to tell your boss – Michael – precisely how bad things are down here and get him to put a bomb up the arse of this lot here. Make them see sense. I can't patch things up for ever.'

Leah smiled. 'No wonder you're so keen for me to patch it up with him . . .'

'Do you mind?'

She shook her head. 'This is work, not personal. I'll talk to him about this straight away. It's not strictly anything to do with the Ministry, but he can probably get through to the right people. How long do you think you've got before something gives?'

'Months, if we're lucky. Weeks if we're not.'

'It just doesn't bear thinking about.'

'No,' said Syd. 'I'm telling you, Leah, that if we don't secure the flood defence protection systems, like yesterday, all it's going to take is one more major storm to burst this lot wide open. Half of London will disappear under water and there won't be a thing anybody can do to stop it.'

32

When Annie looked back later, years after it was all over, she could see that night marked the beginning of the end. Everything changed after the argument with Kellen and the hours spent with Leah. Everything began to unravel, like a ball of wool rolling away down the stairs. Slowly at first, then gathering momentum until it hit the bottom.

At the time, though, it just felt like another difficult morning. After leaving Leah, Annie went straight to her room, feeling more nervous the closer she got. For a couple of minutes, she just stood outside the closed door, in Kellen's blue shirt and her bare legs, trying to pluck up the courage to go in.

But he wasn't there. Crumpled sheets, the usual mixture of clothes about the place and the cold smell of a room left empty several hours ago. She tried the study door, absent-mindedly picking up her yellow jumper from the floor as she walked past. It was locked. Annie sat down heavily on the bed, her adrenaline draining away. Suddenly, she was exhausted by the mental effort. Hoping that Leah wouldn't mind her not turning up for breakfast, she did what she always did in moments of crisis. Curled up and went to sleep.

When Kellen came back ten minutes later, he found her dead to the world. He stood next to the bed and looked at her. Her face was peaceful and her spiky hair was sticking out at odd angles, as it always did in the morning. The soles of her feet were black from creeping around with no shoes or socks on.

He went straight into the study without touching her.

It was nearly midday when Annie woke up again and she could tell Kellen had been back. The room felt different, as if the air had been stirred up while she was sleeping. It wasn't a good sign that he had left her sleeping. Was he still angry, perhaps? Or maybe he felt they should talk first, sort the problem out rather than papering over the cracks with sex. It would be the emotionally responsible thing to do. Then again, neither of them was particularly good on that front.

Annie stretched. Her neck and shoulders were stiff from a night spent in different beds at uncomfortable angles. And she needed a shower. Her whole body was sticky and felt slept in, and she could do with some clean clothes. Grabbing a towel, she disappeared into the bathroom.

Sitting at his computer next door, Kellen heard the water running. He was curious to know where she'd spent the night after she'd stormed out. He assumed she'd been with Leah, who he knew was back, although it was possible she'd sought refuge with Mary instead. Either way, he was curious to hear what she came up with. He logged off, locked up and went back through to the bedroom.

Annie was drying her hair with a towel with her head upside down, so she didn't notice Kellen to start with.

'Hey,' he said.

She jumped. 'Kellen. You gave me a shock.'

'Is it so surprising that I should be in my own room?'

A bad start. Annie felt bad already, not helped by the fact that she hadn't got anything on.

'I didn't mean it like that,' she said. 'Don't be so touchy.'

'So, where did you get to last night?'

'I—'

'I lay awake for hours waiting – hoping – for you to come back.'

'Look, just let me get some clothes. I feel at a disadvantage.'

'It doesn't usually bother you.'

Annie didn't answer, knowing it was true. She'd been running things through in her head, working out what she'd say and how she'd say it. But now the time had come, she couldn't think of a thing to say. She tugged a plain white vest out of the drawer, pulled on her pants and combats, gave her hair a vigorous brush with her fingers. As she peered at herself in the mirror, she thought how wasted she looked. Her eyes were narrow, her stud seemed too heavy for her nose and the Ogham letter – now so much a part of her that she barely registered it – appeared to be blacker and more prominent than usual.

She took a deep breath, then turned around to face Kellen. 'Right,' she said. 'That's the best I can do.'

He said nothing. Just sat and waited. Annie knew he wasn't going to help her out and that she was going to have to make all the running. She chose the chair opposite him and perched on the edge of it.

'I'm sorry I didn't come back after we'd had that row. I was just really upset.'

'So was I.'

'I know,' she said. 'I just didn't want to end up saying something I'd regret later.'

'Like what?'

'Like, well, anything. Nothing in particular. Sometimes I say things I don't mean. We all do.'

He looked cynical.

'Oh, come on. Everybody does it. You're not making this any easier.'

'So it's my fault now.'

'It's not anyone's fault.'

'All I want to know is where you were last night and why you didn't come back. That's not too much to ask, is it? I was worried about you, for fuck's sake.'

'No, of course it isn't.'

'Well?'

Annie felt a knot in her chest. She didn't want to tell him, but knew she had to. The toss-up was between a slow build-up and getting it over and done with in one go. Like getting into a swimming pool inch by cold inch versus the short, sharp shock of jumping feet first into the water. She went for the jump.

'I spent the night with Leah.'

'Thank you,' he said. 'That wasn't so difficult, was it?'

'No, you don't understand. We slept together.'

For what seemed like hours, he simply stared at her. Annie looked in his eyes, trying to work out what he was thinking, but could read nothing.

'You had sex with Leah? Is that what you're telling me?'

Annie nodded.

He stood up, sending his chair flying behind him. 'Christ!'

'I'm sorry,' she said. 'I didn't mean it to happen. It was just one of those things.'

'Christ.'

She reached out for him, but he jerked away.

'I'm sorry,' she said again. 'I don't want us—'

'I can't believe you'd do this to me,' he shouted at her.

'I made a mistake.'

'I'll kill her.'

'It wasn't Leah's fault,' she said immediately, 'any more than it was mine. It just happened. I wish it hadn't, but it has.'

'So whose fault is it then?' he demanded. 'Mine? Is it my fault? Am I not giving you what you want? Is that it?'

Annie couldn't cope with the way the row was escalating.

'Don't do this,' she said. 'You know what I feel for you.'

'Yeah, right, Annie. You've got a nice way of showing it . . .'

'For fuck's sake. Why won't you listen?' She was shouting now too, no longer sure whether she was angry or worried that they'd gone too far. 'I love you,' she yelled.

The second she'd said it, Annie was mortified. She'd never let herself say those words before. Not to Kellen, not to anyone. And now? Instead of it meaning something, she'd slung them out like a term of abuse.

'What did you say?'

'You—' She broke off as Kellen pulled her roughly towards

him, crushed his mouth down on hers. Annie was suddenly boiling hot, felt a kick of desire as they half fell, half stumbled backwards on to the bed.

It was only afterwards, when he was lying in her arms, that Annie wondered if it all hadn't been a bit textbook. The way he'd reacted first with relief, then hurt, then with recrimination, then anger, then passion. An A to Z of appropriate emotions. Like a man playing a part.

Leah and Michael sat opposite each other in silence in the flat in Weston Street. Everybody else from the Unit had left discreetly, claiming prior engagements.

'I wasn't sure if I should expect you this morning,' he said. His voice was steady and he sounded annoyed.

'Neither was I.'

He looked at her, surprised by her sharpness. 'Do you want to tell me what this is about, Leah? One minute we're celebrating our success in getting Cordou, the next you've withdrawn into total silence. You can't have spoken more than ten words to me on the flight back.'

'There was nothing to say.'

'You give the impression that there's one hell of a lot to say.'

Leah didn't answer. Syd had half persuaded her earlier she was overreacting, and completely persuaded her it would sound as if she was just a woman who couldn't stomach the hard male realities. Leah was sure of her ground. She knew the difference between taking difficult decisions and taking immoral ones, and it was nothing to do with being tough. But she didn't know precisely what had gone on with Cordou and she hadn't asked, for fear of how Michael might answer.

'Leah?'

'What?'

Her refusal to tell him anything was making him angry now.

'Look, either tell me what's on your mind,' he said. 'Or leave. I've a lot to do.'

Leah was bewildered as to how they could be so far apart, so immediately. But, then, lacking emotional experience, she had no more idea of how to bridge the gap between them than Michael did. She bottled out, telling herself it was for the sake of restoring the *status quo*. And, as so many times before, she buried her private feelings and automatically took refuge in work.

Avoiding his eyes, Leah began to tell him what Syd had said. Michael was relieved to have something to deflect his attention away from Leah herself, and leaped into action. He made calls and contacted people. He had sufficient influence to make trouble for the management responsible for the Barrier, even though it was none of his business. In fact, he probably had sufficient power to force them to do some of the things Syd was demanding. But his trump card was the Lightermen. If indeed the Marsh Projects were under threat of flooding, then the Ministry – and therefore Michael – had a legitimate interest. The safety of the Lightermen was paramount and it was his responsibility to ensure they were not at risk.

Now they were over the most embarrassing point, they both continued as if there had been no falling out. Michael updated her on the progress of the Office Français des Biotechnologies, then outlined the Unit's role in tightening the net round the Network. Leah had listened carefully and managed to avoid thinking of Paris or Cordou.

By the time Leah left Weston Street a couple of hours later, she had erased all personal thoughts from her mind. Or, at least, she told herself she had. It was easier. Better not to get emotionally involved, there was no time. She had too much work to do.

33

Friday 10 October

Autumn had arrived, transforming London with colour and smell and light. Late–flowering cherry bushes, their leaves crimson, lined the banks of the Thames. The water speckled blue and white in the rays of the October sun and the greens and browns of the end of the summer were disappearing from the trees, replaced by gold, russet and yellow.

The days were clear and warm, no longer oppressively hot and humid. The insects began to die. Every now and again, there were tremendous electric storms, which lit up the skyline. It looked as if there was a long line of bonfires burning from the mouth of the river all the way to its source in the countryside well beyond London. Sometimes, the winds reached hurricane force, making it too dangerous to be outside. Taxis were overturned, bits of rubbish and boxes were hurled down streets like a tenpin bowling ball at skittles, shattering everything in its path. A couple of people were killed. There was never rain and the episodes never lasted more than about half an hour, but it was frightening. As if nature was biting back.

As October marched on, the threat of winter in the air at the end and beginning of each day became more obvious. Now, there was a heavy frost each morning that left the pavements glistening like ice, and beads of condensation balanced like diamonds on the black metal railings. It would not be long before the cold came. Annie was back in the regular habit of slipping out into the mist while everyone was still asleep, just as she had when she was a child. Listening to the incessant chattering of migrating birds, wheeling and shrieking over the river at dawn. It was the time when she did most of her thinking. About her and Kellen. About Leah and Mary. About what she was doing here at all. Like any significant date – an exam, a court appearance, a birthday – the thirty-first of October was burned into her mind. Annie knew that Mary intended to try to return during the fourth Fire Festival when she thought the door between 1997 and 2008 would be open. Maybe it would. The rhythm of her heart and her feet on the street as she walked around and around helped her to think. She always came back to the same single question. Why?

Every morning, Annie returned to the Pen with the end of her nose bright red and the tips of her ears tingling. Sometimes, she would go to the kitchen and start laying out breakfast for Jonas and Malik, who needed to be up and away by seven. Other days, if Kellen had spent the night with her, she would creep back upstairs and wake him with her cold hands.

Annie had tried to recapture the magic of her first weeks. Get it back, then hold on to it this time. But nothing was the same. It wasn't just Kellen and Leah who had changed, but the atmosphere inside the Pen. It felt as if everyone was waiting for something to happen, although they didn't know what or when. Everyone was going about their business much the same, but with a watchfulness in their eye. And although people still came looking for free drink and food, even the Saturday service was less popular than before. Everyone could smell the tension around them.

Kellen was distant and preoccupied a lot of the time. He was still physically obsessed with her, touching her body, stroking it so possessively that sometimes it was too much and Annie felt invaded rather than worshipped. But, at the same time, she got the feeling that he consciously had to remind himself to make her laugh or tell her how much he cared. That it didn't come naturally to him any more. Their relationship was becoming more private, sure. More exclusive of others. But it was less intimate. She would catch him looking at her so intensely, but when she asked what he was thinking, he always shrugged and said it was nothing.

Most evenings, he'd sit her down and bombard her with questions late into the night. His mind worked so fast and made associations so eccentric, that half the time Annie didn't understand what he was asking. Whereas before he had deliberately not pushed her into talking about the travelling and her past, now there was an urgency to his voice. He asked the same things over and over. Why did she think she was here? Who — or what — had made it happen? What did the sign on her head signify? Did she think she could harness the power to travel backwards and forwards or was it a one-way trip? What about him? Would it be safe or possible for him? On nights like these, unwelcome thoughts of going back sneaked into her mind. She pushed them away.

Annie felt increasingly compromised by the bargain she'd struck with Mary not to tell Kellen what they discussed amongst themselves. But she kept her word and attempted to tell him only those things she had worked out for herself. It wasn't much and she could sense his frustration. She also knew he could tell that she wasn't being straight with him. He simply didn't believe she was as incurious as she was making out.

He kept bullying her. When she got tired, she just wanted to put her hands over her ears and tell him to leave her alone. On two occasions, when he'd succeeded in bringing her close to tears, he'd apologised. Smoothing her hair and holding her tight against him, so she could hear his heart beating, he'd whispered an explanation. He felt that the more he knew, the greater the chance they had of being able to stay together. And he couldn't stand the thought of losing her, he said. It was devotion to her — to them — that made him so desperate to know the truth. For the next few days he would try his best to back off. But gradually, he'd slip back into the same old ways.

These days, she only really felt at ease in the stillness after they'd made love, when they were lying side by side, their fingers, arms and legs entwined, talking like they had in the old days. Then, Annie experienced a sense of belonging that eluded her the rest of the time. At times like these, the thought of going back was too painful to contemplate.

Outside the privacy of their room, Kellen's relationship with Leah was increasingly hard for Annie to handle. After the first awkward encounter, he appeared perfectly relaxed and comfortable around Leah. He was relying more on Lonnie to fill the lieutenant role that had been hers, but otherwise Kellen went out of his way to be nice to her. He didn't refer to the night the women had spent together or make pointed comments. In fact, whenever Leah did make a rare appearance, he arranged things so he was sitting next to her. He even bought her some lilies and left them outside her bedroom door to cheer her up.

None of it made any difference to Leah. She denied there'd been any sort of falling out, but she was jumpy and tense around him. Restricted her conversation to monosyllables. Annie found it upsetting and increasingly tried to avoid being in the same room as them both. See no evil, hear no evil. It didn't help. She couldn't shake the feeling that they were all marking time. That they were all stumbling closer to the edge.

Another week passed.

34

Friday 17 October

'It's open,' Annie yelled. 'You can come in.'

She was sorting out some clothes, so she didn't look up straight away.

'Hello, Annie,' said Mary.

Annie leaped to her feet.

'What a surprise, I mean . . . I'm sorry, that sounded really rude.'

Mary smiled. 'It's all right.'

'It's just that you've never come down to me before. I've always come up.'

Annie was amazed at how pleased she was. They had been spending less time together recently, partly because her mind was so occupied by her disintegrating relationships with Leah and Kellen, and because she knew Mary wouldn't be sympathetic. While Annie felt her priority was dealing with the here and now, she was well aware that Mary would not approve of the level of her emotional engagement in the first place. And the last thing Annie wanted was to have to listen to Mary saying she'd told her so.

'It's really great to see you,' she said. 'Do you want to sit down?'

Mary shook her head and Annie noticed she was wearing outdoor clothes. Brown jacket, a scarf and trousers.

'Are you going somewhere?'

'Not me,' she replied. 'Us. I want to go to Crucifix Lane and I would like you to come with me.'

It was overcast and cold, so they walked fast, their heads down, with the wind snapping at their heels. They arrived in Crucifix Lane just after ten o'clock and, to start with, just stood there and looked around.

'What are you thinking?' asked Annie after a while.

'That we need a cloth or something to cover that,' said Mary, pointing up at the MSU camera above them.

'Good point,' she said and unzipped her jacket. 'We can use this.'

'We need something to get it up there.'

'Why are you whispering? Do you think it can pick up what we're saying?'

'I don't know,' Mary replied. 'But I'd rather not risk it.'

'Who's on the end of the camera, do you think?'

'I imagine it's just the usual surveillance camera for this district,' she answered. 'It doesn't look particularly special. In fact, now I come to think of it, it definitely is that. Your boy used to work for a monitoring company, didn't he? That's why he knew about Crucifix Lane in the first place. He was watching the camera when the unfortunate first traveller came through.'

'Of course,' said Annie.

'Has he ever offered to show you the film of it?' asked Mary.

Annie shook her head. 'And I've never asked. I thought it would be too upsetting.'

Mary frowned. 'It does make me wonder if he has film of us too.'

'No, he can't. He quit his job at the Monitoring and Surveillance Unit in February to concentrate on the Network full time. In any case, if he had film of us he would have told me about it.'

Mary did not share Annie's faith in Kellen's ability to be

open with her, but she stayed silent. Annie cast her eyes around for something to help her get the jacket up over the camera, and spotted an old broom handle lying on the pavement opposite. It looked like a bit of driftwood.

'This should do it.'

Balancing the jacket on the end, she stretched up as high as she could towards the roof of the tunnel and, after a few goes, finally managed to hang it across the lens.

'Well done,' said Mary. 'Now, the first thing is to work out if we came through in exactly the same place.'

'OK,' said Annie, walking to the junction with a tiny side street and stopping. 'Bearing in mind I was a bit out of it, it was roughly here – I could see the row of shops from where I was sitting. Just by White's Grounds.'

She squatted down and pointed at the wall. 'And I'm pretty sure this is where I saw the row of letters before I was unconscious.'

She got to her feet. 'Your turn now.'

Mary moved Annie out of the way.

'Here,' she said. 'Just a tiny bit further along.'

'But to all intents and purposes, the same place,' said Annie.

Mary had produced a bit of chalk from her pocket and made a couple of marks on the pavement.

'Isn't that a bit dangerous? What if someone notices it?'

'I'll rub it out before we leave,' Mary replied. 'It's just to make things easier now.'

'Can I just ask you something?' said Annie.

'Ask away.'

'Why are we doing this now? I mean, why have we waited until today?'

'I didn't think there was any point before. It wasn't going to make any difference to my thought process.'

'Surely this isn't the first time you've been back since May?'

'It is, actually. The physical location is the one thing we are sure about, after all. I thought it unlikely we'd learn any more from it.'

Annie was still looking surprised. 'Well, I don't know how

you've managed to keep away. This place is like a magnet to me. I've been here hundreds of times.'

'Why do you think that is?'

'Just the obvious,' replied Annie. 'A way of reminding myself of where it all started.'

Mary nodded.

'But anyway, you still haven't told me why you wanted to come today.'

'There's nothing special about today,' she said, 'rather than yesterday or tomorrow. But the thirty-first of October. It's supposed to be the month where divine and royal powers are at their most potent, according to the Ogham calendar. It therefore seemed an appropriate time to come.'

Annie rolled her eyes. She still felt a little self-conscious when Mary started talking about the Ogham. It wasn't that she didn't take it seriously, as such. It was more that, despite everything, making decisions on the basis of which month it was seemed as if they were absolving themselves of independent thought. After all, she'd never even been able to stomach reading her horoscope. Still, she tried.

'So, you're still thinking of the next Fire Festival?'

'Yes,' said Mary. 'Although, it would have been more logical for the sequence to have started with the Celtic new year in November – and the first Fire Festival of *Samain* – rather than in February.'

'Logic,' said Annie. 'If you're hoping for logic, then I think we're in deep trouble already . . .'

Mary smiled. 'Yes, well perhaps that wasn't the best choice of word in the circumstances.'

'Is it not possible that there was an earlier traveller, though? One nobody knows about who came through in November 1996.'

'Completely possible,' said Mary. 'And if that is the case, it is therefore also possible that the door will not be open. Not if the cycle has already run its course.'

'But if the key year is 2008 or 1997, as opposed to 2007 and 1996, then that would make a difference.'

'Precisely. So, all we can do is work on the assumption that we will have a chance of returning to our own time during *Samain*. If the door is open in both directions, if we will have access to it simply by being in Crucifix Lane and if we can make use of the power without being destroyed by it.'

Annie shivered. 'Hoping that what kept us safe and brought us through before will see us back again . . .'

'It might be dangerous,' said Mary. 'I just don't know.'

'And we won't know until we take the risk.'

'Precisely. Although, as we've discussed before, it might be nothing to do with either us or him, but a simple matter of timing. That the traveller who died had the misfortune to be pulled through too soon. Remember, we both came through on the last day. Me at the end of *Beltane*, you at the end of *Lugnassadh*.'

Annie stopped talking and starting thinking. In a way, this was all of academic interest. Nothing more. Even though things with Kellen were not as good as they had been – well, were quite rocky, if she was honest – Annie still felt there was something worth fighting for. She wasn't going to walk away from him at the first sign of trouble.

'Have you noticed this before in your visits?' said Mary, pointing at a black mark on the pavement.

Annie looked. 'That scorch mark? Yeah, I have seen it. I didn't see how it could be relevant, though. I just assumed someone had lit a fire here at some time.'

'Perhaps this is where the first traveller came through?' suggested Mary.

Annie looked dubious. 'February was a long time ago. It doesn't seem likely it would still be here eight months later, not given all the flooding and stuff like that. Never mind the usual wear and tear on the pavement.'

'Actually, that's the point,' said Mary. 'First, virtually no traffic comes through here. The occasional taxi, virtually no pedestrians. It looks too threatening. And it's hardly an ideal spot for a fire because of the wind.'

'True.'

'In any case, if it is something to do with him, then it couldn't be washed away by the rain in the usual way.'

'How do you mean?'

'Well, it's not likely to be subject to the usual laws of science. Presumably, like the letters we both saw carved on to the wall, it exists in a different plane.'

Annie suddenly felt excited.

'And the music,' she said. 'I heard the music from the Pen *before* I came through, as well as after. That shouldn't have been possible either. And the sheet of music you saw, but then couldn't get hold of when you tried to pick it up. Maybe there's something like a no man's land between 1997 and 2008 where basic physical truths become hazy. Where vision and sound are no longer fixed in one time or another.'

Mary smiled. 'You have been thinking. Because you hadn't been coming up to see me as much recently, I'd assumed you'd pushed all of this to the back of your mind.'

'So did I, to tell you the truth,' admitted Annie. 'Kellen's been going on at me so much, that I've tried to forget all about it. Because I promised you I wouldn't tell him anything, it's been really difficult. But I have been toying with ideas in my head, although I hadn't realised I'd got anywhere. My subconscious must be in better shape than I thought . . .'

Mary took Annie's hand and gave it a squeeze. 'Well done.'

Annie was astonished to find herself blushing. 'Thanks,' she said.

'You should be pleased with yourself,' continued Mary. 'So, let's pause for thought for a moment. We know where the travelling happens and we think we know when it happens. We've also discovered a handful of similarities between ourselves that might or might not be relevant. But what we have not yet managed to explain is the link, if any, between 1997 and 2008.'

Annie looked cocky. 'Far be it from me to show off,' she said, 'but I do have a theory about this. Well, not so much a theory, as an observation.'

'Yes?'

'There is a synchronicity between 1997 and 2008. That is, the day and the date is the same. The second of August 1997 fell on a Saturday. The second of August 2008 was also a Saturday. You told me you came through on Friday the second of May 1997. You arrived on Friday the second of May. Do you see what I'm getting at?'

'Of course,' said Mary. 'The days and dates have run a full cycle.'

'And, perhaps just as important,' continued Annie, 'is the fact that 2008 is the first year after 1997 of which this is true.' She suddenly shivered. As if someone was walking over her grave. She looked down and could see the goosebumps on her bare arms.

'You've gone very pale,' said Mary. 'Are you all right?'

Annie nodded. 'I just felt a chill up my spine,' she said. 'You know, I wish I had your faith in there being a reason for all of this. I wish I felt the same.'

Mary smiled. 'I do believe we have been brought here for a purpose, either to witness something or to prevent something happening. It's possible we won't even recognise the moment – not understand what is required of us until after it is over. I just don't know.'

'But if that's what you think, then I don't understand why you've stayed locked away in your room all this time. Experiencing nothing, going nowhere. Not if you thought you were supposed to see something important. It doesn't make sense.'

Mary looked at her. 'I don't think it is ours to discover,' she said, after a while. 'If I'm right – and we are to witness something – I think it will be something so absolute, so unavoidable, that it won't matter where we are. It won't be some small local incident we might stumble upon by chance. If, at any stage in the past few months, I'd felt I should be out playing the detective, then I would have done so.'

Annie frowned.

'We cannot always understand the significance of events until after they are over,' continued Mary. 'What seems important at the time, might turn out to mean nothing. And things that appear insignificant, irrelevant even, might turn out to be a turning point.'

Annie looked at her. 'That reminds me of something Leah said. That history was now.'

Mary smiled. 'She was right. Whatever is going on is beyond our immediate understanding. When the time comes – *if* it comes – all we can do is react and do the best we can.'

Annie was still reluctant to let the subject drop. 'But what I still don't understand is how this squares with what you were telling me before about not getting involved. All that stuff about the drowning boy and not perverting the course of history.'

'It's entirely different altering something in the future, where you do not belong, to working within your own time to change things. If you like, one is interference, the other is influence. We should not change the pattern of history in the wrong place. Everything must follow in order.'

'You're making it sound so serious. As if the world's about to end.'

Mary ignored the comment, just stared at her. Annie thought the letter on her forehead looked very dark. Threatening, almost.

'Are you going to come with me?'

Annie shook her head. 'I don't know,' she said quietly. 'I'm sorry.'

Mary nodded. 'You look cold. I think we should go back now.'

'OK. I'll just clean this and get my coat.'

They walked out of Crucifix Lane into the strong wind that was blasting down St Thomas Street into their faces. Neither of them said a word. High in the tunnel, concealed behind the MSU camera, three tiny pinpoints of light flashed red. Recording their departure.

At the Pen, Kellen flicked a switch and the cameras went off-line.

'Well, well . . .' he said to the blank screen.

He had seen Annie leave with Mary a couple of hours earlier and had guessed where they were going. For the past hour and a half he had been watching Crucifix Lane. He'd seen them arrive, cover up the MSU camera, and poke about on the ground at the end of the tunnel near White's Grounds. No sound, just pictures. But very interesting all the same.

Kellen had gone out of his way to encourage the friendship at first, assuming that information would filter back to him from Mary via Annie. Annie had led him to believe that she didn't visit Mary very much, saying it was too boring and claiming the huge age gap meant they had nothing in common except for the obvious shared experience. But watching their body language, Kellen realised they were still much closer than she had led him to believe.

He pulled a joint from behind his ear and lit it. He was amazed at how completely Annie had taken him in. All this time she'd been claiming to know virtually nothing about how the travelling worked and what the letters might mean. And he'd believed her, assuming that Mary had been as tight-lipped with Annie as she'd been with him.

Not that it mattered now. All he'd wanted to know was that Mary Royle was going to attempt a return journey. The fact she'd left her room and gone to Crucifix Lane in the first place was proof enough of that. And now he knew Annie was in on the plans too. Annie had been telling him she didn't want to go back and she wanted to stay with him. But perhaps she was lying about that too. He was almost impressed by how well she'd deceived him. Ironically, it would make it all much easier for him.

His plan was straightforward. He had to persuade Annie to go back to 1997, collect the things he wanted her to bring to him – the documents, medicines, plant specimens – then come back to 2008. Once she was out of his hands, he'd have no way of knowing if she would keep her word. He wouldn't even know if she had made it back at all.

He hoped it wouldn't go wrong, like it had the first time,

and not just because of what he stood to gain. But, at the end of the day, Kellen knew if he didn't take the risk, then he wouldn't get what he wanted. And if it did work, then he would have the power to do almost anything he desired. An unfair advantage, some might say.

Kellen looked at the time. Just gone twelve. It would be twenty minutes at least before Annie arrived back, but he wanted to make sure he was waiting for her. After all, he was looking forward to seeing how she accounted for her morning.

35

Friday 24 October

'Nothing's going to happen to Annie,' Michael said. 'You said it yourself. Kellen's got nothing to gain. If necessary, we'll go in and get her.'

'And Mary Royle?'

'Mary too,' he confirmed. 'I'm not intending to launch a raid unless I absolutely have to. I want every single last piece of information in place before I do anything.'

Leah frowned. 'Surely we have enough evidence already?'

'A great deal, yes,' he agreed. 'But, if we go in now, it might put Mary and Annie in danger, not to mention many others who you believe have nothing to do with the illegal side of things. It would be safer to try to flush Harris and Lonnie Bell out into the open.'

Leah was puzzled by his sudden reluctance to act. 'Is there something you're not telling me, Michael?'

'Like what?'

'Well, your patience seems out of character. I can't come up with any good reason to explain why you won't go in now.'

Michael hesitated. 'All right,' he said finally. 'I have to admit I want to know what Harris is up to with Annie Jones. If we hold off just a few more days, then I think something important might come out of it.'

Leah felt a rush of irritation. It was a common feeling now. Their conversations seemed to have fallen into a pattern. They started off well, quickly became annoyed with each other, then ended up at one another's throats. Neither of them liked it, but it somehow seemed beyond their control.

'The point of the Unit's operation was to obtain the Lightermen blood for analysis and discover who was behind the biopirating. That's what we did. In fact, we'd achieved all of that nearly six weeks ago now. Yet here you are, still sitting on your hands, refusing to finish the job off. What Kellen might or might not be intending to do with Annie is entirely beside the point, Michael, and you know it.'

'Don't you care what happens to her?'

'How dare you,' she said. 'You know perfectly well how much I care about Annie. That's one of the reasons I want you to do something. In any case, if we don't act soon, there's a very real risk of Kellen clearing out and then there'll be nothing left for us to find by the time you do get in there. There'll be nothing incriminating in the laboratory, just perfectly harmless and legal drugs. He'll move his stock elsewhere and junk any significant data.'

'We still have Cordou.'

'We don't,' snapped Leah. 'We have Cordou admitting to buying samples on the black market. We have proof of money leaving his bank and going into an account in Lonnie's name – a *false* name, remember – but we haven't actually got our hands on it. We have got two witnesses who can identify Lonnie with Cordou. The rest is all circumstantial. No evidence to prove that Cordou and Kellen have had contact. The confession you got won't stand up in a British court.'

'Christ, I might have known we'd get back to that.'

'Excuse me?' said Leah coldly.

'Paris. Cordou. His confession.'

'Look, Michael, I've tried to explain to you what I felt about that. You simply ridiculed me. I think we've established, beyond reasonable doubt, that I think less of you for allowing Cordou to be physically intimidated. And you think less of me because I objected to it and made the mistake of telling you so.'

'It's just so naïve.'

'And I find both your derision and your attitude repellent.'

'Yes, you've made that clear.'

'You know,' she continued bitterly. 'What gets me the most is how women are supposed to accept violence as a fact of life. As if there's no morality or choice involved.'

'It is inevitable in this business,' he yelled. 'Grow up, Leah. People don't tell you what you want to know just because you say please . . .'

'I know that. But what did you really achieve with Cordou? I mean, *really* achieve? Sure you forced him to admit to meeting with Lonnie Bell and buying samples. You forced him to admit he had heard of Kellen Harris and the Network. But, when it came down to it, Kellen had covered his tracks too well. Just face it, he ran rings around you, Michael. He was way out in front.'

He slapped her. He didn't know how it happened, but he lashed out. He looked down at his hand and saw it was smarting from the force of the blow.

He was horrified. 'Christ, Leah. I'm sorry.'

Leah put her hand to her face in disbelief. 'You hit me,' she said.

'Leah . . . I don't know what came over me.'

'You hit me,' she repeated.

Michael tried to touch her.

'Don't. Just get me something cold to put on my face.'

He rushed into the bathroom and came back with a wet towel. Leah took it from him in silence. Michael could see the red imprint of his hand on her cheek.

'You owe me an explanation,' she said at last.

Michael misunderstood. 'I'm so sorry. What can I say? I don't know what happened.'

'I don't mean this,' she said. 'I want you to tell me what it is with you and Kellen.'

He looked over her head, unable to meet her gaze.

'I don't know what you mean,' he said, after a while.

'Bullshit,' she said. 'This is your one – and last – chance to tell me why everything you do comes back to Harris. You're obsessed with the man, Michael.'

'I . . .'

'You seem to be on self-destruct at the moment and I'm not prepared to stand by and watch it happen, without at least knowing what the hell it's all about.'

Still he didn't speak.

'I'm warning you, Michael. If you don't tell me what's going on right now, then I'm walking out of here and I will not be back.'

They had been this close to the brink before. But in the past, he'd always ducked away at the last moment and she had let him. Neither of them had ever been quite sure whether it was down to their respect for one another or their lack of it. Michael knew she was serious.

Leah held her breath. She heard the sigh, saw the struggle on his face, saw the resignation.

'We'd better go and sit down,' he said, pulling a bottle of whisky and two glasses from the overhead cupboard.

Michael told her a story of two damaged children in an unhappy family. An absent and wealthy father, an alcoholic and lonely mother, the brothers four years apart. Both 'accidents'. So-called failures of contraception, or so they were told.

The older son was serious, conscientious, awkward with adults. He was competitive and angry and single-minded, with a pronounced sense of right and wrong. He had a formidable intellect and capacity for work, which went largely ignored and unpraised.

The younger son was beautiful and charming. From the earliest age he could manipulate the adults around him into giving him what he wanted. He wasn't academically skilled, but had a native intelligence that got him through. He too was competitive, but jealous and indulged as well and with no interest in right and wrong. He took for granted all the things that fell into his lap.

Michael told Leah of a rare family outing, no doubt intended as an apology or bribe. The shove in the small of his back, the surprise as his feet were stolen away from under him. The rush of fear as he fell towards the river and how shockingly cold the water had been. He described the thudding in his head and the air hissing out of his lungs, the hands reaching down and the panic in the adult faces as they struggled to save him. He remembered recognising no one. They were all strangers to him. Then, at last, the rough concrete wall scraping against his legs as he was hauled out and onto the bank. The coughing, the smell of vomit and earth against his face. The humiliation.

He told Leah how his parents had fussed over him until the helpful passers-by had gone, then how his father had criticised him for being so clumsy and his mother smacked him for accusing his brother. Couldn't he see how he'd scared everyone? So selfish. Always so selfish. It was only when Michael talked about the look of triumph on his brother's face and the memory of the injustice, that his voice began to crack.

Leah tried to block out the image of the cold twelve-year-old, ashamed and alone on the bank. She closed her eyes. Tried not to pity the man for what had been done to the boy.

The rest of the story was easier. How Misha Harris became Michael Searle, leaving England to build a life for himself in the Pacific. How he had changed his appearance, turning his eyes from brown to blue, his hair from black to brown. The loss of weight and the surgery which so altered the look of his face.

By the time Michael had finished talking, the whisky was three-quarters drunk. Leah walked over and crouched down in front of him. Took his hands in hers.

'I had no idea you even had a brother.'

Michael looked down at her pale face and smiled. 'No,' he said. 'But you understand now. I can't let Kellen go.'

She nodded. Then refusing to let herself think of the possible consequences of what she was about to do, Leah leaned up and kissed him.

36

Saturday 25 October

Over the next few hours, Michael and Leah hammered out a compromise.

He agreed he would launch the raid on the Pen on Sunday 2 November. And she promised that she would make sure she had finished everything she wanted to do there and was out by Friday 31 October. He didn't want her to go back at all, but she'd insisted. She wanted to try to make sure that Vicky, Jonas and Malik did not get caught up in the Unit's operation, although she had no idea how she was going to do that without rumours getting back to Kellen. Most important of all, she told him, was to persuade Annie to leave with her. When she was honest with herself, she didn't think Annie would be prepared to leave Kellen.

Leah spent so much time reassuring Michael that she was going to be all right, that she couldn't tell him how scared she really was. Since getting back from Paris in September, she had become convinced that Kellen knew about her. Nothing tangible she could point to, more the way that lots of little things seemed to add up to something bigger. The way he always asked her opinion at any group meeting, the way he always seemed to be keeping an eye on her or wanting to corner her for a quiet chat. He'd even left a bouquet of white and yellow lilies outside her door, explaining to everybody else that he was trying to cheer her up. He was worried about her, he said. White lilies for purity, yellow for honesty. Leah had no doubt it was intended as a warning. Still, he said and did nothing. On a couple of occasions, it crossed her mind that it might just be his way of getting back at her for sleeping with Annie. Smiling as he wielded the knife.

But she stuck it out. She was determined not to give in. Not until she'd got through to Annie. She'd tried to talk to her a couple of times, but had got nowhere. Leah realised things were not entirely perfect between her and Kellen, more from what Annie didn't say than what she did, but the time never seemed to be right. On the surface, Annie was completely loyal and committed to him and Leah simply couldn't get up the courage to try to come between them. She knew Annie would hate her for it.

The atmosphere had got worse in the last couple of days. Kellen was away, but he'd clearly set Lonnie on to her instead. On Wednesday, she'd found him sniffing around outside her room, so blatantly that it was obvious he intended to be seen. Wherever she went, he seemed to be right behind her, never saying anything, just following her with his eyes from room to room. She felt as if she were being stalked.

At ten o'clock on the Saturday night, a text message flashed up on her phone. It was from Michael telling her to get out. Kellen had discovered something and was on his way back. She had to pack up and leave immediately. He'd explain when she got to Weston Street.

Leah got her head in gear straight away. Didn't panic, didn't lose her cool. First, she scribbled a note to Annie saying she wanted to see her urgently. She ran and pushed it under the bedroom door, praying that she would come back and be the one to pick it up. Back in her room, she shovelled the contents of her chest of drawers into a bag.

Leah jumped out of her skin at the knock on the door.

'Can I come in?'

No answer. Annie tried the handle.

'Leah?' she called. 'Are you in there?'

After what seemed like minutes, Annie heard footsteps, then the sound of the key and the door opened.

'I got your note, so—' Annie broke off when she saw the state of the room. It looked like a bomb had hit it. Clothes, books, papers everywhere.

'What the fuck's going on?'

Leah locked the door again behind her, then went back to what she was doing.

Annie followed her. 'Has something happened? You look awful.'

'What time is it?'

'Nearly midnight.'

Annie was shocked by the mixture of exhaustion and adrenaline in Leah's eyes. She grabbed her arms, as if she thought she could shake an answer out of her.

'Leah,' she said. 'What's wrong? You're scaring me.'

'I can't pack with you hanging on to me like this.'

Annie let go. 'Then tell me what's going on.'

'This won't take long,' she said. 'Sit down for a moment, you're making me nervous hovering over me like this.'

'But why are you packing? Where are you going?'

'I'll be done in a few minutes.'

Annie moved the bag and flopped on to the bed with a sick feeling in the pit of her stomach as she watched Leah sort out papers. She put one pile into the bag, then dropped the remainder into the wastepaper bin and struck a match. Within seconds, the whole lot went up in flames.

'Fucking hell,' shrieked Annie. 'Are you out of your mind?'

Leah stepped back and held up her hand to protect her face from the heat, while Annie clambered on the bed to open the shutters and let the smoke out. By the time she'd done it, Leah was pouring water on the flames.

'What is all this about?' Annie yelled.

Leah reached a hand to help her down, but she ignored it.

'It's the only sure way to destroy papers,' Leah said.

'Well, I think you've succeeded in annihilating those.'

She felt light-headed from the shock of it and thumped down on the bed, her legs half buckling under her. Without saying anything, Leah sat down beside her and took her hand.

Annie suddenly felt very sad, although she didn't know why. There was a prickling sensation at the back of her throat and in her eyes. She swallowed, to stop herself from crying.

'What is going on, Leah?' she said, at last.

Leah squeezed her hand. 'I don't know how to start.'

Annie's heart had started to pound. She knew she wasn't going to like what Leah was about to say.

'No prizes for working out I'm leaving. I guess the most important thing to say at this point is . . . all I hope is that you will understand why I did the things I did.'

'What things?'

Leah ignored her. 'I'm going to miss you—'

'Why will you miss me?'

'—but you could come with me.'

'Stop, Leah. You're not making sense. Come with you where?'

Leah took a deep breath. 'It's not safe for me to be here any more.'

'Safe?' repeated Annie.

'We have to be honest with each other now. It's our last chance. I've been dreading this moment, trying to work out the best way of saying this, but it's even harder than I thought it would be.'

'What could possibly be so bad? I know you've not been happy for a few weeks now. And I'm sorry if that's my fault in any way. Kellen just seems to have monopolised my time recently, so I've not been around much. But, whatever it is you have to say, I bet we'll be laughing about it in a minute.'

Leah shook her head. 'Annie, listen to me. Meeting Kellen, moving in here, it wasn't just one of those things like I told you it was. I was working under specific instructions to get to know Kellen and find out anything I could about the Network and how it worked.'

'Instructions?' said Annie. 'Shit, you're making it sound like some sort of undercover operation . . .' She expected Leah to laugh. She didn't. Just carried on as if Annie hadn't said anything.

'Since April, I've been working for the Industrial Intelligence Unit of the Ministry of BioProspecting and Patenting. For some time, they had suspected Kellen was involved in illicit bioprospecting activities. They needed someone on the inside who could monitor everything about the Network and its operations and report back.'

Annie stared at her. 'You're serious, aren't you? You're trying to tell me that you've been spying on everybody and writing it down in a little black book? Come on, Leah. You can't expect me to believe that.' But even as the words were coming out of her mouth, Annie knew she was hearing the truth. All the unexplained absences, the way she could suddenly shut down, the fact she had so many facts and figures at her fingertips. Not the sort of information that could be picked up by just anybody.

Leah twisted her plait. 'I was recruited by the Ministry for the IIU back in April, when I was still working at the Barrier. They needed a hydrologist because their first project concerned a group living in the Marsh Projects, which is, as you know, extremely vulnerable to flooding and changes to the river environment.'

'The Lightermen,' said Annie It just slipped out. She'd been trying not to agree or engage with anything Leah was saying.

'It wasn't hard getting close to Kellen,' she continued. 'You know what he's like. Anyway, I engineered a meeting around Easter. Within weeks, he'd suggested I should come and live at the Pen and work for the Network full time. I agreed, pretended to resign from my now non-existent job at the Barrier and moved in.'

'You told me you hadn't ever been lovers.'

Leah jerked her head up. 'Is that what you think?'

Annie's voice was hollow. 'I don't know what to think.'

'We weren't lovers, for crying out loud. Kellen wouldn't have minded, but I made it clear I wasn't interested and that was the end of it.' She waited for Annie to interrupt – challenge her, shout at her – but she said nothing. 'Look, I know this is hard for you. But you've just got to accept Kellen is not the man you think he is. It's all an illusion. Like all these tapestries and fake concern for those less fortunate than himself, the quasi-religious nonsense, there's nothing to any of it. It's all bogus. The only person Kellen cares about is himself.'

'That's not true,' Annie shouted at her.

Leah shrugged. 'For six months I've been recording anything of significance that happens here, getting to know people and passing information back to the Unit.'

'About me?'

'I'm sorry, Annie.'

Annie suddenly kicked the door. Leah jumped and looked at her in alarm. Annie refused to meet her eye.

'The important thing is,' Leah continued as calmly as she could, 'that Michael's suspicions were well-founded. Rumours had been circulating for months that Kellen was involved in a big biopirating operation scheduled to take place at the beginning of August. Everybody in the Network knew the visit to the Marsh Projects was special. Even without the secrecy surrounding the exact details of timing, the sheer volume of equipment and medicines gave it away.

'We received reports from our undercover agents in the Projects that the Lightermen were being intimidated, having refused to give blood. A week before the operation itself, an old man was badly beaten as a warning to everyone else that they'd better cooperate. As a strategy, it worked. Kellen got the blood, which we tracked to Paris by—'

Annie snapped. 'Stop,' she shouted. 'I'm not going to listen to any more of this shit.'

Leah leaped up and charged across the room to her. 'God, I know this must be a shock. I know how much he means to you. But at least hear me out. Please?'

'Hear you out?' she yelled. 'You want me to sit here and listen to you denounce Kellen as some sort of criminal. Listen to you boast about how you've been spying on us all for months. For fuck's sake, Leah. You're supposed to be a friend.'

'I am your friend,' she said. 'That's why I'm telling you. You've got to come with me. I can't leave you here.'

Annie shoved her away. 'Come with you,' she shrieked. 'How can you possibly imagine I'd go anywhere with you after this?'

'He knows, Annie. Kellen knows about me and what's been going on. I don't know what he's going to do but, believe me, he will react. He can't afford not to. Him and Lonnie. Think about what he's been asking you to do for him? Can't you see it? You know how things have changed around here. Look around you. It's all falling apart.'

'No,' shouted Annie, putting her hands over her ears. 'No, no, no.'

Leah grabbed an envelope from her coat, scribbled something on the back, then thrust it at Annie.

'Take it,' she said. 'It's all in here.'

Annie didn't move. Leah leaned forward and pushed the envelope into the pocket of her trousers.

'Read it, Annie. For your sake as much as mine. There's a number there telling you how you can get hold of me. Please call me. Any time, day or night.'

She grabbed her bag from the bed, then unlocked the door. 'You take care,' she whispered.

Annie heard the sound of her feet running quietly down the corridor. She could picture her on the stairs, sprinting across the main hall, letting herself out of the side entrance and disappearing into the dark. Annie thought she could hear her running along the cobbled street down below. But it was probably her mind playing tricks.

Still she did not move. Just stood in the centre of Leah's abandoned room, tears rolling silently down her cheeks.

37

Sunday 26 October

Annie sat with her knees drawn up to her chin, watching dawn bleach away the remains of the night. She felt as if she'd been anaesthetised from head to toe. Her hands were frozen, stiff and rigid like claws, and her legs were numb from sitting in the same place for too long. She'd been waiting all night for Kellen to come back.

A storm had blown up at about two o'clock. Annie had found it comforting to be surrounded by so much angry noise and confusion. It so matched her mood. At about three, the wind had stopped and the rain had started. Now the last few raindrops hung suspended like beads of glass on the bare twigs and branches of the trees. On the bridges crossing the river, Annie could just make out the swish of water caught in the tyres of buses and taxis.

She pushed her fingers through her hair. It felt like fur now it was longer, like the coat of an animal. She wandered into the bathroom and splashed some water on her face. A pale, dead face looked out of the mirror at her. Her eyes were rimmed red and the mark on her forehead seemed even more prominent than usual. As if she'd been branded.

Her tongue and mouth were sticky from lack of sleep. She cleaned her teeth so roughly that her gums started to bleed. For some reason, the pain made her feel better, strengthened her resolve that she was doing the right thing. She leaned over and spat. The red was startling on the white surface of the basin.

Annie didn't remember leaving Leah's room and coming back to her own. All she had been thinking about was Leah's envelope feeling as if it was burning a hole in her pocket. She had intended to hand it over to Kellen without even looking. But he still wasn't back. She took it out. Put it on the table. Looked at it. Time passed and he still didn't appear. She eased the papers out, held them in her hand, smoothed them down and started to read. She concentrated on every detail and, when she had finished, she immediately started again from the top, then again and again, until she knew the contents off by heart. Finally, she put the papers back into the envelope and the envelope back on the table.

Annie accepted the evidence. Predictably, Leah had been thorough and had compiled an overwhelming dossier against the Network. Some of the incidents she was referring to Annie had even witnessed, although without understanding their significance. Only the conclusion was wrong. Leah had failed to separate Kellen from the Network and vice versa. She'd made the assumption that because the crimes were being carried out under the cover of the Network, the only person who could be responsible was Kellen himself. But Annie had checked and rechecked the information, gone over all the days, dates and times, and reached a different conclusion about who was behind it. It wasn't like Leah to make a mistake, but Annie could only presume that her feelings had got in the way of her judgement on this one.

Annie was not looking forward to telling Kellen what had been going on behind his back. He'd be hurt and angry to realise he'd been betrayed by someone he'd trusted. She would do her best to support him. Annie knew she should make contact with Leah. Tell her where she'd gone wrong. But she was too angry, couldn't even bear the thought of hearing her voice right now. She'd leave it. Maybe she'd feel calmer later in the week.

When Kellen turned up a couple of hours later, Annie was still sitting in the same place staring at nothing.

'Annie?' he said, dropping his bag by the door. 'What's up?'

She started shaking. Uncontrollable shaking. She could see the look of alarm in his face but simply couldn't stop herself.

'Hey,' he whispered. 'Annie. What's going on here? Are you sick?'

Annie shook her head.

'You're hurt. Someone's hurt you?'

'I'm OK.'

Kellen reached out and touched her hands. 'You're freezing,' he said. 'I'll go and get something to warm you up. Just wait here. I'll be right back.'

He threw a blanket over her shoulders, then disappeared. Annie didn't move. When he came back five minutes later, he had a cup of coffee for her.

'Drink this,' he said, putting it into her hands.

Annie couldn't feel a thing. She knew it was hot because of the steam coming off the surface, but her hands didn't register the heat.

'Thank you,' she said.

'Tell me what's happened. Please.'

'Leah's gone.'

'Gone? What do you mean, gone?'

'She left last night. She wanted me to go with her. And, I have to say, we did not part on the best of terms.'

Kellen pulled up the other chair and sat down in front of her, so close that their knees were touching.

'Go on,' he said.

'She gave me some papers. Said I'd understand when I'd read them.'

'What sort of papers?'

Annie ignored the question. 'I thought she was a really good friend, Kellen. Someone special. But all the time she was simply pretending and spying on me, you, all of us in fact.'

Kellen put his hand on Annie's leg. 'Have you got the stuff she gave you?'

She nodded.

'Then why don't you give them to me now. I'll read them while you finish your drink, then we can talk. OK?'

'Help yourself. They're right there.'

Kellen turned around and saw the white envelope lying in the middle of the table. For five minutes, the only noise in the room was the sound of pages being turned. Annie raised the cup to her mouth, sipped, lowered it again until all the coffee had gone. Put the empty cup on the table. Mechanical gestures. She could taste and feel nothing.

'What's this scribbled on the back of the envelope?' he said.

'That's the number where I can get hold of her. She said I could call any time.'

'Do you know where she is?'

'I don't want to see her.'

Kellen was massaging her hands now, as if he was trying to rub the pain out of them.

'And what time did all of this happen?'

'Midnight.'

Kellen looked at the time. 'Shit,' he muttered.

'Does it matter?'

He lifted her hands to his mouth and kissed the tips of her fingers. 'No,' he said softly. 'I suppose not. It doesn't say anything about who she was actually working for anywhere. Did she tell you? Think hard. It's important.'

'She did say. Some secret Unit attached to the Ministry of BioProspecting and Patenting. The IIU or IUU or something like that.'

'But who was she reporting to specifically? Think, Annie. Did she give you a name?'

Annie dredged her memory, running through the conversation with Leah until she picked out the word she wanted.

'Michael,' she said. 'Michael somebody.'

'I wonder . . .' he murmured to himself.

'Do you know who she was talking about?' asked Annie, noticing the odd expression on his face.

Kellen was spinning from the shock of what had crossed his mind. Was it possible?

'Kellen?' she repeated.

'Sorry,' he said. 'Yes, I think she's probably referring to a man called Michael Searle. He's one of the rising stars of the Ministry.'

'Do you know him?'

'Only by hearsay. I've never actually met him.'

After a couple of moments, Kellen stopped thinking and made himself concentrate on Annie again.

'You must feel bad,' he said. 'Even without everything else, I know how close you were to Leah.'

'Yes,' she said in a quiet voice.

'But the thing is,' he continued, 'you shouldn't worry about me. This doesn't come as a total surprise. I already knew something was going on with Leah.'

Annie stared at him. 'You did? Why didn't you tell me?'

'I didn't want to say anything until I was sure. I knew you'd be really upset and after that time when you slept together, well, I didn't want you to think I was just trying to make trouble because I was jealous.'

Annie smiled indulgently at him. 'I wouldn't have thought that,' she said. 'Everyone could see you two weren't getting on any more – and I admit I felt guilty that I might have contributed to that – but you were always nice to her. Leah was the one who withdrew.'

'Hey, don't feel guilty. Now you know what she was up to, you know you're not responsible for the atmosphere. Things would have come to a head sooner or later.'

'I guess,' said Annie.

'But, what I don't understand, is why last night? Has something been going on while I've been away?'

'She just said she wasn't safe any more.'

'Well, did she give the impression something was about to happen?'

Annie slowly shook her head. 'Not really.'

Kellen got up and started to walk around the room, tapping his fingers on the side of his jeans.

'What are you thinking?' said Annie after a while.

'That we're both avoiding the central issue here.'

Annie stood up too. The blanket fell from her lap on to the floor. 'What do you mean?' she said, although she knew perfectly well.

'Do you believe her, Annie? Do you believe all that stuff she wrote? That's the only thing that matters right now.'

'Kellen,' she started. 'I've been trying—'

'Christ, no,' he interrupted. 'You do. You think she's telling the truth—'

'No!' she said, half shouting to stop him. 'No, of course I don't. How could you be capable of the sorts of things she's talking about?'

'But then—'

She put her hand across his mouth. 'What I'm saying is that the evidence she's put together is very convincing, but she's just put two and two together and come up with five.'

'I don't understand what you mean.'

'Because you run the Network, and the Network is implicated, Leah's drawn the conclusion that you therefore are the one behind it. The drugs, biopiracy, all the rest of it.'

He still looked blank.

'Shit, Kellen, think about it. Who's the only person, apart from you, who's got both access and opportunity – and the temperament – to be involved in something like this?'

Annie felt overwhelmed with sympathy and could completely understand why he didn't want to face the obvious. Not only was he realising that the reputation of something he'd worked so hard to build up had been damaged, possibly beyond repair. But now he had to accept that someone he trusted had betrayed him. Just like her and Leah.

Annie put her hands on his waist. 'It's Lonnie,' she said. 'Can't you see it? Lonnie's clearly been using the Network – and you – as a cover for his own activities. I'm sorry.'

Kellen dropped his head. Annie couldn't see the expression on his face, but she could tell that he was upset.

'I know,' she murmured, pulling him closer to her. He felt like her child, now. She wanted to make it all better. 'I'm so sorry.'

38

Friday 31 October

Leah and Michael were finding their way with one another. Small, cautious steps.

Leah felt as if she was thawing out. For Michael, all the emotions were new. Unburdening himself of his past had been an enormous act, but learning to wriggle out from under its shadow would be a far greater challenge. He still drank too much and still lost his temper without even thinking about it. But they managed to talk and listen, uncovered parallels and similarities in their childhoods and attitudes that helped them to believe there was a chance, in the long term, of being comfortable with one another.

In the short term, Leah's main concern was negotiating Michael safely through the days leading up to the raid on the Pen on the second of November. She wanted to keep him on track, keep him operating logically and prevent him from either harming Kellen or himself. At the back of her mind was always the fear that Michael's scars were too raw to heal. Revenge had driven his entire adult life. Both for the humiliation of the near-drowning and the death of any chance of happiness or contentment. Michael held his brother entirely responsible for the state of his soul. He couldn't see that he had, in some way, handed it to Kellen on a plate. Leah wanted to shake him. Remind him that nearly twenty years had passed. That, by building Kellen up into a monster, he had only made him more powerful.

Leah still thought Michael was making a mistake not going into the Pen straight away, but now she understood his reluctance. Since everything had always been leading to his ultimate confrontation with Kellen, he'd barely thought of what would happen afterwards. What he might do or feel or think. There was only blank space.

They argued about it, in the same way they'd argued when Leah admitted she had given Annie details of some of the evidence they'd got on the Network. Despite his anger, she'd managed to convince him that she'd done the right thing. After all, how could she hope to influence Annie without giving her something specific to go on?

'What if she doesn't believe you,' Michael had asked. 'What then?'

'She will,' Leah had said. 'I know her.'

But as Wednesday turned into Thursday, Thursday turned into Friday and still Annie didn't call, Leah started to lose faith.

Only two more days to go.

Saturday 1 November

Mary was uneasy. She felt every one of her sixty-three years.

Six hours ago, at seven o'clock yesterday evening, Annie had turned up. At last, she said, she had reached a decision. She was going to travel back with Mary to 1997. At first, she'd been delighted. It was, after all, the news she had been hoping for. But there was something about Annie's enthusiasm that made her realise something was going on. 'What made you change your mind?' she asked her. What about Leah? Or Kellen? What did they think? Little by little, Mary dragged the story out of Annie. The fight with Leah, the accusations against Kellen, the fact she had not seen Leah for over a week. Finally, Annie admitted that Kellen had persuaded her to go back now, in order to make preparations for returning for good.

Mary had so many objections, she hardly knew where to start. Annie tried to argue that it was just like moving flats.

You went backwards and forwards, moving things from one place to the other, until you were ready to shut the door and hand back the key. It didn't sound like Annie talking as much as Kellen. 'He wants you to do something for him, does he?' she asked. Annie denied it, but from the way she shuffled in her seat and her defensive tone, it was obvious that Mary had hit the mark. Mary couldn't get through to her. Even when she accused Kellen of gambling with Annie's life, she simply shrugged and said it wasn't like that.

They reached a sort of stalemate. Neither wanted to fight and they were both nervous. Knowing she'd only alienate Annie if she continued criticising Kellen, Mary decided the best she could do was to hope she'd be able to dissuade her from attempting a third journey, once they were home in 1997.

Since they had both come through in the early morning, they decided to leave the Pen just before six o'clock to go to Crucifix Lane. They talked about where to meet and what to take, what they might expect when they got there. And when they hugged each other goodnight, it was with a sense of nostalgia for the times they'd spent together in Mary's room in the past few months. Already, it belonged to their past.

Mary looked around the room, which seemed very empty without Annie. She sat back in her chair and listened to the rain and wind rattling the shutters. As the hours passed, Mary sat wondering if, after all, she was wrong about why they had been sucked forward in time. Nothing had happened. She had witnessed nothing. She thought of the Ogham calendar, the start of the Celtic new year, how November was the time for settling and reckoning, forgetting the past and starting again.

One more day to go.

Sunday 2 November

One floor below, Annie lay with Kellen in a tangle of legs and arms and hair and breath, all mixed up together.

Four o'clock on Sunday morning. In a matter of hours, the sky would be getting light and she would saying goodbye to

Kellen for the last time. 'Not for the last time,' he kept saying. 'It's just for now. Think of it as a holiday.'

'But what if I can't get back,' she'd asked him. What then?

Annie looked up at the familiar chimes and streamers on the ceiling and wondered what the hell she was doing. The last three months had been the best of her life. If Kellen was wrong – and she couldn't find the way through from 1997 for a second time – then what did she have to look forward to? An empty flat, an old man who no longer recognised her, no job and the knowledge she would spend the next eleven years regretting the choice she was about to make. Missing Kellen, wondering what he was doing without her, scared that he would forget her and move on.

Annie closed her eyes to hold back her tears.

Six o'clock at the Primary Control Centre at the Barrier. Everybody had been working flat out all night. Tempers were frayed, people were triple-checking controls they'd already checked a thousand times before. Nothing now would make any difference, they all knew that, but activity stopped the thinking. Nobody wanted to imagine the one and a half million at risk, the extent of the devastation, the destruction of all water, electricity and gas supplies if London flooded.

For the previous thirty-six hours, Syd had been monitoring the weather forecasts and sea tide level information from the meteorological offices, the weather ships in the Atlantic, the rigs in the North Sea and recording stations on Stornoway. With every hour that passed the situation got more serious. The exceptional surge tide was moving across the Atlantic at over 100 kilometres an hour, heading for the east coast of Britain.

She hadn't waited to see if the northerly winds would drive the zone of water down the North Sea or blow it off course, but had immediately ordered all flood protection systems to be set in motion. The Port of London navigation service was alerted, all shipping and pier operators warned, the navigation signals changed and emergency measures adopted. Every official agency was warned that the Barrier was being closed. The three falling radial gates on the north bank and single gate on the south had been permanently shut since September. One by one, the remaining gates went up into place from the outside in.

Syd had rushed backwards and forwards, issuing orders, sending messages and monitoring every piece of information coming in, however insignificant it seemed, in a desperate attempt to predict how much water might be forced up the Thames if the wind didn't change direction and speed. Four hours ago, news had started to come in of the collapse of the flood defences downstream. Millions of tons of water were already flooding up the Thames. So far, only twenty deaths had been recorded, but Syd knew it was only a matter of time. Despite the bulletins now being broadcast on radio, television, Internet and entertainment screens, warning people to stay inside and take precautions, she knew that most people did not believe they were in real danger. None of them understood that London could be destroyed by water. Terrorist bombs, chemical weapons, maybe. Not a flood. This was England, after all. In the twenty-first century.

Syd looked at the screens, knowing that greed, complacency and a failure to act in time had led them to this point. The greatest natural and man-made disaster London had ever seen. She rubbed her tired eyes and glanced at the time. Nearly six o'clock already. There was nothing left to do now but wait.

39

Sunday 2 November

Annie had no idea how long they had been standing like this. Arms around each other, heads on one another's shoulders, swaying slightly in the middle of the room. As if they were at the end of a long, very gruelling dance competition.

On Mary's advice, Annie was wearing the clothes she'd arrived in. White vest, green army hipsters, trainers, blue fleece. Her rucksack was packed ready by the door. She looked different, though. As if she'd been away somewhere or been through an experience. She was slightly thinner in the face, her black hair was three inches long rather than cropped all over, and the black symbol on her head stood out even more than it had against her pale skin. The new long, black coat Leah had helped her choose before they fell out, was hanging on the back of the chair.

'I love you,' she said.

He stroked her hair. 'Me too.'

'What if—'

He put his finger on her lips. 'Hey, you'll be back,' he said. 'Nothing's going to go wrong. I promise you. Before you know it, we'll be lying in our bed together, in our room, remembering how painful it was to be apart. It will all be over.'

She didn't believe him.

★   ★   ★

At the bottom of the stairs, Annie turned. She had a Polaroid of Kellen in her pocket – as well as one of her and Leah taken at the Barrier – but she wanted to carry her own visual memory in her mind. Something more personal than a photograph. The tilt of his nose, the way his curls surrounded his face, all the things that made him special.

He was a black silhouette, with the light behind him. Annie couldn't see the expression on his face. He raised his hand to say goodbye. Annie did the same, then walked away.

'Are you ready?' said Mary.

Annie nodded, not trusting herself to speak.

It was cold outside and the rain was still falling. Everything was soaked to its bones. Gutters were overflowing and a fast stream of water forced its way over the cobbled stones and down towards the river. The two women, their hoods pulled right down over their heads, slipped and skidded on the wet streets, carefully finding their foothold like children climbing on rocks at the seaside in summer. In the distance, they could hear the persistent blast of sirens on the river, but they took no notice. Regular warnings were as much a part of the contemporary landscape as car alarms in the old days. It never meant anything.

Once Kellen was sure they were out of sight, he ran back to the room, grabbed his jacket and slipped out of the side door into the street. He could have looked at Crucifix Lane on the screen, but he wasn't prepared to pass up the opportunity of seeing it happen for himself – if anything did happen – despite his promise to Annie to let her go alone. He'd stay out of sight and hope that it didn't take too long.

Mary and Annie turned right into Cathedral Street, heading for the subway that would lead them to London Bridge. As they walked, Annie was aware of the weight of her rucksack thumping on her back. Since she'd arrived at the Pen, she'd stopped carrying a bag around with her all the time. Now she felt literally burdened down by her past. The heavy keys to the flat, the purse of old money, other bits and pieces she'd not needed for three months.

The footway was closed as usual, so they cut through Montague Place up into Bedale Street. Annie would have liked Mary to talk to her, anything to help calm her nerves, but there was little point. What could she say that Annie did not know already?

In Weston Street, Michael had received a message from the agent covering the Pen.

'They've just left,' he said.

Leah looked at him. 'Who's just left?'

'Mary and Annie, followed some distance behind by Kellen.'

'God, they really are going to try to get back,' said Leah. 'I didn't think Annie would do it. Not when the time finally came.'

'Kellen must have persuaded her.'

The Unit's raid on the Network was scheduled for eight o'clock that morning. Everything was in place and ready to go. But Michael and Leah had been talking over for days what they would do if the opportunity arose to talk to Annie before then. They both knew logically it would be stupid to make any sort of approach, to either Kellen or Annie, at this eleventh hour. At the same time, the chance to confront Kellen face to face was too much for Michael to pass up. And Leah was both angry and hurt at Annie's failure to get in touch with her. She couldn't let her go without at least trying to talk to her one last time.

Without a word, Leah shut down the computer system as Michael set the alarms. They snatched their coats and ran out of the door, for once paying no attention to the security cameras.

If they had stayed on-line for just a couple of minutes more, they would have got Syd's message telling them to get to higher ground. The Barrier was giving way.

★　　★　　★

The two women arrived in Crucifix Lane at twenty-past six, just as night was turning from black to blue. Annie felt nauseous. She forced herself to swallow.

'What do we do now?'

'Wait,' replied Mary.

'Where we came through?'

'I think so, yes.'

'Do you think it will be obvious if anything is going to happen? Perhaps the letters will reappear on the wall? Perhaps—'

'Annie,' said Mary. 'I don't know.'

'I'm sorry,' she said. 'It's just because I'm nervous. Up until now I've been thinking mostly about how I'm going to feel without Kellen. How awful everything will be back in 1997 on my own. But now we're here, I'm frightened. Of what might happen to us.'

Mary put her hand on Annie's arm. 'I know,' she said.

'Are you?'

'Yes.'

'Of dying? Or of how much it will hurt if—'

'I don't think this is really helpful,' she said. 'You are still sure you want to go back? No last minute doubts?'

Annie leaned back against the dirty brickwork. If Kellen said stay, then she'd stay. But she thought of the excitement on his face when they were talking about all the things she could bring back, the thought of the list in her pocket, the way he'd made her feel she'd be doing something important. She couldn't let him down.

'No,' she said firmly. 'I've got no doubts.'

Mary smiled. 'Good.'

Michael and Leah came out of Weston Street into Snowsfields and over the junction with Bermondsey Street, the rain pounding down on them. Ahead a man was walking fast, his head down. Michael felt his heart seize.

'That's him,' he said.

He was amazed at how calm, how level, his voice sounded.

'It'll be better if we split up,' he continued. 'You follow him. I'm going to loop around the back and cover the top end of Crucifix Lane, where it joins Druid Street.'

'Why do you think he isn't with them?' Leah asked. 'Why is he following them?'

Michael wasn't listening. The only thing in his mind was Kellen.

Leah saw the expression on his face. 'Don't do anything stupid,' she said. 'Please.'

'I won't.'

She watched him go with grave misgivings.

Michael ran through the Bermondsey Street tunnel. The orange lights in the roof stripped every last vestige of colour from his face, making him look even more drawn and pale than usual. At the end, he turned sharp right and took the short cut through Holyrod Street. He knew there were plenty of corners and tiny spaces in the railway arches by William Curtis Park, where he'd have a good view of what was going on at the same time as being able to stay out of sight.

Michael kept below the level of the wall at the bottom of the park until he could see Annie and Mary standing at the far end of Crucifix Lane. He was surprised to see what Mary looked like. Because Leah had told him that she was sixty-three and never came out of her room, he'd imagined her as a timid, wizened old lady. He'd never expected her to look so formidable and self-possessed.

He looked at his watch. 06:24:10. Nearly dawn already. He settled down to wait, barely registering the sirens screaming on the river. In the shelter of his hiding place, he didn't notice the wind had picked up again.

'Hey, look who it is,' said a voice behind him. 'It's been a long time, Misha.'

It was the shock of hearing Kellen's voice that forced Michael's throat to constrict. Not the cold barrel of the gun pressing into his neck.

'It'd probably be best if you just put your hands up on the

wall in front of you,' said Kellen. 'Where I can see them. It would be such a shame if I was forced to do anything.'

Michael did what he was told.

'I have to say it. You really are totally unrecognisable. Eyes, hair, body, the lot. It was only when Annie told me who was controlling Leah, that I started to do a bit of digging. When I discovered that nobody seemed to know anything about this Michael Searle character until he arrived in London a couple of years ago, I got interested. His past was a complete blank. People said he'd come from Australia or New Zealand, but they didn't know what nationality he was. At that point, the unthinkable started to cross my mind. That Michael Searle might conceivably be Misha Harris.'

'Rather a leap of imagination.'

'Not really,' he said. 'Who else would hunt me down with such persistence and single-mindedness. It always felt personal to me.'

Without warning, Kellen suddenly smacked the weapon against Michael's head. He felt his skin split and a streak of blood trickle down from behind his ear. He wondered where Leah was, if she had any idea what was going on. Not that it mattered. His only hope at this point was to get within sight of Annie. He'd no doubt his brother would kill him, if it suited his purposes. But he was prepared to gamble on the fact that Kellen would not risk shooting him in front of Annie. Not if he still needed her on his side.

'She'll see through you.'

Kellen laughed sarcastically.

'Oh, I don't think she will. Annie's really very much in love with me. Can't do enough for me . . .'

'What do you want from her?' Michael demanded.

'Want from her? Why do you assume there has to be an ulterior motive? Maybe I just like her. Maybe I'm head-over-heels in love with her . . .'

'If you loved her, you wouldn't be prepared to risk her life by sending her back.'

'Hey,' said Kellen. 'It's her choice. Nothing to do with

me. She's the one who decided to keep Mary company. All very loyal of her.'

The complete lack of emotion in Kellen's voice turned Michael's stomach.

'You're a liar,' he said, unable to keep the disgust out of his voice.

'Temper, temper,' said Kellen, then again he whipped the barrel of the gun across the side of Michael's head.

'Sorry. Bit clumsy today.'

Michael reeled from the blow. He could see a circle of red in front of his eyes and flashes of white. He held on to the wall to keep himself upright, waiting for the spinning to stop.

Suddenly, he realised his lower legs and feet were wet. Keeping his head as still as possible, he glanced down and saw he was kneeling in a couple of centimetres of water. Druid Street was now covered by a layer of water, black and polluted from the dirt of the city streets.

Michael went cold. At last, he understood the significance of the sirens blasting repeatedly on the river. He was no longer thinking of Kellen but of the investigation he'd set in motion after talking to Syd, to find out exactly how bad things were at the Barrier. He could picture the report now, sitting unopened on his desk, where it had been for over a week.

'London's flooding,' he said urgently. 'We can't stay here.'

'Yeah, right.'

'Look around you,' Michael shouted. 'Can't you see?'

'Hey, we're always being told we're on the verge of going under,' said Kellen dismissively. 'It never happens. But then again, I'd forgotten you have a little bit of a problem with water . . .'

Michael could feel the water lapping against his knees. Syd had explained how it would start slowly at first, the pressure building until it reached breaking point. Then the river would suddenly become like an enormous tidal wave, sending high-speed torrents of water into the streets.

He knew they couldn't wait. Crucifix Lane would be turned into a gigantic storm drain. They had to get to higher ground. Michael leaned forward, rolled himself back on to his heels, tightened the muscles in his arms and, with the sound of the seconds ticking down in his head, suddenly launched himself backwards into Kellen. Kellen was taken by surprise and knocked off balance. Before he could recover, Michael jumped the low wall and escaped into Crucifix Lane.

From her vantage point in White's Grounds, Leah heard the shout at the same moment as Mary and Annie. She poked her head around the corner, trying to see what was going on. Annie and Mary spun around and saw a man, with blood running down the side of his head, coming straight at them.

Mary stepped back in alarm.

'We've got to get out,' Michael yelled. 'All of us. There's no time.'

Annie stared at him. 'Who the fuck are you?'

Michael grabbed Annie's shoulders.

'Get off me,' she shouted. 'Leave me alone.'

'You don't understand,' he shouted in her face. 'It's going to flood. We've only got a few minutes to get away.'

'Annie, listen to him,' shrieked Leah, running towards the three of them. 'He's telling the truth. Listen to the sirens. Remember? All the things that Syd told us would happen? The Barrier must have given way.'

'Where the fuck did you come from,' she said to Leah, 'and who is he?'

'This is Michael.'

'The Michael who's been on Kellen's case? Yeah, right. I'm hardly likely to listen to anything he has to say.'

Leah shook her. 'Didn't you read what I gave you?' she said. 'Well, didn't you? How could you be so stupid?'

'I read it,' said Annie.

'Well, why didn't you call? How could you not call?'

'I didn't trust myself, for fear of what I might say to you. I was − I am still − too angry about what you did. And, in any case, it was for nothing. None of it was anything to do with Kellen. It was all down to Lonnie. Kellen confronted him. Lonnie admitted it. Now he's disappeared. Kellen doesn't know where.'

Leah pushed her. 'Your capacity for self-delusion is incredible,' she shouted. 'How could it possibly be Lonnie? Nothing happens in the Pen without Kellen's say-so and you know it.'

Annie ignored her and turned on Michael.

'And you,' she said. 'What is your problem with Kellen? You people just can't believe that anyone isn't as pointless and vindictive as you. Why couldn't you just let him be?'

Despite his desperation to get everybody out of the confined space of the tunnel, Michael saw Kellen out of the corner of his eye and knew they'd all have to see it through first.

'Why don't you ask him yourself?' he said.

Annie followed the direction of Michael's eyes.

'Kellen,' she said, running up to him.

Mary looked coldly at him. 'Why are you here?'

Kellen ignored her, just turned to Annie and took her hands in his.

'Hey, are you OK?' he said, his voice thick with concern. 'I tried to stop Michael coming after you, but he slipped away from me. I know I promised to stay away, but I couldn't just sit by and do nothing. I'm sorry if it was the wrong thing.'

'No, I'm glad you're here,' she said, kissing him.

Michael turned away in disgust.

'Annie was just explaining how we'd got you all wrong,' said Leah. 'How you were the victim of deception. None of it your fault. How you were taken in by Lonnie—'

Kellen interrupted her. 'Yes, Leah,' he said. 'Of course you would know all about deception, wouldn't you?'

'How dare you? What I did was completely different.'

Something suddenly occurred to Annie. 'How do you know his name, Kellen?'

'Who?'

'How did you know he was Michael?'

He laughed. 'Well, it had to be this Michael Leah had told

you about,' he said. 'I mean, who else could it be. Especially with his little spy trailing along behind him.'

Annie tried to stop it, but a sliver of doubt wriggled into her mind. 'But you didn't know Leah was here until just now,' she said.

Kellen tried to put his arm around her shoulder. 'Hey, what is this? It doesn't matter, does it? The issue is that this is the man who's been trying to destroy the Network.'

'Tell her, Kellen,' Leah demanded. 'Tell her why you know who he is.'

'Ah, so you two are closer than I thought,' he said, intercepting a look between Leah and Michael. 'How sweet. Love blossoming in such a barren landscape.'

'This is starting to scare me,' said Annie. 'Please tell me what she means.'

'They're brothers,' said Leah. 'Kellen is Michael's younger brother.'

Annie felt as if she'd been hit in the face. Her heart was thumping. She turned to Kellen, struggling to keep the panic out of her voice.

'Is this true?' she said.

'Of course it's not true,' he said, reaching out for her.

She stepped back, trying to read the look in his eyes. 'Why didn't you tell me?'

'I didn't tell you because it's not true. Look, Annie, I told you. I haven't seen my brother for over fifteen years.'

Annie looked from Kellen's face to Michael's, trying to see a resemblance. She could see nothing.

Leah grabbed hold of her arm. 'What did he tell you?' she said. 'Not about the accident, I bet? Not how—'

Michael stood still looking at his brother. After all these years, turning out to be nothing more than a mere man. Not a monster, not a demon, just a person. Strange to learn, after all this time, that his desire for revenge was not as strong as his desire to survive. Although maybe before Leah . . .

He quickly put his hand on her shoulder.

'It doesn't matter now,' he said. 'We've got to get out of here.'

Leah broke off, looked down to see the water was now up to the level of the curb.

'Annie,' she said. 'Please. You've got to come with us. Mary too.'

'You asked me to come with you before,' Annie said, trying to hold back the tears. 'I said no then. And I'm saying it again now.'

'You must—'

Leah's plea was interrupted by the echoing boom of thousands of tonnes of water. The noise reverberated in the tunnel like an invading army. The eastern suburbs and urban suburbs were already submerged, the buildings and people swept away on the fierce currents. All London was drowning. The area within the Peripherique would be next to go.

The five of them stood transfixed as the thundering grew louder and louder until the wall of water exploded into the tunnel. Too late to run. Mary grabbed Annie's hand, pulled her back against the wall.

'No,' yelled Michael.

He was sucked under with Leah. The last thing Annie saw was Kellen being hurled high into the air like a ragdoll, then thrown back into the angry tide.

'No,' screamed Annie. 'Please no . . .'

40

Saturday 2 August 1997

When Annie came round, Mary was gone.

The light was shimmering. Everything was out of focus, all a little hazy and ragged around the edges, as if she was waking up from a long sleep and her eyes weren't quite ready to face the day.

The pavement beneath her was dry, although the tarmac was darker beyond the tunnel, suggesting it had perhaps rained a little in the night. It was very muggy, very warm. Annie looked down at her clothes. Everything looked exactly as it had at the moment the fog came down. Green trousers, not ripped, blue fleece with the coffee stain on the collar, black trainers and rucksack. There was no sign of her new coat. She turned her hands over to see if there were any scratches or cuts. Nothing. She ran her fingers through her regular No 2 haircut. And there, sure enough, was the tramp in his cardboard box, sleeping off the effects of the booze. Two bottles were lying next to him on the ground.

For a while, Annie just sat against the dirty brickwork, breathing in the foul summer air, her mind functioning but her emotions shut down. When she closed her eyes, all she could see was Leah and Michael being swept away by the water, the horror on Kellen's face as the black current dragged him under, Mary's calm expression as she took her hand. And all she could hear was the booming of the flood, the shouting and the sirens, the fear in Kellen's voice. She played the scene played over and over in her mind, unable to stop, until she thought her head would explode.

Annie didn't bother to check the Polaroids in her bag. She knew they would not be there. There was a lump in her throat now, like a fist. Her skin was stinging from the tears on her face, although she hadn't even realised she was crying. She pulled her knees up to her chin, dropped her head on to her arms and howled.

In Crucifix Lane, the August sun broke through the cloud.

When she heard the taxi, Annie had no idea how long she'd been crying. Thirty minutes? Three hours? Both seemed just as likely. She turned towards the noise. First, the distinctive throb of the diesel engine in the distance, then the screech of tyres as the black cab took the corner with Druid Street too tight. Annie watched the driver yell abuse at a cyclist, then accelerate aggressively to jump the lights at Bermondsey Street.

Some things hadn't changed. In fact, nothing at all had changed. Like the children coming back from Narnia, Annie understood that time had not passed while she had been away. But like them, she knew that even though she looked the same on the outside, inside her spirit was different. She was no longer the person she had been before. Annie thought about all those people who wished they had the chance to live life over again, the people who said if only they'd known what lay ahead, they would have lived their life differently. Done more. Been better. For Annie, the chance was there if she decided to take it.

It was an extraordinary feeling. To be experiencing this particular day as if for the first time, but with the knowledge of how things would turn out. Mary had been right that there was a reason they had been sucked forward to 2008. Time was a series of interconnected steps, each leading one to the other. All those seemingly inconsequential decisions, all the wrong paths taken, all the mistakes, all the good intentions that would finally result in the most devastating flood London would ever know. All those thousands dead. Like Scrooge staring at his own neglected and forgotten grave, Annie accepted that she had been shown the future in order to prevent it.

Suddenly, she felt full of energy. Like she could take on the world. If she worked hard and got involved, maybe she could have an influence. Be someone who mattered rather than a nobody wasting her life on the sidelines. That way, Leah, Michael and Kellen would still be alive on the third of November 2008, not . . . Well. Annie got up and dusted herself down, the sudden movement disturbing the tramp. She watched him shuffle in his box, then roll over and start snoring again.

'If only you knew . . .'

The first thing was to find Mary. When they had talked about how they might get back to 1997, they couldn't decide if they were likely to find themselves standing together in Crucifix Lane on the second of November or alone on the day each of them had left. Annie felt a flurry of nerves. What if something had happened to Mary and she hadn't made it? She shook her head, refusing to contemplate it. Why wouldn't Mary have made it if she had? Mary should have arrived back three months ago and be expecting her to turn up today. Easy. All she had to do was go to the bookshop.

As Annie walked out of the shadows into the street, another thought occurred to her. She was missing Leah – was grieving for Leah, in fact – but actually she was here somewhere. Eleven years younger, sure, but she had grown up not far from here. If she could track her down, then maybe they could be friends and get to know each other again. Kellen too. By 1997, he was also already living in the area.

The pain took her breath away. Just the thought of his name. Annie didn't want to let herself think of how her faith in him had been taken at the very end, how trust had turned to ashes in her hands. If she did, she knew she'd start crying and would never be able to stop. But buried inside her, somewhere beyond words, Annie knew was redemption. That if she met Kellen now, before it all went too far, then maybe he could still be the man she had fallen in love with – not the man Michael, Leah and Mary had shown him to be. She took a deep breath. Maybe.

Annie walked on down Crucifix Lane, glancing at the shops, the poster on the wall of Shand Street advertising the club Reboot. As she drew level with the newsagent, an impulse made her stop. She might as well check. The door rattled as she pushed it open and the familiar smell of newsprint hit her. The shop looked so old-fashioned, with its window covered in scribbled for-sale cards, and cardboard boxes full of crisps stacked floor to ceiling.

'Yes please?'

Annie leaned over the counter and read the date on the nearest paper. The *Guardian*, Saturday August 2 1997. She nodded.

The shopkeeper looked at her.

'Sorry,' she said, backing out of the door. 'I've just remembered I don't have any money on me.'

She carried on to the corner. Astrocat looked precisely as Annie remembered, the name painted down the door in swirly white handwriting, the display of crystals, incense and zodiac necklaces, the peacock feathers hanging down inside. This time, a light blue spine caught Annie's eye. *Secrets of the Ogham Oracle*. It made her laugh. All the things that had been under her nose all along and she'd never noticed. Annie tried the handle, but it was locked. The sign said it was open at ten. She had no idea what the time was, but it couldn't be too far off that now.

As she sat patiently on the step, Annie wondered what – or who – had been behind all this. She didn't believe in God. Or, at least, not *a* God. Destiny? Fate? The Earth protecting itself? She had no idea. But she had a strange feeling in the pit of her stomach that somehow, deep within her, she might, one day, understand. If only she could find the eyes to see.

Annie turned her face to the sun and in the distance, at last, she saw Mary coming up the street towards her. Annie stood up, waited and waited as Mary got closer and closer until she was standing in front of the bookshop. She looked exactly the same, except for one thing. The black mark on her forehead was no longer there.

Annie felt a rush of affection. Relief, too.

'Welcome home,' said Mary, holding out her hand.

Annie took it. 'Yes,' she said. 'I've come home.'

Acknowledgements

My thanks to all those who were involved with *Crucifix Lane*: my agent, Mark Lucas, for advice and encouragement, and his assistant Sally Hughes; to everyone at Hodder & Stoughton, in particular my publisher, Sue Fletcher – for her enthusiasm, patience, professionalism and champagne – and her assistant Bettina Jamani; to all friends at Ashmead School for their support, in particular Ali Perrotto, Chris Vincent-Bennett and Annette Yoosefinejad, without whom life for most of the summer would have been impossible; to my brilliant cousin, Dr Philippa Towlson, who not only checked and corrected my science, but did it in record-breaking time – it goes without saying that any errors that have slipped through are entirely my responsibility; and to my youngest groovy sister, Beth Mosse, for help with research, for good laughs and she knows what . . .

As always, my love to my parents, Richard and Barbara Mosse; to my sister Caroline Matthews; to Matt Seaton; and, most of all, to my children, Martha and Felix, who were as loving and helpful as any eight- and five-year-olds could possibly be: one day, they will understand how grateful I am and how exceptional they are.

Finally – as ever – Greg. For all these years together. For everything.

Kate Mosse
London, 1998

Under Construction
PAMELA JOHNSON

Everyone says it's crazy: renovating a dilapidated house in North London is no job for a young widow with teenage daughters. But it's three years since Greg died, Amy needs a new start. A team of builders tears the house apart around her. As they rebuild it, Amy develops an intimacy with Conor the Irish joiner. Where in her new life can she accommodate a relationship with a married man, father of four young children?

Conor and Amy can exist only in the pockets of time and space they slip into, unnoticed: London cafés, windswept Dungeness, the West coast of Ireland, and the infinite space of Amy's imagination. In reconstructing her life, Amy treads a fine line between creating something and destroying it.

This poetic first novel explores the intimate spaces one woman constructs as she recovers herself.

'Irresistibly readable, with a striking storyline. Pamela Johnson writes with great feeling and wit'
HELEN DUNMORE

'The slow, yet dizzying slide into love makes for a compelling read'
JAMES FRIEL

Pamela Johnson writes, lectures and broadcasts on contemporary visual arts; she also publishes poetry. She lives in London with her husband, son and daughter.

S

SCEPTRE

DAVID HUNT

TRICK SHOT

Photographer Kay Farrow is devastated by the death of her mentor and friend, photojournalist Maddy Yamada, in an apparent hit-and-run accident. What was Maddy doing in San Francisco's Mission district, notorious for drugs and rough sex?

Maddy's legacy to Kay is her precious camera collection, and in it Kay discovers an unfinished roll of film, a series of photographs that give off the unmistakable aura of evil.

The Goddess Gun Club is expensive, exclusive and secretive. Ugly rumours emanate from behind its barricaded gates. In avenging her friend, Kay finds herself peering through the lens at a sinister and decadent organisation and led into uncharted waters of sexual excess and depravity.

'Following her own vision (and nudged on by Hunt's hypnotic prose), Kay conducts an investigation that goes down some very dark alleys and leads to some very bleak truths. But in the inverted imagery of this strange world, the blacker it gets, the lovelier it looks.'
New York Times Book Review

'[A] very impressive first novel . . . unusual, chilling and highly recommended.'
Daily Telegraph on *The Magician's Tale*

HODDER AND STOUGHTON PAPERBACKS

A selection of bestsellers from Hodder and Stoughton

Under Construction	Pamela Johnson	0 340 71798 X	£6.99	☐
Trick Shot	David Hunt	0 340 68894 7	£5.99	☐
These is My Words	Nancy Turner	0 340 71778 5	£6.99	☐
Casanova	Andrew Miller	0 340 68210 8	£6.99	☐
Leading the Cheers	Justin Cartwright	0 340 63785 4	£6.99	☐
Snap Happy	Fiona Walker	0 340 68227 2	£5.99	☐
The Lydian Baker	David Wishart	0 340 71529 4	£6.99	☐

All Hodder & Stoughton books are available at your local bookshop or newsagent, or can be ordered direct from the publisher. Just tick the titles you want and fill in the form below. Prices and availability subject to change without notice.

Hodder & Stoughton Books, Cash Sales Department, Bookpoint, 39 Milton Park, Abingdon, OXON, OX14 4TD, UK. E-mail address: order@bookpoint.co.uk. If you have a credit card you may order by telephone – (01235) 400414.

Please enclose a cheque or postal order made payable to Bookpoint Ltd to the value of the cover price and allow the following for postage and packing:
UK & BFPO – £1.00 for the first book, 50p for the second book, and 30p for each additional book ordered up to a maximum charge of £3.00.
OVERSEAS & EIRE – £2.00 for the first book, £1.00 for the second book, and 50p for each additional book.

Name _____

Address_____

_____

_____

If you would prefer to pay by credit card, please complete:
Please debit my Visa/Access/Diner's Card/American Express (delete as applicable) card no:

Signature _____

Expiry Date_____

If you would NOT like to receive further information on our products please tick the box. ☐